YOUR SECRET TO KEEP

YOUR SECRET TO KEEP

RACHEL LABERGE

PLAYLIST

ROOM FOR 2 | Benson Boone

Better | Khalid

Rewrite the Stars | The Greatest Showman Soundtrack

I Know Places (Taylor's Vrsion) | Taylor Swift

Bobby Sox | Green Day

Tiny Moves | Bleachers

Late Night Talking | Harry Styles

King of My Heart | Taylor Swift

Better Together | Jack Johnson

To Love | Suki Waterhouse

That's Where I Am | Maggie Rogers

Head On Fire | Griff, Sigrid

The Joker and The Queen | Ed Sheeran & Taylor Swift

Then Because She Goes | The 1975

Go on Then, Love | Said The Sky, The Maine

LeBron | A Day to Remember

For all my autoimmune and chronically ill pals, just trying to get from one day to the next. I see you.

To Doris Burke, Michelle Tafoya, Erin Andrews, Lisa Salters, and Pam Oliver for showing me there's a place for women in sports.

To the man who interrupted my conversation to tell me I was a "LeBron Whore" this book is NOT for you. I do not wish you well.

Letter from the author

If you hate a content warning, this is your chance to flip the page. This isn't for you. Hurry... get to the next page... Move along!

Last chance!

YOUR SECRET TO KEEP may have topics which readers find distressing such as sports related injuries, anxiety, panic attacks, depression, autoimmune and chronically ill symptoms, and mentions of death of a parent. I always aim to be transparent and authentic with representation in my books—YOUR SECRET TO KEEP features my own lived in experiences for both mental health and autoimmune disorders.

YOUR SECRET TO KEEP includes explicit language, on page sexual content, and is meant for readers 18+.

Take care of yourself...

Xoxo - Rach

Character art by Juni Given, @junidraws_

Prologue
Brooks

Want to know a secret? I don't think I'll ever love anything, or anyone, as much as a basketball court. It's my first true love; it's never fucked me over or fucked me up. Even after the painful losses—half-court shots and lucky bounces that crack your heart in two—the court still welcomed me back. Challenged me. To play. To practice. To pour myself into it.

All I need is basketball.

Maybe it's the paparazzi reminding me that my too-recent-ex-girl-friend is already living with another NBA player? I love how they scream that shit when I'm walking into the stadium. Or maybe it's the rush of the win streak? Either way, it doesn't matter. Tonight, it's the truth.

The Jags have won ten straight games and it's looking like the eleventh is only a quarter away. It's March in the NBA—aka, get your shit together or watch the playoffs from the couch. There's only a month left of the regular season and I'm here to make sure it's not the end for *my* fucking team.

The whistle blows and we're into the fourth quarter. I create some space, exactly where I know my point guard is going to put the ball—I smirk as soon as it hits my hands. I look left just as I pass the ball right, confusing my defender for a split second—only long enough to get the ball off my fingers. Jalen snags it, just like Coach planned. He dribbles once, using the step to move closer to the corner, and puts up a three-point shot.

He looks at me and fucking winks as he jogs back up the court, the ball still hanging in the air. Cocky bastard. I'll make fun of him for that later. But when the ball swishes through the net, the crowd erupts, loudly enough I can feel the vibrations on the court—I can't help but smile.

Jalen pounds his chest, soaking it in but not missing a beat on the defensive play. He swipes at the ball, poking it away and cataloging his third steal of the night. I sprint, eyes on the court, moving as fast as I can to get to the basket. I turn just in time to catch the pass, dribble it a single time, and dunk it.

Energy zips through the air like something you can reach out and grab on to. It's everywhere. It hangs over the court then weaves through the players—everyone can feel it. I can almost fucking taste it. My heart thuds heavily but I feel light on my feet, as if I'm floating, while teammates offer high fives and chest bumps.

This is it. Nothing gets better than this.

The opposing team is trying to get the game under control but it's not working. We're leading by thirteen in the fourth quarter. They inch closer to closing the gap, but then the ball is hot in our hands, and we can't miss.

I jog backwards as they try to bring it up the floor. The player in front of me is desperately looking for the play to develop, needing to get the ball past me and to the right side of the court. It's a last second decision, but I want to go for the jugular. Right as the opposing player is trying to bring it past half-court, I pivot at the last possible second, stepping forward and swiping at the ball.

I know it's a stretch, me stealing the ball this way, but fuck if I'm not going to try. In a split second, it feels like time stalls. When the tip of a single finger touches the ball, poking it away, I put my head down and go to run.

Pop.

Silence hits me like a suckerpunch. The cheers from the crowd and yelling from my teammates are nowhere to be found. I hear nothing besides the echo of the pop that reverberates through my body. Instead of running forward, I awkwardly fall and roll to my back, grabbing for my knee.

Non-contact. Pop. Tingling.

My heart splinters on the basketball court. I'm cracking in two as the trainer runs over to me. When Coach leans down, his hand pressed to my shoulder, his eyes lock on mine and I don't need a test to confirm what I already know.

I just tore my ACL.

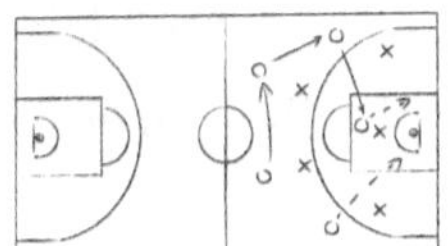

Three weeks later

The room is dark. Too dark. Or maybe it's just enough? Whatever I was binging on Netflix ended an hour ago and my TV automatically turned off. The best part of the darkness is how it doesn't bounce off my metal brace. The reminder of everything falling apart at a record pace.

I'm not cleared for air travel, which means my team is a thousand miles away for a game without me. Not that I'd go anyway. A few days after surgery, when the stitches were still fresh and the bruising still purple, I went to the arena. As I crutched by the court, my body wouldn't let me get any closer. Like we were the same side of a magnet, the push had me trying to get as far as away as I could.

I was walking to Coach's office when I lost my battle with the push. Stopping in my tracks, my hand on my chest, I looked for air that wasn't there—begged for a tiny fucking breath to get me to the next second. It was like the universe was playing with me, giving me a fraction of the oxygen I desperately tried to find, only to point out how much I needed it. Like it was in my grasp, but I couldn't reach further. A cruel fucking game.

If it hadn't been for one of the assistant coaches, I would've fallen onto the court, most likely doing more damage to my knee or a different body part. Instead, my coach watched me struggle and helped me sit down. He tried to talk to me, but I couldn't hear him. There was nothing besides the echoes from the life-altering pop on that fateful day. It crawled through my body, making its presence known in every fucking cell.

I never did make it to Coach's office. He came to my place that night, with a physical therapist specializing in injury recovery and a voice soft enough to know I looked like shit.

I could barely look at Coach then. The way I can barely look at myself now.

People still send flowers, food, surprise packages. They call and text. Teammates and friends in the league check in on me, reiterating how this isn't the end—there's a chance I'll come back even better. Some of them knock on the door but I don't answer. No matter what they say or do, it still feels like I lost the one thing that made me.

All I had was basketball.

Chapter 1
Brooks

"I hope your pillow is warm and clammy for the rest of time—that's how terrible this drink is." I try not to gag as the taste of peanut butter whiskey lingers on my tongue.

The drink, which I think is supposed to be the equivalent of a peanut butter and jelly sandwich, is borderline offensive. I chug my water, trying to rinse my mouth of the syrupy sweet aftertaste.

"It's not that bad!" Clay protests, taking a sip of the drink, swishing it around his mouth, and to my horror, swallowing it.

I push my empty water glass forward, giving him room to refill it. To be fair, it's the first dud of the bunch when it comes to what he's tried out on me tonight. Clay is a longtime friend and bartender at Oasis, an almost-too-hipster bar downtown. Usually, the drinks he puts in front of me are delicious.

Not tonight.

"Peanut butter whiskey is having a moment," he insists, talking with his hands to emphasize his point.

Moment or not, it's disgusting. I don't need peanut butter alcoholic beverages.

Thursday night energy, the weekend in everyone's grasp, has people filtering in for dinner and drinks. I'm wearing a baseball cap, sitting at the edge of the bar on a stool which barely looks like it's meant for a guest.

That's the point. I don't want to be seen.

Tonight, I want to be Brooks Pittman, friend of the bartender—not Brooks Pittman, NBA player recovering from an ACL injury.

Even on my good days, I'm plagued with thoughts of how many NBA players don't come back from an injury like this... not really. The worst part is how I've supposedly done this in seven months, basically record time when it comes to an ACL recovery—most athletes need nine to twelve. Technically, I *am* recovered. According to my team doctors and physical therapists, I should have full strength, mobility, and range of motion and explosiveness on the court. I hear them, but I'm not sure if I believe them.

"Don't be such a drama queen," Clay says. "I've made way worse drinks than this one." He dumps the rest of the cocktail in the bar sink.

I take another swig of water, still trying to lose the taste and reply, "Fucking doubtful."

A clicking sound pulls my mind from the terrible drink and over to a woman about to sit a few barstools away. Her hair falls on her shoulders like rays of sunlight, quite the contrast against a black leather jacket. With high cheekbones and pale pink lips, she's gorgeous, but it's her legs which make my eyes go wide. Her golden and smooth skin pull my eyes from where her dress ends all the way to her high-heeled shoes. There's quite a bit to take in; I'm guessing she's almost six foot tall in the heels and maybe 5'9" without. A forest green dress hugs her body, showing the curves of her hips and stopping mid-thigh, while the muscles flex as she gets situated.

She turns, catches my eyes, and offers a polite smile before running her hands through her hair, like she's situating the loose curls. For the next few minutes, she alternates between looking at the door and stretching her neck from side to side. Clearly, she's waiting for someone.

Clay lets her gets comfortable before approaching and asking what she'd like to drink.

"Can you surprise me? Nothing too sweet, but everything else is fair game," she answers while shaking out her hands.

He reaches for a glass and asks, "What are your thoughts on peanut butter?"

Before she has a chance to respond, I interrupt. "No. Just say no. Trust me."

Her face softens with amusement, and I can feel the blood rush to my face. I'm not one to interject myself into other people's business, but no one needs to be exposed to whatever cocktail Clay is trying to get on the menu.

"Nothing too sweet and no peanut butter." Her voice is light as Clay gives me a look that screams, "Stay out of it."

A few minutes later, mystery woman has a drink in front of her—something with bubbly wine, judging by the glass—and a man sits next to her. He's wearing a Tom Ford suit, one my stylist sent me as a pre-game outfit option, and suede loafers. I roll my eyes when I realize his hair is prepared to withstand wind gusts up to 45 MPH—the gel is excessive. I try not to stare, but out of the corner of my eye I see his face twist—not in a good way—when she stands to greet him. I don't know what this man's issue is. She's a fucking smoke show.

He orders a scotch on the rocks with a splash of water, and I can feel Clay about to stroke out. This particular bottle of scotch runs about $4000 each and is not meant to be tampered with. He pours the scotch over ice, his face grimacing as he adds the water, and says something like, "It's your funeral," when he serves it.

My phone buzzes in my pocket.

Jalen

I'm so excited for you to get back on the court

this is our year

i can feel it

I swallow past the lump in my throat as sweat dots my forehead. The season started a week ago, but I'll make my debut in two days. Whenever I imagine stepping back on the court or checking into a game, all I can think of is the night I tore my damn ACL. My nightmares are montages of the pop I heard and felt. The pop that threw me into a dark depressive hole—one I'm trying to stay far away from.

My stomach flips from the anxious walk down memory lane. I try to switch my train of thought, but it's no use. I think about the hours between now and when I'll be back on the court in my purple and gray Jaguar jersey. How can I be so terrified of the thing I love? The thing I was devastated to lose?

Honestly, it feels like the injury was due. Like things had been going too well for too long? My team was kicking ass every night, but more importantly, we were having a blast. The game almost felt too easy at times. Maybe this was how the universe puts me back in my place?

I thought the drinks would help with the anxiety, but Clay had other plans—horrible plans.

"What did you just say?" The mystery woman's voice grabs my attention. I turn to find her looking at the guy next to her, but she's tilting her head.

"I'm sure you're nice and all, but you don't look anything like your pictures. And don't you think the heels are a bit much? You're clearly tall enough without them." His voice is loud enough to try and get a reaction from those around them.

Holy shit.

She scoffs and looks down at her drink before pressing her lips together.

"If you want to talk dating profiles, I think you left your crippling small dick energy from your bio, *Randall.*" Her voice scrapes over each of the letters in his name—sarcastic and pointed.

Clay lets out a slow whistle and a high top near the bar lets out a laugh. It's not that we're eavesdropping, it's just impossible not to listen.

"Wouldn't you like to know about my dick?" the guy snaps, standing from the bar stool, clearly trying to get under her skin.

"I'm sure it's a real short story." She uses her hand for emphasis, with only an inch in between her thumb and forefinger. "Wouldn't even count towards my reading goal for the year." She turns back to face Clay and beams when she hears the laughs from around her.

I quietly laugh because that was fucking gold. She seems annoyed but pretty unbothered. The guy puts three crisp $100 bills on the bar, his hand smacking the surface loudly. "I'm surprised you even know how to read," he spits, and then he utters something that sounds very much like "dumb bitch."

I'm out of my stool and in front of him in just a few strides. His eyes go wide as he takes me in, and I can tell from his expression he knows who I am.

I tip my head towards the door. "Get the fuck out of here."

"You're Brooks—"

"Sick of your shit? Yes. Go." I keep my voice level, flat, and to the point.

The guy says nothing as he turns on his heel and heads for the door. Some of the guests clap and cheer as he exits the bar. I catch a look from Clay, one that asks, "What the fuck are you doing?" but I choose to leave him wondering.

"Lia, your table's ready," the hostess calls, not realizing the other half of the date just got laughed out of the place.

"Ugh, actually, I don't think I need the table anymore." Lia's voice is disappointed, low, and like a punch to the gut. She touches the elbow of her jacket, rubbing the spot over and over.

Naturally, I do something ridiculous. I lean my arms on the bar next to her and ask, "Want to have dinner with me?"

Chapter 2
Lia

DID I PINCH THE inside of my arm to make sure I was indeed awake when Brooks Pittman casually gave me a drink recommendation? Yes. Did I think I was seeing things when one of my favorite NBA players appeared to be sitting at the same bar I was? Also, yes.

Brooks Pittman waits for me to answer. Do I want to have dinner with him? Absolutely. One hundred percent yes. I press my lips together, giving myself a sliver of space to decide and not make a complete ass of myself.

"You want to have dinner with me?" I ask, trying to sound like I've said these words before.

"Yes. Come on." He reaches his hand for mine.

I blink slowly, afraid to move because this doesn't feel real. I'm worried I'll do something to jostle myself awake and into the real world, out of the dream I must be having.

I gently put my hand in his and he squeezes it, which pulls the breath right from my lungs. I look from our hands to Brooks, and he smirks. Maybe I've had so many horrific dating interactions I've built up enough karma to have something like this happen? Something amazing.

The hostess leads us to our table, and I try to act like this is normal and not a fantasy I've dreamt of. A jolt hits me when I think about texting Shelbie. She has no idea who Brooks Pittman is—she's not a big sports person—but she'll scream when she hears about my comeback to that dating app disaster before casually going on a date with an NBA player, in true best friend fashion.

Should I try to get a photo of us at dinner? Honestly, I don't know if anyone would believe me if I told them this story. The sound of a glass being set down brings me back to the table where it's only Brooks and me. When did the hostess even leave?

I try to keep the nervous laughter to a minimum when Brooks locks his eyes, the color of warm caramel, on mine.

"I'm Brooks," he waves, and I'm still waiting for him to say this is a joke. But then he continues. "Even though this isn't the date you had planned, I'm comfortable saying I'm probably better than whoever the fuck the guy was."

Smiling and laughing, now at Brooks Pittman instead of as my standard defense mechanism, I reply, "I know who you are." I take a long drink of water, thankful for the ice.

"You do?" His face is etched with doubt, evident by the raised brows and side-eye glance.

I need to choose what kind of woman I am in this situation: the one who simply knows he's a professional athlete, or Lia Stone: lifelong Jags fanatic and sports obsessed.

Slowly breathing in, I choose to be myself and go for it. "Brooks Pittman, shooting guard for the Jersey Jaguars. You played college basketball at The University of Alabama, where you basically bullied and willed your team to make the tournament your senior year." I sit back and get comfortable—each word has Brooks jaw falling a little bit more. "You took the Tide all the way to the Elite Eight and lost with a buzzer beater half-court shot. Heartbreaking. And when it comes to the Jags, you typically play the two, but I think the team has a better point differential when you're at the three."

"Oh. My. God," he says, shaking his head in disbelief.

I don't typically like to show off my knowledge of how the basketball positions translate to numbers for player sets and rotations, but I think my drink got a little ahead of me. My heart beats too quickly, rattling in my ears. I take another drink of water, considering the small speech I just delivered. "How was that?"

"Pretty good. I think I love you," he praises and laughs—like, really laughs. The sound, full and radiant, has me matching the energy with a grin.

Shrugging my shoulders, I reply, "Just a fan." I act like his love comment won't be running around in my brain for the rest of time. Like, remember when Brooks Pittman said he thought he loved me?

Brooks opens the menu and muses, "Well, I only know your name because of the hostess, so it looks like I have some catching up to do."

I give him an out. "You don't have to stay if you already had plans or whatever. It won't be the first time I was disappointed by a date."

"Believe me, this is a much better plan than having the bartender feed me disgusting drinks he's trying out for the winter menu. And you can't tell me you think I'm better at the three and then leave me hanging."

Brooks is wearing a navy shirt—it's kind of odd to see him in non-Jags colors, but athletes don't go around living in a team color palette. His muscles press against the fabric, ones I've seen on TV but never in person—never like this. His hair is dark under his backwards hat and he is the definition of a man crush Monday.

"Thoughts on the lobster wontons to start?"

Looks like we're doing this.

I'm on a date with Brooks Pittman.

Chapter 3
Brooks

THE RESTAURANT IS EMPTY besides the staff cleaning up for the night. I knew it was late, but had no idea it was *this* late. Our laughs fill in the cracks between the sounds of dishes being stacked, chairs being scooted in, and employees finishing their shift.

I can't stop staring at Lia. She's unreal. It's cliché to say she's unlike anyone I've ever met, but it's the fucking truth. We were talking about basketball defensive sets and specific offensive plays; she asked questions that some of my teammates probably haven't even wondered about. She's smart, confident, and it's such a turn on.

It's surprising how she made me want to share. It's not that I'm some sort of recluse, but there's an internal brick wall I've built, reinforced, and sometimes restructured. Lately, people who cross that brick wall are few... even for a night. I'm not saying I want to tell her my deepest darkest secrets or anything, but the brick feels more pliable than it usually does.

Her eyes are a fierce shade of green, like fresh pine trees in the spring sun. I'm not sure I've ever met someone with blonde hair and green eyes. For some reason, it fits perfectly with what I know about her so far.

And her laugh. She laughs like she means it, kind of loud but in the best way. She doesn't cover her mouth or try to stifle it. She gave me her number an hour into the date, and if that isn't a good sign, I don't know what is.

Lia recrosses her legs and one of her heels catches my eye. Black. Strappy.

"I can't believe someone tried making you feel bad for wearing those. You look so fucking good," I blurt out.

Her cheeks flush as she smiles through the compliment, and it warms my chest.

Pushing the button on the side of her phone, Lia's eyes go wide. "It's after midnight. I should get going. I'm teaching yoga tomorrow morning. Well, technically, *this* morning." She grabs her purse and holds it in her lap.

"Wait, I thought you work at a bakery?" I ask, making sure I have my details right.

Lia stands and answers, "Yes. I work a few odd jobs. Kind of in between a main source of income right now."

She puts her hand in mine as we walk out. The staff tell us goodnight, and if I wasn't a regular, I'd feel bad. The valet has already pulled my car to the front, considering it was the only one left.

"Do you need a ride?"

"My place is only a ten-minute walk. It's fine," she says, tipping her head toward her direction of home.

There's no way I'm letting her walk this late—not in those heels and not alone. I'm sure she can handle herself but driving her isn't a problem at all. Plus, I really fucking want to.

"I don't doubt that, but you don't *need* to walk. I have a perfectly open passenger seat for you." I open the car door, gesturing inside.

Lia's lips press together in a thin line. She looks from my car to the direction towards her place, then back to me. It's like she's looking for a reason to say no.

"Please get in the car, Lia," I press, holding the passenger door open.

"If you're sure." She slides into the passenger seat, and I close the door.

The drive is only a few minutes, but Lia launches into a conversation about a rival NBA team. She's trying to get me to dish on players—are they as bad as she thinks? I'm belly laughing at her honesty and border-line ruthlessness. I love it. Lia is a perfect surprise for tonight. I don't think she knows this, but she was the distraction I desperately needed.

"I'm over here," Lia explains and points to an apartment building ahead.

I pull over and get out of the car.

"Are you really going to walk me to my door?" Her cheeks are pink and scrunched with a grin.

I put a hand to my chest. "Absolutely. Proper date etiquette is important to me."

We walk the short distance from the street to her apartment building and I follow her all the way to her door. There's no lobby or central building; instead, everyone has a door facing the outside—sort of like a multi-floor motel. When we hear people screaming, some from inside their own apartment and some from the mostly open hallway, Lia doesn't turn to me or say anything, almost like this is the norm. Paint peels from the walls and garbage bags sit outside some tenant's doors.

This place is a bit rough around the edges—not that I'm judging—and I'm thankful she let me walk her back. She stops in front of a door and I'm relieved that no one is outside, hanging around, at any of the apartments near hers. Maybe she has good neighbors? I can only hope.

"Well, this was unexpected and sort of amazing," Lia admits, her eyes almost sparkling under less-than-stellar lighting. I've never known anyone who looks this good under fluorescents.

I take a small step forward. "Yes. Here's to Randall being a complete dick bag." She laughs at the jab, and it warms me from the inside out. "I feel like I owe him a thank you card or something."

Lia rolls her eyes. "That man deserves nothing. Thanks for turning my night around." She leans in closer, her lips perfectly pink, and all I can think about is how badly I want to kiss her.

I can't remember the last time I had a date like this. Easy. Fun. Where I'm sad to see it end. One where they aren't asking me for basketball tickets halfway through or if I can introduce them to someone I was recently photographed with. It seems like my presence is enough and she doesn't need anything else from me.

Fuck it. I'm going for it.

Slowly I close the space between us, giving Lia time to back up if she wants to. Placing two fingers under her chin, I tip her face to mine and put my lips to hers. Time drags, but the second our lips touch, it's like a spark of energy hits my bloodstream. Any ounce of tiredness is immediately replaced with the possibility of more time with her.

My heart beats quick and light—I can hear it in my ears. I bet she could feel it if her hands were on my chest. The thought of her touching me that way has me needing more.

Her tongue sweeps along the seam of my lips and when I open, Lia lets out a sound that could bring me to my knees. It's like a half moan mixed with a laugh—I want to bottle it and keep it forever.

My hands move to her hair as I walk us back until she's flush against her apartment door. She takes her hands and grabs the front of my shirt, pulling me closer to her. I let my hands run down her side, ending on her lower back, at the top of her ass.

"Your hands. God. They feel too good." Lia breaks the kiss as she leans closer to me, and I let them fall an inch or two farther. Her voice is breathy, shallow, and quiet which makes my dick strain against my pants.

I have a handful of her ass as I kiss down her neck. There's more for me to grab than I can hold onto and it's ridiculously hot.

Fuck.

She hitches one of her legs and I grab her thigh, digging my fingers into the skin. Her hips push forward, her back arching from the door, and I press my mouth to the top of her breasts. I pepper them with kisses before letting my tongue drag across. Tasting her.

A door slamming above us brings me back to the fact that we're in public. We pull away and Lia looks at me, her fingers touching her swollen lips.

"Do you want to come in?" Lia reaches in her bag for her keys.

Yes. A resounding yes. But as I'm about to answer, there's a pull at the pit of my stomach. It's the restraint I wish I didn't have.

"I do, but... fuck. I can't believe I'm about to say this." I pull at my neck and catch her eyes with mine. "I haven't felt like this in a long time. I kind of don't want to ruin it. Like, I want to take you out—for real."

Lia steps in, grabs a handful of my shirt, and places a soft kiss on my mouth. "Then take me out, for real. You have my number," she insists while putting the key in the lock and opening the door.

"You got it," I reply as she steps in and stands in the still-open door. I kiss her one last time and pull away.

"Good luck on Saturday. You're going to be great," Lia murmurs while closing the door.

For a moment, I awkwardly stand in front of her apartment. She knows I'm going to play for the first time in a long time and didn't bring it up until the very end. It could've easily become the focus of our night, but it didn't.

Fuck. It makes me like her even more.

Chapter 4
Lia

My phone wakes me from a mid-day nap—a necessity, considering I've recently been bartending until two in the morning and teaching yoga classes four hours later. Last night was my first night off in weeks.

Part of me hopes there will be a text from Brooks waiting for me—my favorite athlete turned man of my dreams with a single impromptu date. My stomach flips when I think about how I offered my phone number—right in the middle of dinner. Will he use it? I have no idea. Part of me feels last night was a one-time thing, but a small piece is holding out that it's more.

The screen shows an incoming call from a number I don't know, not my alarm. I wipe the drool from my mouth and answer.

"I'm looking for Lia Stone," the voice on the other line says.

"This is her." I stifle a yawn and stretch while holding the phone.

"My name is Megan, and I oversee the Jersey Jaguars' media team. This is a bit unconventional, but you interviewed for a position a few months back, correct?"

How could I forget? It was practically my dream job—one which focused on social media and connecting fans to the players—and even though I thought I nailed it, they offered the position to someone else. Oof. I hated that day.

"Yes, that's right." I stand and my muscles pull with tightness from my awkward sleeping position on the couch.

"I'm hoping you're still interested in the position. The original candidate didn't work out. You were our second pick, only by a single vote. You were *my* first pick for the position."

No way.

"Is this a joke?"

Megan laughs on the other line. "No, I'm completely serious. Like I said, I know this isn't typical."

It takes everything in me not to scream yes or say *I'd* pay to work for *them*—that's how bad I want this opportunity. Plus, there's the whole mask of professionalism one is expected to wear.

"The catch is, we need you to start as soon as possible, like tomorrow. Saturday."

"Tomorrow? Wow."

"If you can swing it, we're happy to include a signing bonus for the quick pivot."

I take a slow breath, acting like I'm mulling it over, but I knew I was going to say yes as soon as the question was asked. I'd even do it without the signing bonus, but that's a significant perk. My position was eliminated at my previous job five months ago, but what they meant was they were going to keep hiring interns every six months and not pay anyone what they're worth for the work. The hours were crippling, and the pay was abysmal, but it was consistent and helped me stay afloat.

"Can you send a formal offer to review, including the signing bonus?" I asked as casually as possible.

"Absolutely. Clicking send now. Call if you have questions, but we'd love an answer as soon as possible."

After ending the call, I open my laptop, refresh my email inbox, and watch as the offer comes in. I click the attachment, my fingers trembling above the track pad as I read through the offer I know I'm going to agree to.

My mouth drops when I get to the bonus—it's not life-changing money, but it will give me some breathing room. Maybe I won't have to fit in a consistent yoga morning schedule, or take random shifts at the coffee shop or bakery? I sigh out a breath, and it's as if some of the stress goes with it.

In this moment, I wish I could call my parents. Tell them the good news. But it's impossible—I've been missing them for over a decade. The way my mom would rub my back after school, listening to me tell her everything that happened. The way my dad would make breakfast for us on the weekends.

In the art of trying to play it cool, I call the one person who will be as excited as I am.

"An unsolicited phone call? Who even are you?" Wes, my younger brother, jokes as the sound of squeaking shoes on the basketball court fills the background. "I thought you were a millennial."

I laugh because, even though he's a senior in high school, he gets me—the last thing I ever want to give or receive is a phone call. This news is a perfect example of when it's warranted.

"Hush. I know, but I couldn't text you this. Guess what?!" I prompt him. From here, I can envision him holding a basketball on a hip while pressing the phone to his face with the opposite shoulder.

"You've been awake for fifty hours straight and are starting to hallucinate?" Sarcasm drips from Wes' words.

I gasp like he's guessed correctly, and then say, "Nope. And that happened *one time*. Let it go."

"I'm about to start practice, so you have thirty seconds to cut to the chase or we'll have to pick this up later. Your choice." I hear him dribble a ball.

"I got the job!"

"Which one? It's hard to keep them straight."

"With the Jags. Apparently, their original hire didn't work out, and I was next in line. I'm about to accept the offer, but I wanted to tell you first."

"That's amazing! Like actually legit." I hear Wes tell my news to some of his teammates who must be standing around him, and a band of warmth spreads through my chest. "I want to hear all about it, but Coach is going to kill me if he sees I'm on my phone."

"I'll see you Sunday morning," I say and I'm sliding back into the couch, grabbing my laptop.

My phone buzzes again.

Shelbie

> okay if you don't dish on your date with what's his face

> i'm keeping your tip money from the other night

> not really but come on

Me

> are you working tonight? i'll come in

yes

> i'll wear my best don't-even-think-of-sitting-there face if someone tries taking the edge bar stool

What about Brooks? The thought nags, buried under pure joy and elation. It's not something I can even get into right now—plus, he hasn't reached out. There's no way I can even consider that as part of my decision for this job. Even if he's charming, gorgeous, and a complete gentleman, I learned a long time ago you have to look out for yourself because no one else will.

I set my phone on the side table, taking a deep breath. Closing my eyes, I feel the air stretch my rib cage and sigh it out. The way my lips pull up is like it's coming straight from my heart. This is something I've wanted, down to my bones, and I'm not the kind of girl who has gotten a lot of what she wants.

Replying to the offer letter, I formally accept. When I'm confident the email has sent, I close my laptop and jump from the couch. I dance around my tiny studio apartment to a song playing on my phone.

This is a win I've needed.

For a long time.

Chapter 5
Brooks

I MIGHT THROW UP on the court. We're shooting around before tip-off and my stomach feels like it's made of steel knots—there's no give. I miss the easiness that surrounded my team before I went down with the injury.

I haven't played in a professional game in two hundred twenty-five days and it's like I'm sweating doubt at this point of our pre-game routine. We're in a shooting line, passing to a three-point shooter then handling the ball to go to the basket for a layup. This is usually my favorite part, considering it's the most familiar. Every basketball player runs this warmup—it's one of the first you learn—and for a moment it takes me back to the sixth grade court, my high school team, and then to The University of Alabama's Coleman Coliseum.

I should be able to do this with my eyes closed. Instead, I find myself holding my breath and awkwardly picking up my knees as if I'm trying to stretch. The tape under my warmup joggers feels odd, like everyone can see remnants of the injury I didn't know if I'd come back from.

When some players tear their ACL, they come back with a brace. I tried that but couldn't get the hang of it. Plus, it seemed to draw attention to the thing I want everyone to put in the back of their minds, in hopes it'd give me the chance to do the same.

My leg is taped, something much easier to get used to—also easier to remove in case it's too much. This is the same tape pattern and brand, done by the same trainer, that I've been using for weeks. But tonight, it itches and keeps picking at my brain.

"I know what you're doing," Jalen says while standing behind me in the layup line. Luckily, a ball hits my fingers and like muscle memory, my body moves towards the basket.

His eyes catch mine after and he offers a knowing smile. I should be thankful I have such a good friend on the team, but right now I wish it were different. Jalen and I got drafted the same year, me in the first round and him in the second, but it felt like we'd been playing together since the days of community center gyms and jerseys hanging past our kid knees. He's the type of point guard who can feel out everyone on the court. I love playing with him.

He stands next to me. "Take a breath. You're going to be fine. If it doesn't feel right, tell Coach and he'll take you out."

I listen to him, sucking in air but the metal feeling from my stomach is taking up too much room. Jalen is one of the people who knows me like this—he can catch on to what's happening without me saying a word.

"No one expects you to play your typical minutes. Ease into it." He hands me a ball from the rack, as all the players have their own and take turns making whatever shots they want.

"I hear you."

"I know you *hear* me, but do you *believe* me?"

This smart mouth asshole. He knows me too well.

"I'm trying to," I answer honestly.

He shoots a three from the corner, his favorite spot, and it goes in without touching anything besides the ropes of the net. I look at him and he's holding his shooting motion, eyes locked on mine, showing off.

I laugh and Jalen grins, getting the reaction he was hoping for.

He dribbles the ball and stands next to me as I shoot a mid-range jumper. "Do we need a safe word for when you've had enough, or are you good?"

Closing my eyes, I shake my head, trying not to laugh again. "No safe word necessary. I've got this."

I run back and forth near half court, dribbling the ball, and the arena is buzzing. With only a few minutes until game time, seats are filling as the energy builds, spreading from one fan to the next.

Someone is shown on the Jumbotron, and the crowd goes wild.

Zack Andersen and his fiancé, Emilie. Or my half-brother and future sister-in-law. Or maybe it's my half-sister-in-law? Is that a thing?

He catches me watching the Jumbotron and I look to the suite. Zack jumps up and down and everyone around him follows suit, including my mom and half-sister Riley. I've met people with endless energy, but Zack is on another level. He's like a golden retriever that never loses their puppy energy.

My heart warms at the sentiment. I only learned about Zack and Riley a little more than a year ago. I had no idea what life would be like after uncovering this type of emotional bomb, but it's been fairly positive. The universe seemed to know I'd need more support for the injury because they came at the perfect time.

When it works, I go to family dinner. Sometimes my mom even joins. I'll never forget the way my life seemed to snap together the first time I watched Mack, my dad's wife, and my mom cook together. There are a lot of ways this could've gone and I'm fucking thankful for all the amazing things this has brought me and how everyone has handled it.

I wave at the suite, and it makes Zack jump more, if that's even possible. The crowd gets louder when they see our interaction, and even more so when Zack indicates he wants the crowd to make more noise.

All I know is I feel a lightness, my lips pulling up, like I might be able to do this. Like I'm finally starting to believe my teammates and doctors.

The main lights dim with only a few minutes until tip-off. I pass the ball to a ball boy and jog to the bench, sitting down next to Jalen. The nausea has lessened but is still residing in my body.

He reaches his arm around my shoulder, squeezes for a quick second, and says, "I still can't believe you're related to Zack Andersen. You lucky bastard." He laughs, jostling my shoulders. "Wait, did you give that girl tickets for tonight? Mystery date girl? The one woman you've told me about since you finally shook Rebecca loose."

I look at my shoes, pretending to tighten the already-perfect laces. "Lia? No. I haven't texted her yet. Need to get through this game without puking on the court in front of nineteen thousand people before I invite her to one of these."

I choose to sidestep the Rebecca comment. If you wanted to look at a dysfunctional relationship, that would be a solid example. I can't tell you why I kept going back after she cheated. Or why I agreed to an open relationship when it was the last thing I wanted. *Or* how I acted like I'd participate by dating or sleeping with other women. It's been about a year since we broke up for good and almost as long since I've heard from her. The two of them—Jalen and Rebecca—hated each other and sometimes it felt like I was a referee.

"That's fair, but don't let her meet some other loser on a dating app before you lock down another date. It's tough out there."

I cackle. "How in the hell would you know that? Mister 'I married my high school sweetheart the month after graduation.'"

I might give him shit but anyone with even mediocre eyesight can realize Jalen and Stephanie, his wife, are truly the type of people meant to be. It's nauseating how happy they are.

"Maybe mystery girl can make you as happy as Steph makes me?" he asks, nudging my shoulder.

Maybe. I'd be lying if I said I hadn't dished about the entire date to Jalen. I knew I was doing the opposite of playing it cool, but I kind of had to when the press took some photos of me out with Lia. The best photo is one someone took, and probably sold, of me standing in the restaurant and telling her fuck of a date to leave. I've only been known as one of the golden boys of the NBA, so I enjoyed people seeing me in a different way.

"We'll come back to your dating life after we get the win. Let's kick some California ass tonight, huh?"

I take a deep breath and smirk. "Let's do it."

Jalen and I pop up, doing our handshake before we take our places for the anthem.

Chapter 6
Lia

I PINCH MYSELF TO make sure I'm indeed awake. The pain is a welcome reminder I'm standing in the broadcast booth as the Jersey Jags are about to tip off.

"I know this is kind of bonkers, getting a rundown of the functions and places in the arena on your first night, especially during a game," Megan chuckles, smiling in a way that I know she means it.

I'm familiar with this set up because I'm basically standing on the edge of a dream. I went to college for journalism and broadcasting, trying to find a way to get my hands on any and every opportunity to cover sports. This booth is the endgame, and I know this media team job is the first step in that direction.

"I know you've got some experience with this, so no need to tell you much more than this is where it is. You're welcome to hang in the back during games you're not working, as long as it's not too crowded."

I do my best to hide my Pennywise-like grin, brimming with excitement that starts at my core and reaches my bones. The idea of being able to attend these games for free? I've died and went to heaven. Being allowed in the booth? I'm going to pass out.

When Megan looks to me, she says, "Actually, there isn't anything that's off limits. Besides the training room when there's a new injury, and the locker room before we get the 'all clear.'"

Maybe the terrible date with Randall moved my karma in the right direction. Honestly, it's the least he, or the universe, could do after that disaster.

Megan moves to the window, taking in the entire court and arena. Something happens and the feel of the crowd cheering starts at my feet, the ground almost rumbling, and travels up my body.

We look at the Jumbotron and see Brooks. My stomach bottoms out and I do what I can to not let the look he's wearing push me back on my heels. Well, technically my sneakers. I'm wearing a pair of newly thrifted black wide-leg pants paired with a lilac chiffon button-up. I wouldn't say it's Jaguar colors, but this is what you get when you have short notice and no budget to find business casual attire. I'm wearing my trusty black and white Nike Dunks, the pair I found at a consignment store a few months ago.

The Jumbotron cuts from Brooks to one of the suites and back again.

"Oh, I forgot Zack Andersen was coming tonight. We'll have to pop in and get some photos of them tonight." Megan looks at me, like she needs me to remember, and I nod.

Zack Andersen—long snapper for the Upstate Cosmos—is Brooks' half-brother. The story broke probably six months ago. Part of me almost asked about it when we were on our date, but it felt too personal.

"The plan is for you to watch the first half of the game tonight—consider it part of your signing bonus—then I'll come get you for the second half and post-game coverage," Megan explains while turning and leading us out of the booth. "I'll show you to the staff hospitality suite and let you get settled."

I don't say anything because I sort of can't believe this is happening.

"You good?" she asks.

"Ugh, erm.. yes! Totally good. Just taking it in."

A smile spreads on Megan's bold and red lips, the kind that feels genuine, and she stops for a moment. "I knew you were a fan, but I love that you're a *fan*. I have a feeling we're going to have a blast working together."

She shows me to the suite and tells me to take whatever seat I'd like. There's food, drinks, and a spectacular view of the arena.

I sink into one of the deep leather theater seats and try to relax my body. I didn't know what to expect from a game day orientation, but this quite literally feels like a dream come true. Cracking open a Dr. Pepper, my go-to beverage, I lean back and let the bubbles hit my tongue.

I'm thankful no one is around to watch when I kick my feet like a toddler as they announce the starting line ups.

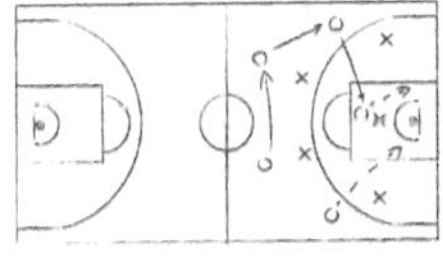

The energy is electric, enough to almost be recharging me. I can't remember a time when I felt more awake or excited to be at work. I follow Megan around as she introduces me to some of the entertainment staff who I'll work with from time to time, and everyone seems kind and respectful. She has this air of confidence that follows her throughout the arena, no matter who she's talking to. Staff, and team members, address her by name. It's obvious they respect her and it's a breath of fresh air.

Five years ago, most professional sports teams were ahead of the curve if they had thirty percent of women on their staff. The trend is heading in the right direction but there's still a ton of work to do. It's not just about being let in the room, but looking to women for contributions, making impactful decisions, and leading key projects.

It's wild that I've watched the first woman call an NBA Finals game in my lifetime. Doris Burke, also the first female analyst to work in the booth, is out here blazing a trail—one I'm hoping has enough room for me.

I walk behind Megan as we head to the court, pushing down the wave of emotion about to make me cry. One, it's still not hitting me that I'm getting paid to step on a place I damn-near view as sacred. Two, watching Megan walk in like she's meant to be here, she's earned her place in this organization, has me wanting to fist pump.

We're standing in the corner but are on the floor—a place I've dreamt of getting tickets for, but this is as close as I've ever come. It's the fourth quarter and there's only a minute left. The Jags are down by one and there's not a single fan who is sitting in their seat.

"Jalen, pick up the pace!" Megan screams through her hands as the point guard dribbles the ball up the floor.

She looks at me, only for a second, and offers a smirk—one that says "you're not the only fan here." Jalen passes the ball and it's like watching a choreographed dance where each person is hitting their marks. Each player on the court touches the ball as they try to set the best play.

Brooks gets the ball near the free throw line and jukes his defender, throwing him off and providing enough space to take it right to the basket. He could've shot a layup but instead he dunks it, and it's like the arena has grown legs and is about to launch us into space.

I clap like I would if I were watching the game at home, leaving out the list of expletives I'd use—I'm not sure of the vibe quite yet.

Jags lead by one and the team has the ball, bringing it up the court toward us. This is one of the best teams in the NBA and if the Jags can pull off this win, it'd be a great sign for the season.

The Knights try to get the ball in the paint, but the Jags keep double teaming, and the center can't get a shot off. There's about ten seconds left in the game and the shot clock is about to expire. The center heaves a desperation pass to a guard in the corner, ready to shoot a three, but Brooks steps out of his defensive position and is in the perfect place to steal the ball.

When the ball hits Brooks in the hands, it somehow gets louder than the previous play. There's only eight seconds left—a two-point basket basically seals the game or gives the opposing team a chance to send it to overtime, while a Jags three pointer would mean a win.

Instead of going into the paint and hitting the easy layup, which is enough insurance to add a win to the record, he stops at the three-point line and shoots. The arena holds a collective breath, fans from both sides, and I swear I can hear the ball swish through the net.

Jags are now up by four. All they have to do is play the 'don't foul' game and Brooks' comeback will end in a win.

Jalen runs over and hits Brooks in the chest as the rest of the Jags players crowd around them. The coaching staff and bench are pure chaos in the best way, like the game is over even though there are technically four seconds left. The referees get everyone back in position, eager to get the rest of the game played and end the celebration early.

The Knights are out of timeouts when they try to inbound the ball, and they're unsuccessful as Jalen steals it and dribbles out the end of the game. Everyone's watching him, but the person I'm watching is Brooks.

He's near the corner of the court, where they'll run into the tunnel in a few minutes. His hands are resting on top of his head and he takes shallow breaths—I can see his chest moving from here. When he rests his hands on his knees, he wipes his face. Drops of sweat or tears? No one will know.

I swallow past the lump in my throat and look up, stopping my own tears.

Brooks Pittman really is something.

Chapter 7
Brooks

"GET THE HELL OVER here and grab your game ball, Brooks!" Coach yells and the locker room goes wild. It has the vibe of a playoff game and not a regular season win. I know in my heart and soul that I'm lucky to play for a team like this; one that supported me throughout my entire recovery and let me decide when I was ready to return to the court.

I stand and someone starts spraying champagne—that has Jalen written all over it—and Coach yells, "Jesus Christ! Careful with those corks," with his hands up before continuing. "This guy has busted his ass to get back to the court for this team, these fans, and this franchise. The Jersey Jags are out for blood this year, and with Brooks back, we might be able to pull it off!"

The sound is deafening in the best way. My teammates jump around me; you could almost reach out and grab the joy filling this room. I hold onto the ball tighter than necessary, already thinking about how this will go somewhere special in my house—the one I just bought. A suggestion from my therapist to move on from the place where my depression was the worst, the recovery the most difficult, was something I couldn't say yes to quick enough.

I look down at my knee, the tape the same as it was when I had it done before the game. I'm so damn thankful for being able to play almost my typical game minute total. Some teams wouldn't rely on an athlete playing in his first game back when it's down to the wire, but I love that my coaches and teammates trusted me to do what I'm built to.

Put us in the best position to win.

Tonight is one of those nights I'll remember for a long time.

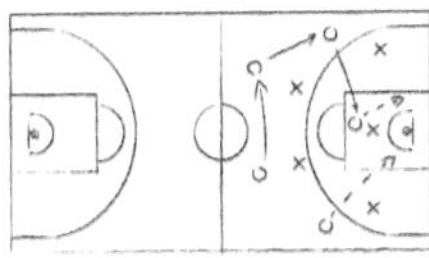

I'm showered and my muscles are tired in the way I welcome after a close game. I know the Jags' media team has come in when I hear Megan congratulating the guys. This means press conferences and interviews are about to start.

My locker is tidy and clean, like always, with the game ball sitting at the bottom until I take it home tonight. I'm making sure everything is in order when I hear Megan behind me.

"Brooks! Couldn't envision a better comeback game." She claps me on the back and a smile pulls hard at the corner of my lips. Megan has been here for the last three years, and I respect how she handles social media for the team. We're never forced to do much of anything, which has us volunteering for more projects she has up her sleeve. She's a blast to work with and knows her shit when it comes to basketball.

I turn to face her but see Lia instead. Well, Lia and Megan together. *What the hell?*

"Brooks, I'd like you to meet Lia Stone. She's our newest hire and will be taking the lead on the project we talked about."

I do my best to keep my expression level as my brain tries to compute what this means. Lia's brows furrow and she looks to Megan for clarification.

"A significant focus this season will be Brooks' return to the game after a severe ACL injury," she explains to Lia. "There's a ton of science and technology which has made the recovery shorter than most and we're hopeful Brooks will show us that in a real-life example… like he did tonight." Megan's voice radiates enthusiasm. "I'm sure a basketball fan like yourself is dying for the chance to spend some time with the one and only Brooks Pittman." A smirk plays on her lips as she looks between the two of us.

"I bet she is." The words fall out of my mouth, quiet, and the right side of my lips tug in a devilish smirk—one I didn't plan for.

Megan leans in, putting her ear closer to me. "What was that?"

I reach out a hand to Lia. "Nothing, just welcoming Lia to the team." She puts her hands in mine and an electric current zaps from my palm and then throughout my entire body.

Lia's cheeks flush pink and the way she looks at me turns my mouth dry.

"I'm looking forward to working together," she offers, enunciating every letter of the word 'working' with a small lean forward. She smiles and gives me a barely-there head shake and I feel like she's thinking the same thing.

Fuck. I think I'm in trouble.

Someone calls for Megan and she gives them the one-minute gesture before looking at the two of us. "You're going to be spending lots of time together over the next few months. Make sure to get to know each other. Also, Brooks, if Zack wouldn't mind, we'd love a photo of you guys."

"You know Zack loves a photo opp," I reply while she's already on her way to someone else.

It's just Lia and I by my locker. I do a quick scan of the room to see if there's anyone I could introduce her to, but the entire team is otherwise occupied with coaching staff and the press is starting to pop in.

"Since when do you work for the Jags?" I ask, my words quick and quieter than I typically am.

"Since today. It happened fast." She grins, and her emerald eyes are fucking mesmerizing. I would probably fall into a forest if I stared long enough.

"You didn't mention it..." My voice trails.

Lia smiles, looking around the locker room before her eyes fall to mine. "No, I didn't bring up the job I lost out on months ago."

Wow. Talk about a coincidence or power of the universe or whatever the hell is playing out here. Whoever is pulling the strings is doing one hell of a job.

She tilts her head and says, "You were great today. How'd it feel?" She glances down at my knee.

"Fucking terrifying." I laugh it off. "But I feel good. Hell of a win." I run my hands through my hair, pushing it away from my forehead. "And you don't have to suck up... we're, like, colleagues now."

Lia gives me a knowing glance.

I lean in closer, just enough that I can say something quietly, only for the two of us. "When can I take you out again?"

She laughs and watches me as she rubs her fingers together. "I'm not sure that's such a good idea now that we're colleagues." She bumps my shoulder with hers.

"You're right. It's not good." I pause, taking in all of her. "It's a great idea." I clap my hands together.

"I'd imagine it's against the rules, and here's what I know about you... you're not one to break them." She lifts an eyebrow, and a side-eye stare lands on me.

"What you know about me, huh? Can't wait for you to learn even more." My phone buzzes in my pocket—Zack. Probably looking for me. "Hey, I've got to get out there, but I'm sure I'll be seeing you around."

Lia thinks she has me all figured out.

It'd be a damn shame if she was wrong.

Chapter 8
Lia

My studio apartment feels bigger than it did before I left. Blush pink walls are illuminated by twinkly lights placed along, and across, the ceiling for ultimate effect. The warmth of home hits me, widening the grin already plastered on my face. My body should be sore, and my feet should ache considering I walked miles at the game tonight, but there's not an ounce of pain to be found.

This apartment has been home for three years and it's come a long way. It was the only place within my sad excuse of a price range, and even then, I've needed a few rent extensions. It was also the only unit available in the building and they were embarrassed to show it to me. I used that to my advantage and got them to agree to let me do any cosmetic changes I wanted, without needing approval.

It's basically a long rectangle with tall ceilings and no doors, besides one to the small full bathroom. The single saving grace of the dilapidated apartment was they'd recently renovated the bathroom due to a water leak that ruined the floors and part of the wall. It's basic—a shower and tub combo, small cabinet over the toilet and storage space under the sink.

Over the last three years, I've completed projects whenever I could find the materials on sale or had worked enough odd jobs to have extra cash. My landlord is a saint; he's never raised my rent, and I've also never had to call him for anything.

The first thing was priming and painting the entire place—isn't it amazing what a fresh coat of paint can do? Since then, I've redone the trim, taken down moldy cabinets and replaced them with open concept shelving, and built out my dream of a bedroom.

I needed to get creative when it came to my bedroom. A regular from my bartending gig helped me assemble and anchor floor-to-ceiling bookshelves after I beat him in a game of pool—his manual labor was the prize. Using the back corner of the studio, we built one long wall of bookshelves, but used the existing structure to box it in. We used a few smaller shelves to create the corner and a makeshift entrance—a curtain used to fill the space between the shelf and the wall. It feels like a separate room compared to the living space. It turned out better than I could've imagined, which means he may or may not been given a discount on his draft beers as a bonus.

I pull the curtain back and fall into bed—the thick duvet like a cloud and the mattress perfectly comfortable. I once worked part time at a mattress outlet for the discount, otherwise I'd never have been able to afford a bed like this. I've always found a way to make things work, including odd jobs like that. I'm the queen of figuring out how to either get a necessary discount or do it myself.

Refusing to fall asleep without washing my face, I peel myself from bed. Once my skin care is complete and matching pajamas are on, I walk to the kitchen, grabbing a mug and a tea bag. Wisps of chamomile and mint hit my nose as I dip the bag in and out of the perfectly temped water. I started drinking tea when I was a teenager because it was cheap and everywhere you go has hot water. During my college years, I'd made friends with a gas station attendant who'd always let me fill my thermos with hot water for free.

I blow on the tea, the steam soothing as it hits my face. I take a cautious sip, careful not to burn my mouth, and walk back to my bed. I set the tea on the bedside table while I get under the blankets—my favorite routine of the day. The down comforter is perfectly heavy on my body.

As I reach for my phone, it buzzes with a notification.

Unknown

> i've been wanting to go here

> think it'd be perfect for a second date

> this is Brooks btw

My stomach flips as my jaw falls open. The morning after our date, or whatever the hell that was, I convinced myself Brooks was simply being nice, stepping in so someone who got ready for a night out wasn't left sitting alone at the bar. Even after our kiss, the one which stole and captivated my breath as it lit a fire in my belly, I told myself it wasn't real. Then I got the Jags job offer, which sort of means dating him—even if he was interested—is off the table.

Me

> if this is Brooks, tell me something only he'd know

> sometimes you think I'm better when I play the three

I press my lips together, running from the smile threatening to take over my entire face. The softness of my overnight lip mask makes it impossible not to move them side to side.

> okay, I believe you

> what do you think about the dinner spot?

Engaging with the fantasy, I open the link to a place I've never heard of. To be fair, I'm not one to go out much, due to lack of disposable income. The only reason I was at Oasis was because LDR, my acronym for Little Dick Randall, suggested it. I had to break into my bonus envelope, tip money from the bar set aside for something fun or tragic, to pay for myself in case he didn't offer.

The dinner spot Brooks sent has my mouth watering. It offers twists on classic dishes like meatloaf, grilled cheese sandwiches, and chicken pot pie. I let myself fall down the rabbit hole, the one where I go out with Brooks. For only a few seconds, I think of his lips on mine, and then he's kissing the soft spot behind my ear as his hands squeeze the side of my hip. A car honk from outside the window startles me, bringing me back to the moment.

you don't really want to date me

plus it's probably frowned upon by my new employer

oh, i definitely want to date you

thought the first date kind of gave that vibe

also, the only policy has to do with interns

which you are not

Actually, I haven't completed a full orientation with the Jags yet. Brooks could be right. But is it professional? Will they still take me seriously? Is it a good idea? I bite my lip and put my head back on the pillows, staring at the ceiling while trying to sort these feelings.

A bubble of rage starts small before filling my chest. Would these be the same things I'd worry about if I was a man? Would a man be taken less seriously in their job based on who they were dating? In most cases, like we know already, the answer is no. Bullshit or not, it's the world we live in, or the world I live in at least. Maybe men get a little more leeway than women but how much am I willing to risk?

Wow, talk about getting ahead of myself.

> you're actually asking me out?

> yes. one hundred percent.

> this time, without the loser you were supposed to be out with

My heart races in my chest like it has somewhere to be. My night with Brooks was unexpectedly fun. Gone were the typical first date nerves, replaced with the suggestion of being comfortable. The idea of him wanting me, like that, has me blushing alone in my studio apartment.

> we'll see

> i can work with that

> because it's not a no

I save Brooks' number in my phone, and when I see our updated text thread with his name associated with it, I let out a small scream and kick my feet.

Chapter 9
Brooks

"Did you see the new media hire? You ever meet someone with blonde hair and green eyes?" Jalen asks.

It's Monday morning and the locker room is empty besides the two of us. We're an hour early since I had the itch to get extra shots up today before practice. One of Jalen's best qualities is how he's always down for extra work.

I shoot him a look while I tighten the laces on my shoes.

"What? She's pretty, that's all I'm saying." He lifts his hands like he's surrendering. "You know I'm taken." He wiggles his left hand, a silicone wedding band on his ring finger.

My shoes are the only thing I can focus on. Otherwise, I'm going to spill the details to Jalen. I have no idea if there's anything to keep secret at this point, but I don't know if I want to take the chance.

We're walking to the court when Megan passes us. "Brooks!" she calls. "Before I forget, can you pop by my office after practice? I want to get our schedules aligned for the project we've been planning."

"You've got it."

"Plus, we can get Lia up to speed."

"Lia?" Jalen asks.

"Yes, she was with me Saturday. The new media hire. Did you have too much fun last night?" She steps in, looking at his eyes for signs of a hangover—something she won't find.

"No, I remember her," he answers, his brain trying to connect the dots.

Megan nods in agreement and says, "She's smart, loves basketball, and seems like she can hold her own. I think it will be perfect."

So do I, but for many different reasons—ones I don't share aloud right now.

Megan's phone rings and she pulls it from her pocket while already walking past us. "We can chat more later." Her phone is to her ear before I have a chance to respond.

"Why does your face look like that?" Jalen presses, ducking his head and focusing on me. "Lia. Why do I know that name?"

"It doesn't look like anything." I try to keep us moving but Jalen isn't having it. He puts a hand on my chest to stop me. Trying to shrug him off, I say, "You probably know a lot of names."

"You, my guy, are the worst liar," he laughs. "Your face is red, and your forehead looks all clammy." He feels my forehead with the back of his hand, then emphasizes shaking off the sweat when he pulls it away. His eyes light up and he snaps his finger. "Lia is the name of your mystery girl!"

I suck in as much air as my lungs will allow, resting my hands on my hips. My neck tenses as I look at the ceiling, trying to get as much time as possible before I decide what to tell him. Finally, I look at Jalen and I know he's right: I'm a bad liar.

"Yes. Mystery girl is the new hire." The words are barely out of my mouth before Jalen's hand covers his mouth as his brows scrunch and eyes go wide. "Her first day was yesterday," I continue. "Apparently, whoever they hired first didn't work out and they moved on quickly. I didn't even meet the other hire."

"Wait, so Lia's working on the whole 'Brooks return to the game project?'"

I shrug my shoulders. "Apparently? Guess I'll learn more after practice."

"You lucky bastard," Jalen jokes. "Didn't you say she was incredible? I'm not getting why you look like someone stole your hard-earned bag of Halloween candy..."

"I asked her out and she said *maybe*. The job makes this complicated. We're coworkers."

He nods in understanding and luckily starts walking so we can get to the court. "I've never thought of it that way, but I guess it's true. I mean, is it against the rules or what's the deal?"

"I don't know. Not worth knowing if she doesn't say yes." I start doing circles with my arms, stretching out my shoulders.

It's not like I'd ever try and go out with an executive. Not to sound like a toddler, but I met Lia before she accepted this job. Shouldn't there be an asterisk for this sort of thing?

Jalen stops, shifting his weight to one leg. "Brooks. Don't be a dumb ass. Get all the information and *be ready* if she says yes." He puts a finger in my chest. "All I know is y'all will be spending a lot of time together. Could be a blessing or a curse..." He laughs when we step foot on the court.

It finally feels how it used to: my happy place. The place where I can sort through everything and figure shit out.

Fuck, do I need it.

"Brooks, you ready for me?" the trainer calls from across the court, a foam roller in one hand and a roll of tape in the other.

"Don't you come a step closer with that foam roller," Jalen yells, shooting a ball from half court which hits the rim and the sound of bouncing echoes. "It took me days to be able to walk right after whatever torture you inflicted."

I laugh at Jalen being dramatic and the feeling of being home hits me. This court. These people. It's light and comforting all at once.

It's the thing I've missed most.

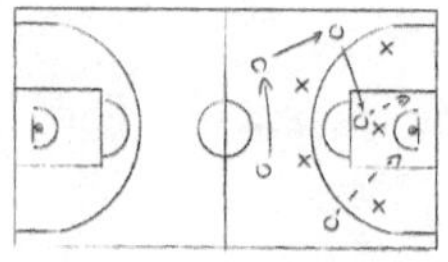

Is Lia kidding? Her lips, full and shiny, are one hell of a distraction as I meet with her and Megan. She's wearing a black dress with a collared white button-up shirt underneath it. Where you might expect to see high heels, she's wearing black combat boots. Might be an odd combination but it fucking works.

Now, do I know anything about fashion? No. Does that stop me from cataloging this outfit as one of the hottest I've ever seen a woman wear? Not a chance.

Megan has a printed calendar, with a matching version in our email, and is walking us through dates. Everything is color coordinated; my name is in green and Lia's in red, to show when and where we'll be working together.

The calendar looks like Christmas came early. This meeting has made it clear how much the two of us will be working together. I flick my eyes and try to catch Lia's from across the table while Megan flips to another page, another month. Her eyes are like emeralds and when they land on mine, she scrunches her nose and gives the smallest head shake that only I know means "quit it."

"Brooks, your job is to give as much access as possible to Lia. Open up. No recluse behavior." She points a finger at me before chuckling and shaking my shoulder.

She's talking about my puzzle phase. When I got out of surgery, all I wanted to do were puzzles. I wasn't cleared for any physical activity, so I soaked up every single minute of finding corner pieces and squinting over a puzzle table. They gave me purpose; something to do, complete.

I became a *little* obsessed. Maybe I still am. I think about the table I had custom ordered for my library back home with a current puzzle waiting for me.

"Open up. You got it," I say without looking from the calendar.

"Lia, you'll be responsible for getting footage for content. Both planned and candid. Once we get going, you'll see what works and what people like to see."

She tucks a piece of straight blonde hair behind her ear and asks, "What's my expectation for travel or away games?"

"Honestly, we'll take as much of you as we can get. All expenses will be covered. If you can let me know which games are a yes, no, and maybe, I'll start getting those pieces going as far as passes, hotel rooms, all of it."

I swear, there are pink hearts flashing in Lia's eyes. I know what she's thinking: you're going to *pay* for me to go to basketball games?

"For this project, I'm thinking four to five months," Megan continues. "At least to the anniversary of the injury. Ironically, there's an away game on the same date."

The devil works hard but the PR team for any professional sports league works harder. All kidding aside, I like our commissioner. He was courtside when I got hurt and made time to check on me, swallowing past his own emotion when we knew what it was, just needing the formal tests to confirm.

Lia coughs. "Months or weeks? Not sure if I heard you..." Her voice trails off.

"Months. You'll be able to be involved with other projects too, giving you a break from this guy. We have an opportunity to showcase the doctor and medical team who completed the new procedure, and this guy always is good for the team image." Megan gestures to me. "He's easy to work with."

Chapter 10
Lia

BUTTERFLIES FLUTTER AND HIT the edges of my ribs when I think about Brooks turning his phone off airplane mode and immediately texting me. I don't know much about him, outside of basketball stats, and only managed to fall into a rabbit hole of his past girlfriends once since our dinner, but I want to know more.

It's my second week with the Jags and the team has had three away games, which kept them on the road for the entire week. I wasn't expected to go to any of these so I could meet the rest of the media team and get used to the Jags processes. Plus, I was able to grab a few bartending shifts and make some extra cash—never a bad thing.

I also spent some time researching the ethics for someone in my position who dates a player from the franchise they work for. I was hoping someone would point out a law, or a court case, where it would paint my decision in black and white. No such luck as I sit here in a world of gray, thinking about the series of events.

Here's the thing: I want to go out with Brooks Pittman. Again. I want his mouth on me. His hands. I want to press into his body like I did outside my apartment. Put my hands on his broad chest, his wide shoulders.

> let me know what you decide

> sleep good

I want to tell him to drive over. Or to drop his address. But I don't. Instead, I go with the most vanilla and safest of responses.

> you too

Don't mind me, I'm just over here being the most boring person on the planet. I scoff and put my phone somewhere I can't see it. My fingers touch a patch of skin on my forearm until they find the roughest part behind my elbow. I rub lotion into the spots—the sanitizer water at the bar is probably the culprit. I catch my reflection in the bathroom mirror and notice a few red spots in the corner of my eyes. Leaning forward, I see some of the same dry skin on my lash line.

I wash my face twice, once with a balm cleanser and then with a gel, before reaching for my go-to moisturizer. My skin has always been sensitive, and this helps keep it hydrated without any agitation. I even put a few dabs on the dry spots on my arms.

Before climbing into bed, I roll out my yoga mat to do a few flows before bed. My hands and wrists have been sore, most likely from bartending, and I feel my best when I keep moving my body.

Once my muscles are happily fatigued and my lids are heavy, I roll the mat and crawl into bed. I try to hold on to the tired feeling, to fall asleep quick, but my heart races thinking about Brooks.

The way he looks at me.

The way I seem to be on his mind.

The way I want him even when it'd be better not to.

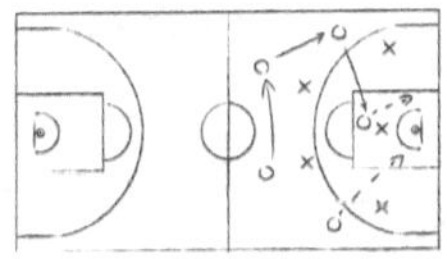

Today, my job is to film content at shoot around. Using a handheld Nikon, I get stills and video of Brooks doing the typical drills before he splits from the team to work with a specialist.

It's like an obstacle course—different levels of short boxes, mats and circles. The coach demonstrates, without breaking a sweat or needing to stop talking, how Brooks should be able to get through it all on one leg and then the other.

"Piece of cake," Brooks brags, clearly in my direction.

Brooks starts with his strong side, the knee that wasn't surgically repaired, and he gets stuck trying to tap in and out of a rope shaped like an oval on the court. When he puts the other leg on the court, he smiles at the camera and goes back to the beginning.

"This is tougher than the ones we've done before, Brooks. Plus, you might be tired from the game last night. Try it again." The coach claps his shoulder and encourages him to keep going. My heart hangs in the space in my chest, wondering if this embarrasses him. Should I keep filming? I mean, even if it's filmed, we don't have to use it. I guess that's the whole reason we're doing this—it's all about the ups and downs.

Brooks gets hung up at the same spot, but getting farther around the circle before falling back and putting both feet on the court. He takes a short walk, hands on his head, but the smile doesn't leave his face.

I take a chance and decide to jump in. "I don't want whatever cake you were talking about." I pull the camera down so he can see my teasing smirk.

Brooks lets out a laugh, his strong shoulders moving, "It's harder than it looks."

"Okay, Mister 'Piece of cake.'" I roll my eyes and turn them back to the screen, still recording.

"If it looks so easy, why don't you try?" Brooks walks forward, his hands now resting on his hips, the sweat on his chest dampening his lilac Jags practice shirt.

I look at the coach to see if this is against the rules. I'm not sure I signed a physical waiver when it came to my Jags paperwork, but who cares.

"Can you record this for me? Want to make sure we document how the new hire outworks the professional athlete." I offer a friendly wink before handing the point and shoot camera to a staff member.

I do a few quick stretches as I stand at the start of the drill, envisioning the path I'll take to reach the end. "Ready to see how it's done?" I call playfully.

Brooks laughs and tilts his chin to the ceiling as some of his teammates look over from their own practice circuit.

I look for the red light on the camera, making sure we're recording. There are two ways this could go, and both are great content opportunities. The first is I don't get through the drill, and Brooks gloats and laughs with the staff and maybe some of the guys. The second, and what I think will happen, is I get through the entire drill and we get to watch Brooks' reaction on camera.

"Whatever you say, Lia." He rests his arms on his knees, bending down a little like he's trying to get a better look.

Fuck, he can look at me like that any time.

I take a deep breath and start the drill. My core is strong and holds me up, thanks to the hours of yoga and standing behind the bar, while I move through the rope and lines on the court. I'm light on my feet and thankful for the shoes I picked out today—comfortable but cute sneakers.

When I hit the point at which Brooks struggled, I can feel his eyes on me. I thought he'd try to psych me out or startle me with cheering, but he keeps quiet as I pass the part he got stuck on.

The rest of the shapes and tapping in and outside of the tape on one leg fly by, and at least I got further than Brooks. It's only by a few seconds and I tap onto the court. Before I can say a single thing, the specialists start clapping and cheering for me. I know they're embellishing because of the camera, but it's going to be absolutely perfect footage.

"She schooled you on the first try!" one of them cheers while Brooks walks to me, clapping his hands slowly.

Guys offer me high fives, which I take, and a sense of belonging is right within my grasp. I'm not just going to be the media girl; I'm turning into *Lia*. This is the sort of feeling which warms you from inside your chest to the top of your skin.

Brooks is the last one to offer a high five and he steps in closer than anyone else. "Impressive. I wonder if I should start doing yoga?" He pulls one lip into a lop-sided grin, and fuck, it could end me. That grin should be a crime.

I wonder if he practices that smirk. It's like what we've all read about in romance books or watched Disney princes and princesses do our whole lives. Brooks Pittman has it down—and I mean *all* the way down.

"You should." The roof of my mouth is like sandpaper.

"Only if you're teaching me." Brooks drags out the 'you' from the middle of the sentence.

"I *am* a yoga teacher. That could be arranged." I realize I'm only a few inches away from him, the space full of sparklers and zips of energy. "Think you can handle it?" I tease, pushing a finger into his chest and feeling his muscles.

Brooks leans closer until it's only our shared breath separating us. This is too close for colleagues, but I can't move. I try to say something but when I open my mouth, there's nothing. He breathes out and his eyes jump from mine to my mouth and back again.

I'm the one who can't handle it. He's leaning in and I'm hopeful that if there is a god of knees, they're looking down on me, willing my wobbly excuses to keep myself standing.

The squeak of basketball shoes on the court yanks us back to the present and each of us take a step back, putting more room between us.

I look around. Did anyone see that tiny moment? Am I going to get in trouble before I even get to do anything? Relief washes over me when I notice everyone doing their own thing, including the person with the camera, which hangs around his neck.

Close call. And from what I can tell, I fear that won't be the only one.

Chapter 11
Brooks

THE TRAINER IS TESTING my range of motion while I look at the clock; there are only a few hours until game time. I don't know if I'm just tired from the week of road games and travel, but my knee hasn't felt right. There's no pain, tenderness, or swelling but the crippling feeling of anxiety is permeating out of my pores.

"I think you're tired from returning. Nothing structural," the trainer assures me, crouched down as he watches me point and flex my toes while feeling different parts of both knees. He looks away like the doctor does when they are listening to your heartbeat. His words and touch are soft, like he's afraid to scare me away from being told the truth about my knee.

"Okay. I trust you," I say as he stands, his eyes not leaving mine, and I wish I sounded more convincing.

"But I don't think you trust *you*. Listen, you ran at that recovery, but it's different from playing in games, especially on the bender we were just on. This is your call. I can chat with the coaching staff and let them know you need a minutes restriction, or you can be a last-minute restriction."

I narrow my eyes at him and he knows what I'm thinking.

"Or I can pretend you were in here with zero concerns and you're in control. I know you're not dumb enough to put yourself at risk, so take a seat tonight when you need it, ok?"

I nod and offer a sad excuse for a smile. It's almost more frustrating to know nothing is actually wrong and it's all in my head. This isn't new. No matter how many times someone told me the surgery was a success—that it went better than they'd ever imagined, I was on schedule for the quickest return to the game after a torn ACL, and probably safer than most—doubt still crouched in the corner of my mind.

"Honestly, it's typical fatigue. Don't hold back. You go out at one hundred percent for the minutes you can manage, or you don't go at all." He points at me, and I nod in agreement.

You're fine.

The knee is fine.

This is normal.

I tell myself over and over, trying to get the anxiety to dial itself back while I finish the rest of my pre-game treatment.

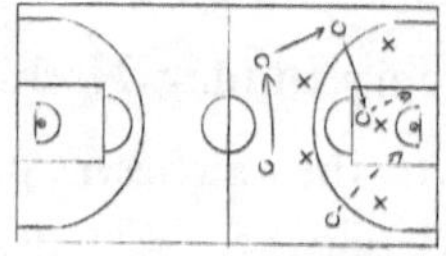

I'm in the tunnel doing some stretches when Lia walks towards me. She's wearing a white top, with flowy sleeves that move when she walks, and deep purple pants. It's like she color-matched the Jags' jersey to get the perfect shade.

"Happy to see me, huh?" She lifts the camera around her neck and snaps a candid photo of me.

I don't know how she does it, but she brings this lightness that slinks around. "I'm always happy to see you." The words fall out of my mouth before I have a chance to reconsider. The pink that floods her cheeks is so damn gorgeous.

She stands next to me and says, "Alright, this match-up should be no problem, right? I mean, they've got questionable shooters, and I think they have a few ball hogs which disrupts the offense."

My eyebrows raise because, no matter what, sometimes my brain isn't where it should be. I can't let go of her comment on touching balls.

Lia bumps into me, rolling her eyes. "Still a middle schooler at heart, like all men," she laughs.

"I do what I can," I reply, shrugging my shoulders and switching my legs for my Achilles and calf stretch, pushing my foot into the wall, toe up and heel down. "You're right. We should win tonight."

Dramatically putting the camera in front of her face and using the view finder, Lia teases, "Okay, Brooks Pittman, number seven, how's it going?"

I love how her voice changes from talking about the match-up to her social media voice, the one that might be heard on the Jags account. Plus, she's been so damn good that Megan has given her room to do what she creatively wants.

"Good. Excited for the home crowd tonight." I offer her, and the camera, a warm look.

"And how's the knee?"

I don't know why the question hits me the way it does. Lia is always asking how I'm feeling, how I'm moving, how the knee is. This time, it takes all the air from my lungs, stealing it like a thief and leaving me breathless.

The doubt, with its barbed wire edges, crawls back, growing with each second until it takes residence in my chest. The very same doubt I've tried to push down, cover with optimism and keep my brain and body busy. All it takes is a single question from Lia to unravel all of it.

Lia slowly pulls the camera down from her face, holding it at her chest. She's looking at me with those wide eyes, emerald and velvety, as the rest of her face damn near pales.

When I don't say anything, she emphasizes stopping the recording with the camera, letting it hang in front of her with the wide black strap on her neck. Her eyes find mine again, and it's like she's a fresh spring meadow that I could run straight into. If I'm honest, I wish I could run away right now.

"Are you okay?" she whispers.

I nod my head, a weak attempt to say I'm fine while I look past her to the court.

It's a soft touch, her fingers on my forearm for only a second, that has my eyes snapping to hers. "Brooks, what's wrong?" Lia presses.

The words are simple, straight forward. I'm surprised by how my body leans forward, wishing her hands were still touching me. I want to tell her everything. It feels like she could make this better.

"My knee feels weird." I look down, lifting my knee to my chest. If I look at her while I share this, I'm afraid I'll get weirdly emotional. "Checked with the trainers. They say it's normal. Fatigue."

I can't believe those words come out of my mouth. While I'm trying to think of how I can take it back, Lia shakes her head and moves in closer.

"I can't imagine playing after an injury like that." She frowns slightly, her eyes on mine. "I'm sure it all feels kind of weird."

I glance for a millisecond, and her face is nothing but kindness and caring. For fuck's sake, she's someone I could melt into.

"Just nervous. It's like, even though everyone says it's fine, it's still hard to believe." I talk so fast that I run out of breath and suck in air at the end of my sentence.

"The yoga teacher in me wants to remind you to breathe," Lia says calmly, taking a deep breath herself which inherently makes me want to copy her.

We breathe in. And out.

She crosses her arms, looks around to see if anyone is paying attention, then leans in closer. "Listen, you know your body best. Don't overdo it."

Lia talks in a way that makes you want to pay attention. It's comforting and the right amount of stern.

"You got it." I try to sound convincing—for her and for myself.

I've never had a problem telling Coach if I needed to sit. Tonight's game won't be any different—I know that.

"I say that from the part of me loving my new job where the whole thing kind of revolves around you, but more so from the Jags fan who's been following this franchise since I can remember." Her words are light and dusted with sarcasm, causing her to smile.

It's like a chain reaction and her words hit me, lifting some of the heavy from my shoulders piece by piece.

"Hey, could you not post my mini freak out when you asked me a very simple question and I couldn't use words?" I joke.

Lia tilts her head, her blonde hair cascading in front of her in waves. "I would never do that." Her words are slow, meticulous, hitting every letter. "You don't ever need to ask me to keep moments like this between us. I'm on your side." She presses a hand to her chest.

She stands next to me, opening the camera's playback. When the video starts playing on the tiny digital screen, she deletes it—no questions asked.

And I believe her.

Lia's on my side.

Chapter 12
Lia

THE JAGS PULL OUT a win at home in overtime, and I love how this place feels. Every staff member has a grin plastered on their face, the fans are ecstatic, and it's like the building has a heavy happiness seeping out of the walls.

I love it. More than I thought I could.

I've been watching basketball my entire life. My dad would turn on the Jags, put on his ratty shirt—the only Jags merch I think he owned—and we'd sit in front of our tiny TV, lamenting over a team we wanted to win but rarely ever did.

My dad taught me the purpose of each player, basic offensive and defensive plays, and the different types of fouls. It was always our thing. Mom would move around us; never upset she wasn't included but in awe that we had such a connection.

When Wes was old enough, he slipped into the living room and wore his own Jags shirt, one he got for a birthday but was quickly growing out of. Game days have always held a special place for me.

After my parents died, game days became the one thing Wes and I kept close. We lived with an aunt and uncle who did their best, but it was barely enough most days. They never had enough money and were always scraping pennies together to make ends meet. I quickly learned how to take care of both Wes and myself, much sooner than anyone should be asked to do. I'd find odd jobs around the neighborhood:

cutting grass, raking leaves, pulling weeds, walking dogs, or any other task they'd let me try.

I had a small music box that was my mom's, and I'd put the dollar bills, and sometimes coins, I'd earned in there. When Wes crawled into my bed in the middle of the night, he'd tell me how he was still hungry or needed something for school. That's when I'd dip into the box, a pink ballerina spinning delicately as I cranked the handle on the bottom.

Wes and I fought when our parents were around, but we simply survived while we were with our aunt and uncle. I wish things had worked out differently, but I'm grateful for the way it brought us together. Wes is one of my favorite people in the whole world and I've felt like that for a long time.

I'm texting him as the team is wrapping up their work for post-game coverage—our players are still doing press.

Wes

tell me you were at the game tonight

I send him a selfie I took earlier. I'm standing on the court, my arm stretched out as far as it could to get me and as much of the arena as possible. It makes me giggle because I'm smiling like my dreams are coming true.

are you kidding me

i can't believe this is your job

when can I come?

Me

i wanted to get through the first week or so before i asked for free tickets

Smiling down at my phone, I think about our interaction before the game. Brooks was practically in tears with worry. The lines were deep in his forehead, his lips the thinnest of lines from being pressed so tight, and his eyes felt like they were afraid to look at anything besides the floor. I had to hold back from wrapping him in a hug, squeezing as tightly as I could. Hugging certainly isn't what colleagues do.

"You want to get some food?"

Brooks stands in the doorway of the completely empty media room—my colleagues don't tend to stick around. Meanwhile, I could get lost in here.

I can see the exhaustion from the game on his face and, for some reason, I want to give him anything he asks for. I don't know if I'm so excited that he got through the game, or if I'm too exhausted pretending I don't want to, but I say, "Yes."

Here's the thing: Brooks doesn't even look surprised.

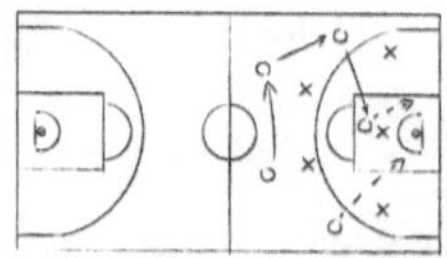

"Do you think they'll give us a vat to go?" I ask as I dip another warm tortilla chip in some of the best salsa I've ever tasted.

"I've definitely done that." Brooks swipes a tortilla through the salsa before popping it in his mouth.

We're sitting in a back booth of a taco spot I've never thought about walking in to. I look around and find most of the restaurant empty. "You come here a lot?"

"It's one of my favorite places and I'm not sure how it hasn't blown up yet. Everything here is authentic and so fucking good," he answers, his hands already in the tortilla chip basket, going for another.

We sit in silence besides the crunching of tortilla chips and the sounds of staff moving around the restaurant. Brooks ordered dinner for both of us, making sure there wasn't anything I was allergic to or didn't like. I didn't tell him that when you grew up like I did, you didn't get a chance to be picky.

"Tell me a secret," he suggests, catching me off guard.

"Only if we can trade them," I counter.

Brooks nods and his mouth pulls into this ridiculously hot half smirk.

I rack my brain for a secret—it's not that I don't have a lot to choose from, but I don't know the vibe. Is this the sort of exchange where we talk about the time I went to class in a bikini for a dare or is it something dark from my childhood? My brain snags on a secret that falls in the middle.

"My aunt thinks chocolate cake is my favorite. Every holiday, special occasion, and celebration she makes a cake from scratch with buttercream frosting. But it's my least favorite." I cover my eyes, afraid to see his reaction.

"Wait, your least favorite?"

"Yes! Like, I'll never turn down cake and I'd definitely try one bite of any kind, but I don't even like chocolate cake all that much. She made it once and I don't know what happened. And then she was so proud every time, I could never correct her."

"How long has this scandal been going on?" Brooks asks, leaning back in the booth with one hand resting on his chest.

I think back to the first birthday without my parents. It still stings when I put myself back in that year. "I was twelve. I'm going to be twenty-seven soon. So... fifteen years."

"You've been choking down chocolate cake for a decade and a half!" Brooks laughs and it's quiet but shakes his shoulders. "What is your favorite?"

"Carrot cake. With cream cheese frosting. My mouth is watering thinking about it," I answer, shimmying my shoulders with excitement.

"Me too. Completely underrated pick." He smiles as his eyes land on mine. It's infuriating how he can pull me to him like this with a single glance. His eyes are like the bottom of a honey pot.

"Your turn," I say, reaching for my glass of water.

Brooks rubs his hands together, shaking them out before stretching his neck, his head dipping side to side. "When I found out that Zack was my brother, I was afraid to meet him—not for any reason other than I thought he wouldn't like me. I was worried we wouldn't get along or he wouldn't think I measured up."

Definitely leaning towards the heavier.

"Zack Andersen? The man is like a walking golden retriever," I say, placing my hands on the table and making a noise borderline too loud.

"I know. I mean, that's what the media showed, but people put on a good act."

"Fair. And I hate to tell you this, especially because I know your ego is already inflated from another notch in the win column, but you're kind of a big deal." I emphatically roll my eyes before they land on his face.

"Sometimes it still doesn't feel like enough." His voice fades from the strong, confident person sitting across from me until it's small enough to fit in my pocket.

"For who?"

"Me. The team. The fans. Take your pick." Brooks shrugs his shoulders before he coughs, getting passed the shakiness in his voice.

This hits me. Hard. The idea of this professional athlete, a multi-millionaire, doing the thing he's probably dreamt of his whole life, and still not being sure if he's living up to the standard.

It's like he's pulling back the curtain from one of the things I keep deep inside myself—the idea of enough. How much of myself can I give to meet expectations? Do I even *have* enough to measure up?

This can't be easy for him to share. I don't say anything but reach over and squeeze his fingers. He squeezes them back and then our hands sort of stay like that—intertwined on top of the table—until they drop off our food.

"This looks... wow." I'm practically drooling as I scan the table, which is full of a variety of tacos, tostadas, and mini chimichangas.

Brooks claps his hands, rubbing them together. "Make sure you get a bite of all three of those tacos. That's your first assignment."

When he ordered everything I had no idea what the end game was, but I love that we're going to be eating it family style, even though it's only the two of us. I've never been one to hesitate when it comes to sharing food, but I know that's not always the case.

"Wait, I just thought of something," I exclaim, my hand hovering above the shrimp taco I've had my eye on since the server set it on the table. "Did you sneak a date out of me?" It's wildly apparent that we're in a dim room, sharing a meal.

Brooks shakes his head, his mouth full with a bite of tostada. He finishes chewing and says, "No." He shakes his head, the middle of his brow scrunched. "Truly, you showed up for me before the game and I wanted to say thank you."

I nod with the shrimp taco in front of my mouth, the smell of lime and cilantro making my stomach hurt with how hungry I am.

"But maybe it was a subconscious plan…" His voice trails off as he cuts off a piece of a chimichanga covered in queso. He tilts his head back and forth, like he's weighing the merits of if it was or wasn't, all while wearing that half smirk that could be the end of me.

Maybe I should be mad? Or feel like I was tricked? But I'm not. Spending time with Brooks is smooth. Effortless. If I wasn't working for the Jags, I'd be dying to go out with him. I can't imagine a world where I don't say 'yes' and let him whisk me away to hole-in-the-wall taco spots or wherever else he wanted to take me. Besides maybe the one where I'm working somewhere I've dreamed of my whole life.

But maybe there's a way to have both?

Chapter 13
Brooks

Again, I find myself outside of Lia's apartment. She puts her key in the door, unlocking and opening it a crack before turning back to me.

She bites her lip and moves her jaw back and forth until she takes a breath, like she's going to say something, but nothing comes. Her mouth hangs open.

"Were you going to say something?" I laugh.

She rocks back on her heels and replies, "I'm thinking about it."

"How long should I wait?" I put a hand on the door frame, leaning my weight to one side.

"I shouldn't say it," Lia insists, almost like she's talking to herself and I'm not standing right here. A dog barks, a glass breaks, and some of her neighbors yell loud enough that it's easy to hear, even when it's the floor above us.

I take in a long breath and murmur, "Then don't."

"But I want to." Her eyes dart from mine to my lips and back again. I'm holding my breath, hoping she's going to say one of the hundred things that would make this night continue.

So far, I've let her set boundaries that I've followed. I don't ever want her to feel uncomfortable and I know the job means a lot to her. If it was my choice, we'd be planning our nights together every night when we were free.

Lia opens the door further, standing in the doorway so still she's like a statue. "Do you want to come in?"

I say nothing but my smile gives me away as I step into her apartment. The alarm bells are going off in my brain, screaming about the scenario I'd hoped would happen but wasn't sure it actually would.

I want to know more about her. I want to see where she lives. Learn more of her secrets.

I take my shoes off, copying Lia, and catalog the details of her apartment. It's a studio, but it's not cramped or anything I would have expected. The outside of this place is kind of rough, needing a fresh coat of paint and replacement light bulbs while address numbers are falling off doors, but her apartment is nothing like that.

Light pink covers the walls and when she says, "Let's get cozy," twinkly lights turn on and her main lights dim. It's fucking adorable.

"This is nice," I compliment, looking around the small kitchen as Lia takes her leftovers and vat of salsa out of the bag and puts them in the fridge.

"Thanks. I've done a lot to make it feel like home. I've been here for a few years."

"Long enough to make it cozy?" I tease a little bit on the last word, thinking about the voice command she used a minute ago.

"Almost. Do you want tea?"

"If you're having some."

She moves around the kitchen. I lean against the counter, thinking about her routines. Is this something she does every night? I see pictures on the fridge and take a closer look.

They're mostly of her and a younger man. Out to dinner. At a coffee shop. In Santa hats on Christmas morning. I'm guessing it's her brother, but who knows.

"Who is this?" I ask, pointing to one of the photos.

"Wes. My younger brother."

"How young?"

"Seventeen. Senior in high school. Obsessed with basketball. He's played on the varsity team since he was a freshman. He's trying to get scouts to come to a few games." Lia talks about him in a way that shows how much she cares about him.

"Is he any good?"

"Yeah, he is. Unbiased opinion. I'd never set him up for failure, like those horrible parents who tell their kids they're the next LeBron James when they're 5'6" and think they're too good to practice free throws or learn how to handle the ball with both hands."

"I mean, I know some scouts. I did once go to college," I laugh as she dips tea bags in and out of the steaming water.

She gives me a side-eye look and insists, "I'd never ask you to do that." Lia shakes her head as she looks at the clock on the oven, seeing how much time has passed.

"You're not asking. I'm offering. If he's good, maybe he'll go to my alma mater and help them win a championship or something."

"He's been dying to come to a game. To meet you. He keeps asking me to take pictures while I'm at work because I don't think he believes it's real." She takes the tea bags out, straining the water in the sink and tossing the bags in the trash.

She carries both mugs into what the living room would be. A love seat and a chair are placed next to each other in front of a light wooden coffee table.

I take one end of the love seat as Lia hands me the steaming mug. When Lia sets her own mug down on a small side table on the other side of the love seat, I know she's going to sit next to me.

My heartbeat races in my chest, all over tea on a fucking love seat. I've completely lost it. I don't have a grip on anything. I set the mug down mostly because I don't trust myself to nervously shake and spill it.

"To be fair, sometimes I don't think it's real either," she offers, holding the mug with both hands, the steam drifting in front of her face.

"I get that. Sometimes I still feel like that. No matter how many years I've been in the league. I'm kind of hoping it doesn't go away. It helps keep things in perspective."

Lia keeps situating herself, trying to get comfortable with her legs underneath her but she doesn't stop fidgeting. She sets her mug down and tries to adjust the back cushion. I lean back and do the "give me" gesture with my hands.

When Lia realizes what I'm trying to get her to do, and she actually does it, I feel like I've won something. She takes her long legs and stretches them out over the top of my lap.

Instead of picking my tea up, I rub one hand on the side of her calf and to her knee. I'd be lying to say I hadn't thought about my hands, and mouth, on her legs. I wonder how long it'd take for me to kiss all the way up them. I laugh and can feel her looking at me.

"What are we doing?" she asks.

I don't say anything at first, but turn and look at her, tilting my head and resting it on the top of the love seat. "I don't know."

"We really should be friends." Lia leans forward, her hands close to mine. "Just friends." Her voice comes out breathy and unconvincing.

"If that's what you want," I reply as she takes a hand and runs it along my arm until it lands on my shoulder. I do my best not to react because her hands on me make me want to do the same to her.

"What does that mean?" she fake-whines, putting her arms around her knees, which are still on top of my legs.

I put two fingers under her chin, tilting it until she's looking at me with the greenest eyes I've ever seen in real life. "It means I don't want to be *just* your friend," I murmur. She doesn't say anything, but it feels like she's leaning into the touch—or maybe I'm imagining it. "But I'll take what I can get."

She lets out a shaky breath and her fingers push through my hair, scratching until they land on the nape of my neck. Her eyes are dark as they roam over me, jumping from one feature to the next.

Lia swings her legs off mine and my heart drops to the bottom of the deepest part of myself. Fuck. I thought she was going to kiss me. Say something I wanted to hear. I look down at my knees, my hands resting on them, and I'm about to stand.

But then Lia puts one knee on the side of my leg and picks the other one up and over until she's straddling me. Both of her hands push my hair back, until they're hooked around my neck. She throws her blonde hair to the side, pressing into me.

"It has to be a secret. If we do this. I tried looking through my paperwork but I couldn't find—"

"They can't fire you for dating me. It may be frowned upon, but it's not in the contract you signed," I insist. The look she gives me, hesitant and curious, has me wondering if that's something I should've kept to myself. "Also, if it doesn't interfere with your work, Megan would never."

"How do you know that?"

Shit. Maybe I shouldn't have said that. Well, I can't turn back now.

"I asked my lawyer. I mean, he doesn't know it's about you," I assure Lia. "I used hypotheticals, but he also signed an NDA, so you have nothing to worry about."

She gives me a tiny smile. Her lips barely move, but I know she's not mad.

"When did you learn this?"

"I called him on my way home from my first game back. After we were in the locker room." The words tumble from my mouth before I have a chance to chill them out. I'm not saying I should've lied to her, but I'm painfully aware of how needy and desperate I sound. I could've said last week or a few days ago, but instead I rambled about the first possible time I knew she'd be working with my team.

Lia presses her forehead to mine and whispers, "I like that you did that."

Before I can respond, her lips are on mine. I smile into the kiss at first, and I feel her smiling back. Fuck, the way I want to make her happy. My hands splay across her lower back as she arches, pushing closer and closer to me. Her tits move into my chest, and I let my hands down further until my fingers are kneading her ass.

Her lips are soft, almost velvety and full. They press into mine and I kiss her back with my tongue touching along the seam of her mouth. When she lets me in, she tastes like vanilla and peppermint, which I'm guessing is from the tea.

Lia tilts her head and I put one of my hands in her hair, feeling through the strands. When she breaks the kiss, I realize she's laughing.

"I'm sorry. Nothing's funny. I'm sort of freaking out. Like, I'm making out with Brooks Pittman on my couch." Lia's voice runs out of her mouth, almost dancing in excitement, and it feels like a compliment.

I put my mouth back on hers, kissing through her laugh and pulling her chest flush with mine. I hold onto her for the way she showed up for me pre-game and how she gave in tonight.

"Tell me about it. I've got Lia Stone on my lap, and I feel like I'm fucking dreaming." Her cheeks pinch when I say her full name.

"I don't know if we're doing this yet," she admits, her mouth claiming mine.

"This is your call, Lia. If I get to kiss you while you decide, that's okay with me," I promise.

I truly would've been only her friend and tried my best to forget our first kiss after our impromptu first date, but it would've been fucking hard. Honestly, what are the odds that a mystery woman shows up in my life, and then her job is to spend time with me—documenting my return from injury? It feels like the universe is pushing us together and I'm going to take it, secrets and all.

Here's the thing: I'll keep any secret necessary. The original Coca Cola recipe? I'm a vault. Nuclear codes? What codes. The truth behind the pyramids? Believe me, I'm the wrong guy.

If it means I get to be with Lia, my lips are sealed.

Chapter 14

Lia

"Yoga is bullshit," Shelbie groans as she takes a long drink of her coffee.

I roll my eyes, laughing, because this isn't new.

"Why do you come if you hate it this much?" I blow on the mug of hot coffee, wondering how Shelbie didn't burn her mouth.

Now I'm thinking about my lips and how they still feel perfectly swollen from last night.

She yawns as she takes her black hair down from the messy bun she wore in class. It reaches past her shoulders and looks much better than it should for just falling out of a scrunchie. That's the kind of luck Shelbie has, though.

Shelbie rolls her eyes. "Because someone went and got a dream job or something and has been impossible to get a hold of."

Ouch. I know she's giving me a hard time, but she isn't wrong.

"When do you sleep?" She slouches back into the booth of our favorite coffee shop, which happens to be only a block from where I teach yoga.

"I've learned how to survive on four hours. What can I say?"

"You're ridiculous. Now dish on the basketball player."

Heat creeps up my neck until it lands on my cheeks. Whatever is between us is supposed to be a secret, but there's no way I can keep this to myself. Shelbie is the human version of a vault.

"Let's see. We're spending a ton of time together for work, it's going really well, and, oh yeah, I made out with him on my couch last night. Like a teenager."

Shelbie clicks her tongue and hisses, "Next time, lead with the make out session. Why do you look so guilty? He's not married, right?"

"Like I'd consider anything if he were married," I scoff, taking a sip of my still-scorching coffee. If anything's remained consistent for most of my life, it's the importance of following the rules. Good girl syndrome runs deep in these bones; it's part of my marrow at this point. "It feels like I'm breaking the rules or I'm being reckless or irresponsible."

"Knock it off, Lia. No one would ever use the word irresponsible to describe you. You're constantly two steps ahead and go to great lengths to get what you want... except when it comes to hot as fuck athletes, I guess." She pauses and looks around the room.

I sit back with my hands in my lap and take Shelbie in. We've known each other since college, and we stayed in the same area. I've never been one to have a bunch of friends, mostly because I feel like I had way more responsibility than other people my age. But then I met Shelbie, being forced to do an icebreaker for a college class where she eloquently looked at me and said, "Can you believe we're paying for this bullshit?" From then on, we've been close. No matter how much is going on, we can easily pick up right where we left off. When she got the job at The Foundry, she immediately told the manager she knew someone who would be interested in picking up shifts.

We're quite the contrast. My hair is blonde, hers black, and my somewhat energetic sunny energy perfectly balances her deliciously dark and snarky self. If you get Shelbie to smile, you've done something right.

It's kind of like romance books, when the main character is rough around the edges but is only soft for her. Shelbie is the grumpy main character who loves me no matter how much I differ from her.

"You need to let loose. Has anyone ever told you that?" she asks.

"You. About a thousand times. This year."

"And yet, you never listen. You've got this job, you'll make real money, and I know that's one of your main stressors."

The honesty is a lump in my throat I swallow past. It's not a secret I'm always scrounging for money, a habit I had to learn when my parents died. Now I'm in a slightly better spot, but I'm always waiting for something to go wrong that will undo any of the progress I've made.

"I googled Brooks," Shelbie admits with her eyes looking at me over her coffee mug. This doesn't surprise me because, out of all things, Shelbie is a sucker for reality TV and celebrity gossip. "I'm happy to report there's not a single Reddit thread about him being a slime ball. Now, his ex-girlfriend, that's a different story. She doesn't get a passing grade from me."

Brooks and I haven't talked about it, but I'll never forget the press conference after he had a horrible game. It was a few games before he tore his ACL, and it was hard to watch. He couldn't get it going. He ended with one point from a free throw, a bunch of turnovers, and one of the worst stat lines in Jags history. Someone from the press asked about his rumored ex-girlfriend. He cleared his throat, went to say something, but then stood and left instead.

I'll never understand why people think that, because someone is an athlete, it somehow gives us full insight into their entire life. We're not privy to that information. Athletes are allowed to be people.

"Yeah, I remember hearing about that. But I don't want to know any specifics. If he wants to tell me about it, he can."

"Here's my advice. Dating someone you work with? Not always a good idea. But this is the gray area. You're not his coach, a trainer, or a manager. If you think something is there, why run from it?"

The other thing about Shelbie is how solid she is at asking questions. She's got a knack for helping you figure out exactly what the issue is, or what you're worried about.

"I'm afraid it's too big of a risk. I don't want anyone to look at me differently."

"First, fuck that. Are you concerned about Brooks' reputation, or yours because it comes with double standards and expectations?" The question must be rhetorical because she doesn't lose speed. "Well, I'm not saying hook up under the basketball hoop during practice, but hear me out... I think you know how to be discreet, and I know for a fact he does, based on how little of him I can find online. Really, when I Google his name there's a lot about some football player who is apparently his half-brother."

"Zack Andersen."

Shelbie loudly sets down her cup and rolls her eyes. "I know *this* guy's name, isn't that enough? I know Brooks Pittman is number seven and plays for the Jersey Jaguars. He wears purple. If that isn't worth something, I don't know what is," she playfully laments.

I can't help but belly laugh. She's right. "You get all the credit. I'm proud of you. Sports knowledge and yoga in the same day? You're on fire."

She offers me a half-smile and I know I've cracked her hard exterior which is always a little soft for me. "All jokes aside, I think you should do it. But if you don't, quit torturing yourself and don't play the what if game. No one's a winner when we do that."

Damn it. She's so right.

"Hey, I have some promo tickets to give away for the Jags. Do you want to go to a game?" I ask, already knowing the answer but wanting to see it for myself.

Shelbie stands from the table and takes a couple steps like she's going to leave. I grab her arm, laughing. "I'm totally kidding. I'll never make you come to a game."

"Yoga is bad enough, Lia."

It's amazing how the light of my life is someone like Shelbie. She sits back down and launches into a story about someone who left her a $200 tip the other night.

Joy radiates through my chest from being able to spend time with Shelbie this way. I've not realized it until this moment, but I'm excited to slow down on some of the freelance work. I'm keeping a yoga class each week but no shifts at the bar, coffee shop, or bakery until I let them know I'm ready to come back.

I've been moving so fast for so long. I can't remember the last time I had a free night—or better yet, a whole day off. It's been years of picking up shifts, home improvement DIY projects, and trying to get ahead.

Maybe it's time to rest. A little.

And maybe I won't have to spend all my potential free time by myself?

Chapter 15
Brooks

I'M COOKING DINNER, THINKING of how quiet it is at my new house. It's not a new build but it's new to me. With my most recent contract extension, and mental health suggestion from my therapist, I made the decision to buy a house instead of paying rent. I've been living here a few months but it still feels weird walking through the rooms, soaking in the space.

The thing about playing a sport for a living is your situation can get awfully tumultuous out of nowhere. You could get traded, lose your starting spot, not get a contract extension, or have a severe injury. Before I put an offer on this place, I had a meeting with the Jags' head coach, owner, and general manager. I wanted them to look me in the face and tell me their honest intentions. Now they could bullshit me all they wanted, but I had a good feeling about our meeting.

I grew up in a cramped two-bedroom house as an only child. We didn't have a ton of space, but my mom gave me everything she could. Let me tell you, it was more than enough. I've met many people who talk about their childhood as a time they'd like to forget, or they reminisce about struggles I'd never experienced. I may have only had a single parent, but we never went hungry, and we were able to do things like go on vacations and play travel sports, like basketball.

I'll never forget when the head coach for The University of Alabama men's basketball team came to my house, with the scout who attended a game the previous week. I was a junior in high school and had been offered a full-ride scholarship to play a game I'd been obsessed with for as long as I could remember.

"How much is this going to cost? Like really?" my mom asks, looking for the catch. "We can cover it. I just need to start planning for it." She looks at Coach, who is sitting across from us in an accent chair in the living room.

"I promise there's no hidden bill or cost. As long as Brooks remains in good academic standing and displays no conduct detrimental to the team, his tuition and on-campus housing will be 100% covered by this scholarship."

It's like it finally hits her. She sniffles and replies, "I already have a college fund for him though," with tears running down her face as her hand rubs my back.

She looks at me, trails from her tears on her face, and it makes me wipe my own eyes with the back of my hand. It feels like I could possibly get everything I've wanted.

"What do I do with the college fund?" she asks.

"Well, you should go on a vacation," Coach laughs. "Now, I'm going to tell you something, but you can't hold me to it—it's only a feeling. When I watch Brooks, I think about how he could actually play in the NBA." He looks between my mom and I, and it's hard for me to grasp what he's saying. "I know that's the goal for a lot of athletes, but the truth of the matter is, it doesn't happen for most of them. Brooks might be able to play professionally, if that's what he wants to do."

My chest is tight and I feel like I could jump out of my skin, but in the best way.

"I have a feeling you will get a few offers like this, and I know we're typically a football school, but I'm building quite the recruiting class. Hope you'll wear crimson and spend your time with us in Tuscaloosa."

As soon as Coach left, I knew in my heart I'd play for him. There were other offers, some for schools more known for basketball, but it didn't matter. Sometimes you go with your gut, and it was the best decision I ever made.

I'm thinking about my mom, so I send her a text. She's been taking a bunch of trips with her girlfriends and is on the edge of retirement. While she could retire now, it's hard for her to stop working—it's been such a key part of her identity. She busted her ass so I could have every-thing I wanted.

I paid off her house with my latest contract extension and started a joint account which she can pull from to take trips. I knew she wouldn't do it without a nudge from me.

My phone buzzes with a notification and I'm surprised when it's not a response from my mom.

Lia

> so, does your dinner invite still stand?

> or was there an expiration date

This fucking grin would be embarrassing if anyone else could see me. I've left the next move to Lia—not wanting to pressure her or have her do anything that makes her uncomfortable. We haven't seen each other in two days, but it feels longer than that. Before I can text her back, she sends another message.

> is this now old milk?

Me

> no expiration

> pretend I didn't mention old dairy

> i know you already read it, otherwise I'd unsend

> consider it forgotten

I laugh as my fingers fly over the keyboard. Only Lia would find a way to work in expired milk when it comes to me asking her out. A true talent.

When I send the message, three little dots appear and then stop. Appear. Stop. I take a picture of the fresh pasta and send it to her.

Again, the three dots appear and disappear. I can almost see Lia squeezing her phone too tight, pulling it close to her face like she does when she's thinking about something.

I send my address and the code to open the gate. I look around my place and panic. Is everything clean? Is there something I should be doing besides making sure I don't burn what I'm cooking? Luckily, I like a clean space and everything is put away, except for laundry that's currently washing. That should be fine, right? She's not going to, like, snoop in my laundry room?

Wow. The way I need to get a grip. It's clear I've not done this in a *very* long time.

After Rebecca, I poured myself into basketball even more than I already was. If I wasn't at the facility, I was volunteering or finding events to help with—anything connected to the Jags. Keeping myself busy was key. The sad part was I didn't even miss her that much once she finally put me out of my misery. She left and it was like this fog had lifted and I could think more clearly. I was always trying to be enough for her, doing my best to make her want to stay. I lost more and more of myself each day that I went out of my way to do things for her which she either never noticed or cared about.

When she finally left, it was intense how much of my mental space was finally free. I was no longer agonizing about what she'd like for dinner, what place she'd be surprised by if I got a reservation for, or what location I could take her for an impromptu getaway. It fucking stung. Like I never knew how much she was stealing from me until it was three years gone.

I turn down the burner to let the food simmer and go to the living room, one of my favorite spots because it's so comfortable, to turn on my diffuser—a gift from Riley. When she, Zack, and my dad came over to the new place, they each brought housewarming gifts. Zack had my wine fridge stocked and Riley brought over a few diffusers with essential oils. She said she picked out the oil blends based on my aura—whatever the hell that means—and others she thought smelled good.

From what I've read, the jury is out on the benefits of essential oils, but Riley gave me a two-minute lecture on the harm of candles. I thought she didn't want me to burn the new place down, but she quickly gave me the run down on the dangers of fragrance and "carcinogens hiding in plain sight." Now, I'm the proud owner of essential oils and diffusers placed throughout the new house. Plus, every time I see Riley, she brings me a bottle of a new blend or something she thinks would be a perfect fit for me. It's nice that she thinks of me.

My dad and Mack came over a week after with a grill in tow. I've never had a grill, so he was excited to show me how to use and take care of it.

Lavender and peppermint oil are filled in each of the diffusers, which I add water to, and turn all of them on. I jog back to the kitchen, not wanting to burn dinner.

I don't think we need to eat in the dining room; that seems way too formal. Instead, I set the bar—the place I eat whenever I'm home. Music plays through the house, a habit I've gotten into. The quiet is something that itches my brain in the wrong way. It jumpstarts all the 'what if' questions and I usually end on a dark path, marked with worry and hypothetical concerns.

Standing in front of the wine fridge, I don't know if I should bring out a bottle for dinner. To be honest, the only bottle I've had from here was the one Zack picked out after he had the company stock it. The wine was good, but I wasn't tasting all the notes that Zack was; apparently it was a rare Chablis, and he liked it because of the 'dusting of citrus and apple.'

I'm Googling the best wine to pair with carbonara when I get a notification that someone has entered the code at my gate. I go to the front door and peek out the peephole.

Lia is getting out of her car, looking around as she walks the path to the front door. There's not much to see, considering the house is tucked back. The press hasn't ever been an issue for me. Besides when the news came out about me and Zack being related, and the time some trashy tabloid found out about Rebecca's bad behavior, things are mostly quiet.

A wave of nervousness hits me, wondering how weird it will be when she knocks and I'm awkwardly standing at the door. I practically run to a chair in the living room, jumping into it and waiting for her to knock. I don't think this is much better.

This is ridiculous.

I'm ridiculous.

My head falls into my hands and I run my fingers through my hair as Lia knocks on the door. I jump like I wasn't standing there thirty seconds ago, and pause before I open the door, taking in a slow breath.

There she is, all smiles in black leggings and a worn-in, retro Jags crewneck which falls off one of her shoulders, holding a plastic container.

"I brought dessert."

Chapter 16
Lia

"WHAT'S THE DEAL WITH this pasta?" I ask after swallowing another bite. This is on par with some of the best food I've ever eaten. The nervousness sits low in my stomach, but the noodles help. "Is this, like, special pasta given to you by the NBA or something? Are you sharing trade secrets?"

Brooks holds back a laugh. "Would you believe me if I said Zack invited me to a cooking class? Well, he hired the chef, and we all learned at his place."

"Who is all?"

"My dad, his wife, my mom, Riley, Zack, and Emilie... his fiancé."

"Okay, that's adorable."

"Yeah, it's very Zack, if that makes sense." Brooks takes another bite of his pasta. "Tell me about your parents."

A soft hole flutters in my chest. It's more of an ache than a type of hurt. That may change day to day, based on what's going on, if the subject of my parents comes up.

"They were lovely people. My dad is the reason I've been obsessed with the Jags since I can remember, and probably why Wes plays basketball. My mom was the kind of person who was so thankful for what she had." Brooks' brows furrow with the way I talk about them in past tense and then his face drops. "It's okay," I assure him. "They died when I was twelve. It's been a long time."

"I'm sorry. No matter how long it's been." Brooks rubs my forearm as he sits next to me at the bar. "I came from a single parent household and that was hard enough, so I can't imagine."

"Thanks. There were some stretches where it felt impossible, but we made it." I let the feeling of pride run through me, even if it's only a moment. I take my final bite of pasta and then push the dish in front of me.

"Well, didn't mean to make dinner convo this heavy, but here we are." Brooks sarcastically laughs, shrugging his shoulders and lifting his eyebrows.

I shake my head and say, "You didn't know. Plus, I like to talk about them, but my friend circle has always been kind of small. I was always trying to find a job, make some money, and that didn't leave much room for being social." I take a drink of the white wine, which might be the smoothest I've ever had.

Brooks gathers our dishes, puts them in the sink, and starts to wash them. I offer to help but he shakes his head no.

A man who willingly does the dishes is so hot. Not that Brooks needs any help in that department. He's leisurely gorgeous, like he was about to have dinner by himself, and I'm trying not to stare. He's wearing joggers that are tight around his thick and muscular thighs, the same ones I straddled the other night. Some could argue he may need to size up, but they would be ridiculously incorrect.

We sit in a minute of silence, which almost feels warm and perfectly heavy, the kind I hope for when I put my weighted blanket over me. When he's done with the dishes, he reaches for my hand and leads me to the living room. His hand surrounds mine and my heart races. It doesn't stop when he grabs a blanket from a basket, sits on the deep couch, and motions for me to sit next to him.

I set my wine down on the side table and sink into the couch. He opens his arm, like I could lean into him if I wanted, and I do. Brooks watches me as I'm getting situated, kicking my legs to the side and letting his arm rest on my shoulder. I can feel the way his eyes follow my movements, like velvet on my skin. It's nice being the tall girl and still fitting on the couch—I'd consider this an NBA player boyfriend perk.

Boyfriend? Oof. I stare at the wine and internally scold myself. Slow down, killer.

A fireplace boasts a fire across from us and there's a few Halloween decorations on the mantle—a ceramic ghost, a few skeletons with their legs dangling, and velvet pumpkins. Honestly, they're all pieces I'd love to have in my apartment.

"Now, did you wear that shirt specifically for me or no?" He offers a smirk as his eyes land on my tried and true Jags shirt.

"Here's the thing: a lot of my wardrobe is Jags stuff and was even before I got the job."

"I can't wait for you to experience a merch drop," Brooks muses while looking at me, and when he sees my confusion, he keeps going. "It's when we get a full run of the new line from whatever company is contracted. Everyone at the organization gets one of everything, if they want it, and then it's how they decide what to keep for retail, or toss, or save for later."

My eyes are probably bugging out of my head like a fucking Pixar character, but I literally do not care.

"Yeah, you're going to love it," Brooks says while he's drawing his fingers along my arm.

Needing to pivot the attention, I ask, "How do you like the house?" He gave me a quick tour of the downstairs when I came in. During our Jags work, he mentioned he'd recently moved.

"I like it. It's a bit much compared to what I probably need but that's okay. The built-in gate in a neighborhood that doesn't get much press is always nice."

And just like that, there's a perfect opening to one of the questions stuck on the tip of my tongue. "You know what, I've been meaning to ask. How *do* you get the press to leave you alone? Make a deal with the devil?" I joke.

"Honestly, when I'm out in public, I chat with them and try to give them exactly what they're after. I think that makes me feel available and not like they need to follow me back to my house, but that's also why the gate is nice. In case anything like that were to happen." Brooks takes a drink of his wine and sets it back down.

I did find it a bit odd that he freely gave me the code to get into his house. And that there was no one on the road or posted up, trying to see who was coming and going.

"Plus, I don't have many visitors."

The jealous part of me, who wants to ask about previous girlfriends and partners, is quieted by the comment. I'm trying to play it cool and grilling someone about their exes is not the move.

"So if you're worried about being caught coming in, I really doubt it," Brooks explains, "but there is a back entrance. I bought a bunch of land behind the house, and I don't think anyone knows it's there."

"Well, if it didn't have a secret entrance, would any of this even be worth it?" I gesture around the massive house before resting my hand on his chest. "Okay, what other hidden gems do you have? Hidden wine cellars? An ivory tower?"

"I do have a library—or, I *will* have one. The shelves are being custom built next week. Obviously, there's a gym with a sauna in the basement. Oh, and the pool outside? It's heated."

My heart damn near breaks open when he mentions the library, but when he gets to the heated pool, the library simply becomes an open tab in my brain as my mind sprints in a much different direction.

"A heated pool? What a dream." My muscles start to relax thinking about the warmth of the water. "You use it a lot?"

"Not really. It's not that fun to swim alone." Brooks is looking down at me and I can feel the flames starting to lick at my skin.

I lift myself, stretching my arms and saying, "You're not alone now." I sound much more confident than I feel. I'm ridiculously aware that I don't have a swimsuit, which means I'm inviting myself to swim with a professional athlete in my bra and panties. I feel a little better as I realize I at least put on a matching set today, which is certainly not the norm.

Brooks leans forward, capturing my mouth with his, and it feels like every bit of breath leaves my body. His lips are warm, soft, and enveloping.

He pulls away and I display great restraint by not reaching to grab a fistful of his shirt and not let him move an inch further. By not pulling his hard muscles into me. But then he says, "You're right. I'm not."

Chapter 17
Brooks

I'M IN THE POOL waiting for Lia, acting like I'm much more chill about this than I am. My heart thumps and I swear it's making waves in the water. I glance at the sliding glass door, waiting for her to walk out to the patio. Outdoor lights, dim and strewn along the trees and pergola, remind me of Lia's place. I can't take the credit—they were here when I moved in.

I wade through the water, trying to stretch my legs while I wait. The fatigue from the other night has faded but it's still there. Lingering. Reminding me of the injury. I'm amazed I was about to push through to play my normal minutes, with no one wondering if I was struggling or not. The trainer caught my eye a few times and came by to stretch me when I was on the bench. Little things like that make me want to keep playing for this team forever; I'd go to war for the training and coaching staff.

In the last few weeks, it feels like everyone came through for me—the trainer, my teammates, and Lia. It was as if she looked through to the corners of myself where I keep my secrets. I know she didn't tell anyone then, and I know she won't now. She's the kind of person you want working with a professional sports team.

She's also the kind of woman I want to myself.

Just as I'm thinking about her, I hear the sliding glass door open and see Lia wrapped in the towel I left in the bathroom. Her blonde hair is in a messy bun on top of her head, and she watches the ground as she walks closer.

"Stop it. It's perfect out here," Lia sighs, and I stare as she takes in the patio. "I'd be out here every night if I lived somewhere like this. Even if it was freezing." She gives me a side-eye look, slow and fucking sexy, as she loses the towel.

For fuck's sake. I'm doing my best not to stare but it's impossible. A light green lacy bra holds her breasts, the pink of her nipples showing through and her softness spilling over. It's paired with a matching pair of panties—I'm betting, or hoping, it's a thong—and my dick twitches. Her skin looks soft, almost like velvet, and her muscles flex when she walks. Her thighs are curvy and strong, and I immediately wonder what it'd be like to run my hands up and down them. My mouth. My tongue.

Then I see a tattoo on the front of her thigh, and I feel like I could pass out. It's a vine, starting at the top of her hip and splayed across her thigh. The ink is delicate, like it's always been part of her skin, but also bold—like you'd never forget it was there. My dick twitches as my eyes roam over her, especially her long, slender legs.

Lia scurries to the steps of the pool and I wish she'd slow down. "Do you have any tattoos?" she asks.

I cough, clearing my throat. "No, but yours is... it's..." There are no words in my head.

She purses her lips and lets out a tiny laugh. "Thank you. Did you know that some vines can survive for centuries? They're one of the most resilient and adaptable plants on the planet."

Lia has needed to adapt. It's a perfect tattoo for her and I love the excitement rolling through her words. She takes the steps into the pool, the water quickly covering her flawless fucking legs and reaching part of her tattoo. Lia's eyes find mine and I can feel the heat from my blushed cheeks.

"Ooh, this is warm," she sighs, the water hitting her stomach while steam surrounds her silhouette. Lia puts her whole body in, letting the water reach all the way to her chin and starts toward me. "My muscles," she groans, "this feels so good." Her eyes sparkle as she moves closer to me.

"It's nice but I kind of forget about it, to be honest. Plus, I'm not home that often during the season. You know how it is," I explain.

"How could you forget about this? It's amazing." The awe in her face is contagious and I'm trying to hold back a smile.

Fuck, she's gorgeous.

"What's that smile for?" Lia asks.

I look around, trying to decide on what to say, and I decide to go with honesty. "Oh, this is for you. All gorgeous, like that," I gesture to her body in the pool, "at my house. Here with me."

As the words are practically falling on top of each other and dripping out of my mouth, it's clear I barely have any game or skill. I can't keep anything to myself. "I'm also aware of how dumb that sounds," I stammer, and Lia laughs as she swims towards me. "It's just that—"

She puts a finger on my lips. "Not dumb. Not even a little bit." Her hand goes from my mouth to the nape of my neck while she stares at me, her eyes like the lights of the pool reflecting off her own evergreen depths. Lia's other hand circles my neck, and I put my hands on her sides, feeling her ribs. She then dips and wraps her legs around my waist, and I hold her to me.

"No, this definitely isn't dumb," I assure, my lips close to hers and our noses almost touching.

My hands roam down from her lower back to the delicate lace of her panties, my fingers dancing along the thin piece of fabric. Lia's eyes lock on mine as my hands shift to her ass, nothing between her skin and mine.

My cock strains against my shorts and throbs with each touch of her. Fuck, the fabric between us is too much.

"Should we talk about this?" Lia's words fill the sliver of space between us. "Whatever this is. You and me." Her voice gets smaller as she continues.

"If you want to." I lean my head back, giving her space.

"You're okay with keeping this a secret?" she asks, searching my face for something.

"I'm okay with whatever has you coming over for dinner. And swimming in my pool." I place a kiss on her mouth. "I'm a fairly private person and I'll keep this a secret for as long as you need."

She leans in, deepening the kiss and putting a little moan on my lips. Fuck. That noise. That mouth.

Lia pulls away, looking at me. "It feels like this job is a good fit for what I'm looking for long term, but so do you."

So do you.

She immediately bites her lip. "Fuck, I don't think I should've said that. I'm not trying to be all clingy and whatever but it's, like, such a surprise we've met and connected, and—"

I kiss her to stop the rambling and tell her that I agree. "You're not clingy. You're being clear and direct, which I like." She puts her hands through my hair and locks her eyes on mine. "If this is your secret to keep, I'll happily do it."

"For now." She says it almost like a question, needing reassurance.

"For now." I nod and let her fall into me, her head finding the crook of my neck.

"We're doing this?" she asks, her lips close to my ear lobe. I lean into her as she nips me.

"You and me, baby."

Lia kisses me with urgency this time, and it feels like the walls have come down. Maybe she was holding back before?

Her arms loop around my neck and I kiss the column of her throat while she leans back, giving me space. The sheer lace has my mouth watering—her nipples, pink and pointed, underneath the fabric. My mouth finds the tops of her tits and peppers them with kisses. Lia pushes her hips further into me and arches her back, letting out a small moan which makes me smirk against her skin.

"Those noises you make. Fuck," I groan as I drag my tongue across the top of her cleavage.

A hand goes through my hair, pulling on the dark strands to show me where she wants my mouth. A woman who can take charge? This keeps getting better and better. I move us to the bench in the pool and put her ass on the ledge.

I wondered if this would feel awkward or muted. It doesn't. Thank god. For me, there's not an ounce of doubt or questioning. I want her. She wants me. It's a risk but it feels like it's worth taking.

I step closer, letting my length hit her center. Lia's eyes light up, wide and a bit surprised, but then she wears a devious grin.

"This ledge seems awfully practical." She puts her hands on the sides of her legs, emphasizing while spreading them for me.

Her lips take mine and she tastes like the wine from dinner. A light breeze rushes through the trees, causing some of the leaves to fall from their branches, and my exposed skin goosebumps for a second.

I move my hips, touching her and pulling away, watching her expression as my dick touches the lace of her panties. Lia leans back, her arms resting on the edge of the pool. She moans each time I touch her, even though the fabric stays between us. When one of her hands reaches down her body until it's under the lace, grabbing a nipple and rolling it in her own fingers, my balls tighten.

"Keep touching yourself like that," I moan before kissing her jaw and down her throat.

She switches and is pinching the other nipple while her head tips back, her eyes closed. "Are you telling me what to do?" she asks, all breathy and needy.

"Are you listening?" I stretch the letters of the word. She nods her head. "Good girl," I whisper into her ear. "Now reach into your panties and touch yourself."

I step back, wanting to watch her. Without hesitation, her fingers rub down her cleavage, running over her stomach and sliding underneath the lace. I follow suit and wrap my hand around my dick. Through the water, I see when her fingers reach her clit. She releases a gasp and closes her eyes, tipping her head to the sky.

"Eyes on me," I practically growl. I don't want her hiding from me.

Lia's eyes, fierce and blazing, pop open and lock on mine. Her eyelashes are thick and flutter. When she sees my hand touching myself, she bites her lower lip.

"I—" She stammers and stops.

"Tell me what you want." I surprise myself when the words don't sound like a suggestion, but more of a demand.

Lia sighs out a breath. "I want you." She bites her lip and lasers a look in my direction. "I want you to touch me."

Chapter 18
Lia

I'M WAITING FOR FLAMES to dance on the top of my skin, even though I'm surrounded by water. Every look Brooks shoots my way is like there's nothing else in the world. Just him and I.

I'm not one to be vocal—or maybe no man has ever given me the space to do so. But I do know that if my orgasm comes from my own touching, that will be disappointing. I need Brooks. Want him. Even if it scares the hell out of me.

Even if I'm not sure I deserve it.

"You asking for me," he murmurs, closing the distance between us, "is music to my ears." He kisses me quick and hard, dragging his lips down the column of my neck.

"I do want you but—" Alarm bells ring out in my brain. They're telling me to be cautious, urging me to soak in the moments instead of speed through them.

He slowly pulls away so he can see me, his eyes roaming over my face.

"I'm not trying to sound annoying but I kind of want to take this slow." I hate how my voice loses steam as the sentence drags on.

"Whatever you want, Lia. I mean that."

"I've done the casual hookup thing, and I don't want to do that with you. I think you could be more." I put my mouth on his, mostly to cover the embarrassment of my vulnerability showing as a quick blush of my cheeks.

I can't believe I just said that. What is wrong with me?

"I could be more?" he asks in between kisses. I can feel his lips smiling into mine, his cheeks bunched, which immediately lessens the anxiety of what I've asked for—what I've shared. I kiss into him, letting his tongue sweep mine, wanting him to take more of me.

Brooks sits next to me then reaches over, grabbing my hips and picking me up. His hands digging into my skin has me holding my breath. He gets me where he wants me, which is between his legs with my back to his chest. I can feel his muscles tense and his erection hitting above my ass.

Pulling my back flush with his chest, he places both hands on my chest, his fingers feeling the lace before grabbing and ripping the bra down the middle.

I gasp before I mutter, "This is my favorite set. *Was*. I guess."

"I'll get you a new set. This same one. New ones. Whatever you want." He kisses the side of my neck and then my shoulder.

His fingers roll a nipple in each hand and I grip his legs, trying to get any leverage. His legs flex when my hands dig in and I draw a moan from him. My body sings as I push harder into him, my shoulder blades pressing to his chest and pushing back. The steam rolls off the pool as air rustles the trees, a quick reminder that it's late October. Goosebumps break out over my skin right as the heel of Brooks' hand pushes down my body, hitting my clit.

Brooks presses his mouth to the curve of my neck. "Is this okay?"

"If you stop, it won't be," I answer, needier than I'd like.

His fingers brush the spot where fabric and skin meet, right below my navel. Before it comes to me begging, he slips his hand in, and his skin on mine has me lifting my hips. The water helps me push myself closer to his fingers, aching for him to never quit touching me.

His other hand reaches across my body, his forearm flexed against my pebbled chest. The steam crawls up, meeting the skin outside of the water, and I let my head fall back into Brooks' shoulder. His fingers dance along the edge of the lace of my panties, teasing me along the side of my thighs.

I take an arm and hook it behind his neck to lift myself a little, aching for the pressure I need. When the lace of my panties rubs against my center, I shiver against his broad chest.

"Fuck. You like this... it's so hot," he groans into the soft spot between my neck and ear.

His words surround me. They almost wrap me in a bubble that's about to pop. He's barely touched me, but I'm already so close. It's the pressure on my shoulders from his strong front, the way he keeps rolling a nipple with his free hand, the way his lips keep dusting my skin.

It's like Brooks knows he's pushing the limit because his hand finds my center and he draws circles lightly, changing the pressure. My abs let out a tiny shiver when he gets it just right and he definitely picks up on it. Each time he makes me buck, I swear I can feel that devilish smirk on me.

Then it feels like the pressure from the water is too much—overwhelming in the best way—my orgasm running up the hill instead of aching away in my low belly. I can almost reach for it. Put my hands around it and squeeze.

Brooks nips my shoulder and picks up the pace, circling, and my hips move perfectly to roll me down the hill. My climax hits me hard. My muscles tense and release, shaking on Brooks' still-moving hands. He licks along my neck and a whimper falls from my mouth before I can't help but let out a scream.

He doesn't stop. His fingers, his mouth—they stick with me the entire time. The orgasm stretches and when I think it's going to slow, it doesn't. Squeezing my eyes shut, I suck in a breath, and when I open my eyes I'm seeing stars. It's like the world is happening around me in slow motion, and all I can feel is Brooks all around me.

My nerves are deliciously raw, and my bones almost feel heavy. Leaning farther into Brooks, I can't help but accept the smile plastered on my lips.

This. What? How? My brain tries to process of the impromptu evening and it makes no sense. How do I feel this good? How has the happiness sort of settled into me?

Brooks breaks the spell with a kiss to my neck. Proving, again, this actually happened.

"I fear I've not been putting this pool to good use… until tonight." He hugs me to him and all I can think is: how is this man real?

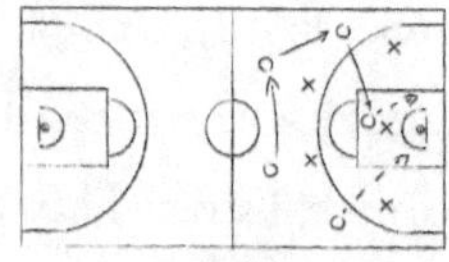

My phone buzzes as I swing open the door to my apartment. The clock tells me it's after two in the morning but my heart races with energy.

Brooks

let me know when you're home

Seeing his name has my stomach flipping like Simone Biles.

Me

home. About to crash

me too. thanks for coming over

thanks for dinner and the swim

> feel free to bring a suit to leave here next time

> or not

When he sends a few devil emojis, I shake my head, my hands covering my eyes. Did tonight really happen? Did Brooks cook for me? Did I swim in his pool in only my bra and panties? Did he actually rip my bra down the middle? Did I let him deliver one of the most earth-shattering orgasms of my life and with only his hands?

Yes. Yes. Yes. Yes, and yes.

I could've stayed the night but that felt too fast. I didn't want to ruin anything, kind of like when you first flip open the page of a new notebook and the pages are crisp and flat. Also, I didn't want to push my luck. Or karma. Or whatever the hell is working in the background to bring Brooks Pittman to me.

I feel the warmth rush over my cheeks—the only confirmation I need.

Falling into bed, I pull the duvet to my chin and try to remember the last time I had a secret this good.

Chapter 19
Brooks

"Going to start calling you Corn Flakes," Jalen teases while he laces his shoes. We're at the gym even though it's our day off, but it feels good. Getting back into a routine has been a key part of my recovery and something that's immediately benefited my mental health. Who would've thought consistency was one of the main things keeping me sane?

"Corn Flakes?"

"Yeah, you flaked last night. The bar? You said you'd come for at least one drink."

Well, shit. I completely forgot.

He stands in front of me. "What happened?"

"I, ugh, lost track of time," I lie, focusing on my own shoes.

Jalen says nothing as I stand, putting my phone away in my locker.

"You're shit at lying. You know that right?" His eyebrows are raised and he's not telling me anything I don't already know. I didn't consider this part—keeping a secret from people who know me, like Jalen.

I mean, there's no way Lia isn't going to tell a girlfriend or two. My brain tries to calculate the risk of telling Jalen *everything*. He's the guy I'd call for anything I truly needed, no matter where I was, and I know he'd come through.

"Why are you thinking so damn hard? Smoke is going to start coming out of your ears," he laughs, proving how well he knows me.

"It's kind of a secret," I admit, looking around the locker room to make sure it's still the two of us.

"You act like I haven't seen you read a romance book on your Kindle on an away game flight. Or how about the time we went and saw the new Grinch movie and you cried at the end?"

The blood hits my cheeks and I shake my head before laughing and covering my eyes with my hands. "Do you ever stop talking?"

"I didn't tell anyone about that. Not even Stephanie. You know she has a book club? They read the same book you were reading, and I didn't even tell her then!"

I take a breath, slow and steady. I need to tell Jalen. One, he'll never quit asking. Two, I'm going to need his advice at some point. After Lia left last night, my nerves kept me awake much later than fucking appropriate. I haven't done this in so long. Whatever happened with Rebecca was years ago at this point and that was a complete disaster. I haven't dated someone in longer than I'd like to admit.

"Fine, fine. I trust you." I push my hands through my hair and they land behind my neck, pulling. "It's Lia and me. We're dating. But it's a secret."

Jalen claps his hands—it catches me off guard and I flinch—and spins in a circle. "Fuck yes! I knew it. I KNEW IT. Tell me she's the reason you bailed last night." He has his hands on his knees, looking at me.

"Yes. She came over for dinner," I answer quietly, nervously looking around to double check it's still just us.

"Man, this is something else. You basically stumble on this gorgeous woman in the wild, and then she gets hired but her main project is hanging with you. Should be easy to keep it low-key, to be honest," he says. "You already have an excuse as to why you'd be together!"

Damn. I didn't even think of it that way. Relief spreads through my chest—telling Jalen is already paying off.

"You know I'll keep all your secrets." Jalen leads us from the locker room into the hallway. "She seems cool."

He's giving me an opening, a place to share, but it's not one I think I'm ready for. Jalen hops onto the court, his shoes squeaking, and it brings the feeling of familiarity—a routine that's part of my chemical makeup—as I take a ball off the rack.

"She's definitely cool," I agree, squeezing the ball between my hands.

I'm thankful it's only the two of us, at least for now. Dribbling, I run up and down the court, all ninety-four feet, over and over as my mind replays last night with Lia. People have come and gone my whole life, but the basketball court has never left me. Maybe that's why I do my best thinking here.

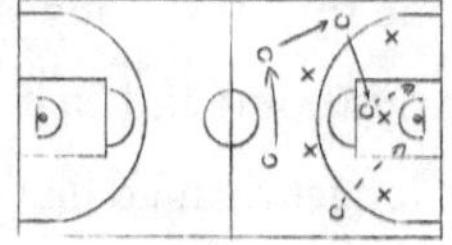

I knock on the door, even though Chris says I can just come in—it still doesn't feel right.

"Brooks! So good to see you," Mack, technically my stepmom, swings open the door, wearing the same big smile I'm used to seeing. "Riley's inside."

When I step in, the warmth wraps around me, a contrast to the snow flurrying outside. It also smells incredible, surely due to a hell of a spread. Pre-game plays on a massive TV in the living room, showing flashes of the Upstate Cosmos warming up. They have an away game today, otherwise I would've been able to make this one. Mack and Chris don't go to many games—they get too nervous watching Zack in person, even though he's a long snapper and chances of him suffering a serious injury are low.

Riley hops off a bar stool in the kitchen, wearing a blue Cosmos jersey, and runs over to me. "Thank god! My mom made enough food for at least an entire starting lineup." She wraps me in a hug, which is a common occurrence at the Hayes household.

She leads me to the kitchen island, where there's a charcuterie board, chicken wings, fries, a few different types of dip, and a bowl of Pop Rocks—Zack's favorite candy and a sort of good luck charm for the family. No matter what, we're all supposed to eat Pop Rocks on game day.

I know if I peek in the pantry, I'll find Sour Patch Kids, my go-to candy. They do the same thing when I play; it might seem small, but it makes me feel like I'm part of the crew.

"It smells great in here," I say, sitting down next to Riley.

"Ah, Chris has been smoking wings all day. He's finishing them on the grill," Mack answers while she stirs a pot on the stove. "I've got the beer cheese dip almost ready."

Riley bumps my shoulder with her and gives me a side-eye look. "Hope you haven't eaten in three days and are that hungry," she jokes.

The door to the patio swings open and Chris walks in with a plate full of saucy chicken wings. I can smell the spice from here.

"You made it! Glad you could come," he booms as he sets down the plate and offers up a cold handshake. We awkwardly stand in front of each other, Chris with his hands on his hips and me sitting back down.

These are good people, but I'd be lying if I said connecting with my dad has been easy. It's like we don't know what to say to each other. I guess that's to be expected considering our relationship is still new and there isn't a roadmap on how to do this.

When I signed my latest contract extension, I bought my mom a new house. While I was helping her move, I found a box in her attic, one that had letters addressed to Chris telling him about me—how I was his son.

Turns out, they had a brief fling while he and Mack were on a break, and my mom never told him she was pregnant. A wild string of events which were only made wilder when I stumbled upon Zack in Mexico. I was there for an NBA game, and we ended up crossing paths.

Everyone has been accepting, kind and open. But sometimes it feels like I fell into something I wasn't supposed to have. It was always me and my mom against the world. Sometimes, it feels like I'm cheating; like I'm not supposed to have these things.

"You were great the other night. Gotta feel good to be back," Riley compliments me, doing her best to soothe the awkward silence everyone in the room must feel.

"Thanks. The team's been solid. Fun start."

"You know what, I appreciate that about you. When Zack threw that touchdown pass in the Super Bowl, I knew then and there we'd hear about it for the rest of time. You're all Mr. Cool." She flicks her hair off her shoulder.

"I mean, if I hit a game winner that wins the Jags a championship, I think I'll like to bring it up." I laugh and shrug my shoulders, knowing my energy and Zack's are similar but not the same. Zack is the kind of guy who could bring up that pass every other day, but you wouldn't find it in yourself to be annoyed with him.

"Maybe this year?" Riley asks, smiling at me with a shoulder shrug.

Probably not. The voice in my head is quick to respond. Sometimes it's hard for me to accept that things like this could happen to me. As if everyone else is meant to win a championship, but not me. Maybe I like to keep expectations low, especially because I feel like I've already lucked out? I wanted to play in the NBA, but I can't believe it's actually my job—maybe I've used up all my good luck or whatever the hell helped get me here.

Mack hands me a plate and tilts her head to the counter where all the food is waiting for us to dig in. "The game starts in a few minutes. Get a plate."

Riley stands and I follow, my mouth watering at the smell of hot smoky wings filling the kitchen.

Chris comes out of the pantry with a bag. "You have to try these. Had a colleague bring cashews back from a business trip in India." He holds the bag out to me with the top open.

The smell of the nuts makes my stomach churn. "I'm okay. Thanks though," I try to politely decline.

"Oh, come on. They're so good." Chris reaches in, grabs a cashew, and pops it in his mouth. He shakes the bag at me with a little smirk.

"I can't—"

"Sure you can," Chris insists, interrupting me.

"No, I'm allergic to cashews." My voice is quiet, but the kitchen is quieter.

A red flush creeps into my dad's cheeks, and I feel like mine match. He slowly closes the bag, keeping his eyes glued to the floor as he walks the nuts back to the pantry.

"Are you allergic to peanuts?" Mack asks, her voice soft but still cutting through the silence.

"No, just tree nuts. Cashews are the worst though."

Mack nods, Riley uses a spoon to scoop a dip on her plate, and Chris doesn't say anything. It's something small, something people close to me have known mostly my entire life, but this is an example of things that get lost in a situation like mine.

"Ugh, sorry. I should know that..." Chris apologizes, his voice soft on the edges.

Lifting my hands up, I say, "No, how could you? It's no problem. I'll pass on the cashews though." I try to laugh it off, giving slack to the tense rope cutting through us.

I'm not angry or disappointed, but it does fucking sting.

It serves as a reminder of all the experiences we've missed out on together.

Chapter 20
Brooks

I'm BACK HOME AFTER celebrating a Cosmos win with my family, which is still weird to say. When I look out the patio door and see the steam rising from the pool, wrestling with the chilled November air, images of Lia rush back. I'm licking my fucking lips thinking of her. I snap a picture of the pool and text it to Lia.

Lia

don't tempt me

Me

i don't know what you're talking about

sure you don't

good Cosmos win today

did you watch?

yeah, i was with my dad

nice to see them

wish no one would've seen Zack's pregame fit though

haha he does love a fashion moment

the pink and white checkers were horrible

damn. thought about getting you a matching blazer

no thanks

but if you want to shop, I think I owe you

i am missing my favorite bra

all lacy

see through

who is tempting who now

what? I'm just trying to remind you

for the replacement

believe me, I'll never forget what it looked like

so you did like it?

what kind of question is that

yes

hell yes

fuck yes

take your pick

i like the idea of you picking out a replacement

I've never wanted to shop more

the idea of me choosing something for you

fuck. that's hot

are you about to swim or are you teasing me

if I said yes, would you come over?

i'm teaching yoga early tomorrow morning

otherwise i'd already be in the car

feels like you're the one teasing me

believe me, wish I was

fuck, you don't know how hot that is

i think i do

but i need to get to sleep, 4:30 am alarm is set

how do i go about scheduling a private yoga session

i'm sure i can fit you in...

you're fucking killing me

night brooks

Chapter 21
Lia

CENTER COURT IS COVERED with puppies, and I think I'm in love. One reason is the dogs running around, and the second is that this was my first pitched idea and Megan agreed to it. If there's one thing people love, it's dogs, and if you have a 6'3" basketball forward sitting with one on the floor and making heart eyes, they love it even more.

All jokes aside, this is a great cause. The local shelter is overrun with dogs to adopt, and while the Jags followers will swoon over their favorite player petting a drooly puppy, it brings great visibility to the dogs themselves. I'm hoping a few find their forever homes today.

My heart warms as the players walk in, not knowing what they're getting themselves into, and immediately brighten when they see the surprise we've been keeping. I didn't even tell Brooks—to be fair, he didn't really ask. That was something we were clear about: keeping work separate from the two of us, especially because we work together closely. Also, if I don't set a boundary, I'll spend time at work thinking about him in ways colleagues should not. His hands. His hands on me. His hands on my—

"All of this is content gold, Lia!" Megan compliments me, immediately stopping my short trip into fantasy land.

I'm filming B-roll content, which are usually pieces to be used later and for other media channels, when I get the pull to look up. *Brooks.* He smirks at me, which I catch in real time—not through a phone screen—and his cheeks pinch a bit. He offers a slight shake of the head and follows his teammates to center court. Some of the dogs start to bark and jump on the makeshift fence meant to keep them contained.

I move with the team as they shake hands with volunteers, taking pictures and signing jerseys. This is just the pick-me-up I needed. I don't know if I've been sleeping wrong or what, but my body has been sore on and off for the last few days. My typical yoga routine isn't cutting it—my muscle are still stiff, especially when it comes to my hands and wrists.

Since the shelter is local, all the volunteers seem to be massive Jags fans. We gave each of them jerseys to wear, picking their favorite player, and we asked the team to sign them as they came in. I'd be lying if I said I didn't smile extra wide whenever someone wanted a Pittman jersey.

Jalen is the first one through the line and immediately steps into the puppy den. He sits on the floor and lets them walk on top of him, licking his face. Since this is a team event, I get to spend more time with players other than Brooks, which is a nice change of pace. The guys are great, especially after Coach made it a point for everyone to meet me. He said, "She's part of this thing, the least you could do is learn her name." If other coaches or male execs in the NBA had this sentiment, we'd be closing a smaller gap when it came to women in sports.

I kneel, getting close to Jalen so I can see his face, right as a golden retriever puppy paws at him and ask, "Do you have a pet at home?"

He tries to look at the camera, but the puppy is awfully demanding of his attention. "No, I don't."

"Hmm, I feel like today could be the perfect day to find one. Don't you think?" It's a joke, but also a suggestion. I don't expect any of the players to take dogs home, but if they did, that would make me ridiculously happy. Jalen laughs and it's sort of the perfect reaction.

I've always wanted a dog. Wes and I asked for one every birthday and Christmas, and the agreement was when I turned thirteen, we'd get a family dog—I think the idea being Wes and I would be old enough to take care of it. My parents were gone before that birthday. I remember silently crying while my aunt and uncle sang to me, candles burning on a chocolate cake. Wes reached under the table and held my hand so tight, I think to keep himself from crying.

There was no birthday wish that year. The things I wanted weren't possible, which sort of sucked all the hope out of me. I needed a time machine and even at thirteen, I knew they weren't real.

Someone playfully bumps into my shoulder, bringing me forward about fourteen years and back to the Jags court. "You good?" Brooks asks.

I put on a smile, the one I've practiced for over a decade. It's best used in public when there isn't room for the tears or the depressing walk down memory lane. "Yes. All good. Just in a daze watching Jalen roll on the ground with the dogs," I reply, watching as more Jags players join in.

"He does seem right at home, doesn't he?" Brooks crosses his arms and I zoom in. Two dogs are pulling at Jalen's sweatshirt drawstrings and another scratching at his tied shoelaces.

Once I've gotten enough content of Jalen, I turn to Brooks. "Tell us about your pet history." I use my best interviewer voice, the one indicating this is content I'll want to edit.

He shrugs his shoulders. "Actually, there's no history. There was a stray cat who would hang outside the rundown court where I spent basically every day after school when I was a kid. I ended up using my lunch money to buy a small bag of cat food and I'd bring a little every day. When it got cold, I convinced my mom to get me a plastic tote, cut a hole in it, and make a spot for it to hide from the elements."

The tears in my eyes are about to spill over. Is this man for real? A woman *must* have crafted him from all the things we love about a person. Fuck, I've got it bad if I think he's the equivalent of a *man written by a woman*, one of my favorite pieces of the romance books I love to read.

"Brooks Pittman, that might be the sweetest thing I've ever heard. You used your lunch money?" I try to keep my voice from sounding too shrill. No one likes a voice like that coming through the speakers as you're scrolling social media.

"Yes. Until my mom found out. Then she started bringing home cat food and helped me with whatever I asked. I think she was praying I didn't ask to bring it home." He laughs and crosses his arms. "No dogs, though."

Brooks looks from me to the dogs hanging out. There's a solid mix of adoptees; everything from a few puppies to senior dogs in all shapes and sizes. We walk closer and he puts his hands behind his back, leaning over the chaos.

"Get in there. Do it for the content," I encourage him. "Do it for the dogs." I mention the tagline I pitched to Megan—let's try and get the other NBA teams to do something similar or make donations to local shelters. She hesitantly agreed, as long as I didn't get my hopes up.

Brooks is hesitant but steps over the barrier like it's nothing—perks of being an NBA player. He's looking at me while stepping into the dark side. Immediately, he finds some older dogs who are off to the side on scattered beds and blankets. It's almost like they're thankful for the break from the chaos. The puppies are with Jalen and some of the other Jags players, jumping and barking; this seems to match perfectly.

I watch as Brooks sits down beside a black and white English bulldog. He's lying on a blanket, and when we get closer, I can tell he's shivering. It's warm in here, in addition to the blankets, so I think he's scared. My heart drops thinking about what could have happened to him to feel this way. His eyes are wide, and I can't stop staring at his sweet facial rolls.

I must wear my brain on my sleeve because a volunteer says quietly, "That's Rocky. He was surrendered a few months ago. His family got a new puppy for a birthday and couldn't keep both. We're guessing he's three years old, so he's basically a puppy himself."

The explanation is a punch to the gut. I fight the urge to let tears spill over and instead run to Rocky where my hands pet him, getting stuck on his velvety ears. I'll never understand how a family can get rid of a pet like that, but according to research while looking for volunteer opportunities, it seems to be fairly common.

"He's great. Just wants a warm place to sleep. Do you have a dog?" the volunteer asks.

I wish. "I don't, but I live in a studio apartment with no yard or anything. He's probably a great fit for me as a person, but not for my current living situation." I've never considered bringing home a dog until now.

It looks like Rocky is warming up to Brooks as he's sniffing the hand that he holds out. A moment later, the bulldog rolls to his back, exposing his belly, and Brooks' lips tug on one side as he provides scratches and pets.

I make sure to zoom in to capture the sweet moment with Brooks and Rocky. These two seem to match with their gentle energy. Walking to the space behind them, I lean down and whisper, "Just a reminder, all of these dogs are available."

Brooks scoffs. "I wish. It's a terrible thing to work a job that keeps me away from home about half the time during the season." He looks at me without breaking contact with the wrinkly dog, who is soaking in all the attention.

"They have dog walkers for that. The volunteers have some great leads on people they'd recommend… I made sure to ask, in case any of you were interested in taking one of these sweet babies home."

I promised myself I'd only hand out short-lived guilt trips today; a little guilt can go a long way. Some of the players already have dogs at home, and I'm not trying to overwhelm anyone.

Brooks looks down at the dog, whose eyes are on the verge of closing. It's like he's in complete bliss. "You seem to think of everything."

"There's no pressure. I'm thankful we can bring visibility to a cause like this. Hopefully we can find homes for all of them."

A few seconds later, a soft snore escapes Rocky, his lips flapping—and my heart melting—with the exhale.

"Jalen, you're responsible for any accidents that occur outside of this area," Megan shouts, as he's taken a puppy out of the fenced-in space and starts rolling a ball towards it. She's laughing, but everyone knows she means it, which is my favorite thing about her—she can be firm without getting a side-eyed glance or the stereotypical "she's too direct" comment.

Megan reminds me how close I am to Brooks, who smells like peppermint. I so badly want to wrap my arms around him from behind, press my cheek to his, and convince him to get this dog. He's the kind of guy you want to touch. Instead, I stand and create some distance before I get carried away.

We get a few group pictures of the volunteers and the team. I even get everyone to do a quick lip sync video for social media, which might be a little cringey, but at the end of the day, some of them are fun to watch.

When I've got all I need, I say my goodbyes to the volunteer team so I can get to work on getting the raw footage post ready—the sooner it's live, the sooner people can adopt dogs from the shelter.

I make the turn from the court into the empty hallway when Brooks catches up to me.

His voice is quiet. "Hey, you have plans tonight?"

I look around to double check it's just the two of us. "Plans to do nothing," I answer, keeping my voice small with several feet between us. "Excited to get cozy and not do much of anything." It's a night I have circled on my calendar because I can't remember the last time I allowed myself to have one like this.

"What if I bring dinner over? We could do nothing together." Brooks lifts a foot and stretches his quad while peeking down the hall that confirm no one is hanging around.

I nod. "I'll text you," I say, trying to hide my smile.

A man that offers to bring dinner? And do nothing? Oof. This is getting out of hand... in the best way.

Chapter 22
Brooks

I'm outside Lia's apartment and nervous energy pricks the tips of my ears. Part of it was due to a random person asking if they've seen me from somewhere, like they almost recognized me, but it's also about who is on the other side of the door. It's alarming to think about how new this is, how I've only known her a few weeks—it feels much longer. My fingers reach down, looking for the tape that's there for practices and game day. There's nothing there, but my fingers run over the place it typically is.

She opens the door, wearing a smile and a matching pajama set—pink with white stripes. I want to wrap her tight, pull her close.

"I brought a few different soups and salads from a place by my house. Thought we could share," I offer as I set the bag on the counter. Again, I'm not big on sharing my food but for some reason it's different with Lia. She didn't ask or assume, but it seems to fit.

Lia takes in an exaggerated breath through her nose. "It smells so good. Thanks for grabbing it." She sits down on the barstool at the counter and lets me unbox everything. I watch as she rubs the same spot over and over again on her elbow.

"Are you okay?" I ask, pointing to her hand.

She shakes her head, like she didn't know she was doing it. "Yes. I'm trying to find a dermatologist who takes my horrible insurance, but I've had no luck. I went to a walk-in clinic and they gave me some cream but it's still super dry. Not a big deal." Lia reaches for a spoon and a container of chicken pot pie soup.

After we've eaten our weight in soup and salad, Lia asks, "Are you ready to do nothing?" Her words are quick and eyes big as I nod. "Come on." I grab my tablet and earbuds before I follow her to her room.

Lia's apartment is cozy—something I want for my own space. Since it's a studio apartment, she's needed to get creative on the room she has. My favorite is how she used bookshelves to create a boundary between the main living area and her bed.

She lifts the duvet cover and slips into bed, propping up the pillows before patting the side next to her. I follow suit and sink onto what feels like one of the nicest mattresses I've ever touched.

"Call me Ms. Ironic, asking you to take it slow and then inviting you to bed." Lia laughs at herself, pressing her hands on the comforter. "Apologies for the mixed signals."

Her voice feels like she's on the edge of self-deprecation. Doubt crinkles the edge of words from a woman who usually seems to know what she wants.

I grab the hand closest to mine and squeeze, trying to reassure her as I say, "You know what? I'm a big fan of mixed signals. Keep me on my toes."

Lia's lips turn up the smallest bit at the corner as she uses her phone to turn on the smart TV. She opens YouTube and clicks a recently viewed video, but it's only the sound of a crackling fire. I think it's meant to feel like we're sitting in a corner of the lodge that shows on the screen.

She immediately starts to defend herself. "Don't make fun of me until you give it a few minutes."

"I think I like this," I say, letting my arms fall on the side of the duvet cover. I swear, I can feel her beam next to me.

"Okay, you brought your iPad. What's the plan?"

"I need to watch some film for the upcoming teams on the schedule. I brought headphones, though."

She looks offended as she protests, "I want to watch film with you! We can put it on the TV."

I quirk an eyebrow. "What about the fireplace thing?"

"The twelve hours of fireplace aesthetic will be waiting for us whenever we need it. I've never gotten to watch film with a professional athlete before." She sits up a little straighter and displays a code on her TV for me to pair my tablet.

I type in the code, seeing a mirror of what's on my tablet screen show on the TV. Before I push play, I stop. I look over to Lia, and her eager face and wide eyes have my heart pounding in my chest. Thumping floods my ears and I take a slow breath, recognizing the heaviness I typically feel becoming slightly less and less. This woman is fun, but the kind of fun that I've been looking for—a kind I was skeptical I'd find.

"What's wrong?" Lia asks.

I turn and reach a hand for her, placing it at the nape of her neck before pulling her lips into mine. Lia opens her mouth, giving me room to really sink into this kiss. I taste her and she puts a hand in my hair, pushing it back.

I pull away so our foreheads are touching and answer, "Absolutely nothing is wrong." Lia quickly presses another kiss to my mouth.

I sit back, propped up on pillows, and push play on the game featuring the top team in our conference. The Jags sit at third, only three games back, but the Denver Gold Rush have a roster that's about to make a serious run at a championship.

The starting lineup is announced as Lia says, "They finally might have all the pieces this season," like she was reading my mind. "I called this three years ago when they created cap space with their young roster. Fans were pissed about letting a few of the veterans sign max deals somewhere else, but they wouldn't be set up like they are now without those moves."

My mouth might be hanging open at her observation on their roster moves and cap space, which at a base level is the amount of money a team has for player contracts. You can go beyond cap space, but it costs the organization a ton of extra money on top of the contracts.

"You said that like you were an announcer for this game." I shake my head and try not to stare at the gorgeous woman who is much more than the fan she claims to be.

"Want to trade secrets? I'll go first," Lia suggests with a hand on her chest. I nod, pause the film, and she continues. "Calling an NBA game? The dream. I practice with old games... turn off the commentary and act like I'm calling them." She tucks a chunk of blonde hair behind her ears and looks at the paused game on the TV. "I majored in Electronic Media Broadcasting and Sports Journalism at my small local college. I love what I'm doing now, but calling games would be the ultimate goal."

"You could do it." The words sprint out of my mouth, a true gut reaction.

Lia scoffs and silently laughs to herself. "You do know that we're just now seeing women in key roles in the NBA, right? Like, it's only been a few seasons of women being referees, in the booth, or on coaching payrolls."

"Perfect timing for Lia Stone to make waves," I boast so mat-ter-of-factly, she tilts her head in surprise. "Listen, there are fans and people who like sports, and then there's you. You have a different kind of love for the game."

"Thank you for the compliment. Very kind of you to say." Lia rubs her hands together and stares down.

I reach over and grab her hands, squeezing, wanting her to look at me. When she does, I insist, "I really think you could do it. You're smart and have the personality for someone in the booth. I'm not just saying it."

She slowly smiles and it feels like I've chipped away a little bit of the apprehension and doubt. "Your turn," she insists.

I look at the ceiling, at the lights littering across while I think of a secret to trade.

"I've always wanted to take a dance class. There was this studio near my house when I was younger. Might've been twelve when I went in and grabbed a brochure. As soon as I saw the cost, I shoved it in my backpack and never mentioned it to my mom."

"You wanted to dance? Stop, I love that so much." Lia turns to me, clasping her hands at her chest and squinting her eyes shut. "You know there's still time, right?"

"Maybe someday," I laugh, shaking my shoulders and getting comfortable as I press play.

"I'd dance with you," she croons, her eyes framed with thick lashes.

Fuck. Why does she have me considering this?

We settle in, the sound of sports commentary and shoes squeaking on the court filling the space around us. When Lia's fingers find mine, I'm not sure I've ever had a better date. This right here? It's everything.

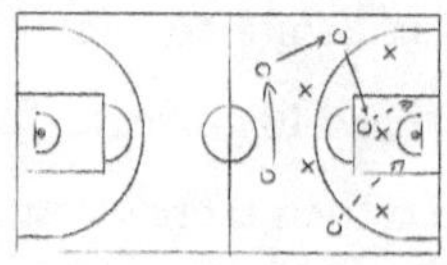

I wake up and it takes me a minute to realize where I am: Lia's; well, specifically her bed. We finished a game, let the next one start, and Lia put her head on my chest. The heaviness of her resting on me made it too easy to fall asleep. The TV has turned off, probably because nothing had played for a while, and I look at my watch to find it's after midnight.

My eyes adjust and I realize Lia is now fully draped across my chest. With a hand looped around my upper arm and her head on my chest, I can't help but soften my shoulders and relax a little bit. I feel her breathe against me, and I can't remember the last time I've felt this—a genuine and honest connection. Everything about this—from Lia wanting to take things slow to having a night together like this—makes it feel like I might've found something worthwhile.

Chapter 23
Lia

"The two of you are going viral!" Megan shouts, practically speed walking onto the court to where Brooks and I are filming content, her heels making sharp clicks.

"What do you mean?" I ask as she happily shoves her phone in front of me, showing me a video that has fifty thousand likes. It's the one where I completed the obstacle course rehab routine that Brooks kept getting stuck on.

"I posted that yesterday," she exclaims. I take her phone and look at the other stats, my jaw dropping at the impressions and views on a single app. We cross-post content from one app to another on a strategic drip schedule. I put it on the first two apps yesterday and we'll post on two others in three days to push the engagement further. Not sure if that makes a difference, but part of my job is to find what works.

Brooks looks over my shoulder, the closeness almost making my ears buzz. "Holy shit."

Pointing between the two of us, Megan says, "I hope you two are having fun because I'm going to need more of this. The two of you guys interacting, just like this." She taps her phone. "Everything I've seen is so natural. You never come off rigid. It's perfect!" Megan claps her hands in excitement.

I try to hide the blush that's about to hit my cheeks. Of course we don't come off rigid—this man has had my nipples in his mouth and given me an orgasm in his pool. When I don't know what to say, Brooks thankfully jumps in.

"I'm having fun, when she's not kicking my ass in rehab and putting it on the Internet," Brooks replies with a wink. He knew I was going to post it, but I'm not sure he saw the final product beforehand.

Megan claps her hands together. "That's what I'm talking about. You two get along so well and it's so authentic."

My chest warms at the observation. It makes sense, considering how easy everything feels with Brooks. I wonder how far the previous hire got with this project. Couldn't have been too far, considering the social media accounts I help manage don't have anything like this in the drafts, and Brooks wasn't playing until my first night.

"Plus, if you're okay with it, we want to add more Lia to the mix. The team is creating a Lia-specific Jags account, and I want to build that out at the same time."

My eyes snap up. "Me? No one cares about who I am," I protest.

Megan raises her eyebrows and scoffs. "Wrong. Lots of people care. The comment section is flooded with fans trying to figure out who you are."

I open the comments, scrolling through thousands of them, and find she's not wrong. There are a ton of tags asking the Jags to introduce me on the page.

"Wow," I exhale. "Okay, so what does that mean?"

"I'm putting a meeting on our calendar with our PR team. We'll go over the basis of what we want you to focus on when posting. I can also give you more resources—maybe an intern to help with posting and filming content? A content editor? What do you need?" Megan asks.

More is better. I love the idea of sinking my hooks in further with the Jags to show them what I'm capable of. "To be honest, I'd like to manage both if it's possible," I request.

"If you can swing it and that's what you want, I'm happy to try that out. We'll also chat with HR regarding additional compensation. This is more work than we brought you on for."

Additional compensation? Have I slipped into an alternate universe—one where success is rewarded, and gorgeous NBA players rescue women from those with the energy of the smallest dick to ever exist?

"Damn. Way to go, Lia." Brooks offers me a high five, bringing me back to the now. "Let me know if you need anything else from me," he requests before turning and heading back to the court. We were filming content before his shootaround started—some random "would you rather" questions that fans had sent in.

I love that he tells me 'good job' in front of my boss.

"If the work becomes too much, we can figure something out," Megan reassures me. "Don't feel like you're signing up to be miserable for the foreseeable future."

Miserable? No way. But I don't tell her that. Sometimes you need to keep things to yourself.

"I've loved everything you've pitched and already completed. Keep doing what you're doing, and we'll get the details for your account nailed down. Good work." She looks at me and I almost tear up from the praise.

Right now, in this moment, I feel like I'm enough. I hold my head a little higher as I stride back to my tripod and cell phone setup on the court. Some of the other Jags players are arriving, but there's still time for us to finish.

When Brooks looks at me, his eyes the color of my favorite shade of coffee, I sigh a breath of happiness.

"I've never thought much about the power of the universe, or fate or whatever, but it's kind of like the Jags have given us the perfect cover to spend time together." He presses his lips together and shrugs his shoulders. "Consider me a believer."

"Back to work, Pittman." I point to the camera and do my best to hide my massive grin and the butterflies taking up residence in my ribcage.

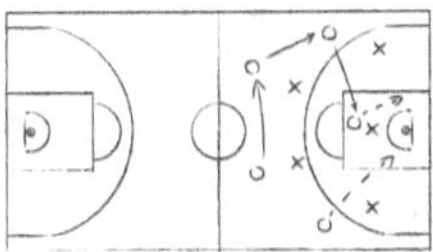

"Why do you look like that? You're freaking me out," Shelbie asks while wiping down the bar. Tonight I'm on the other side, chatting with my managers about taking a break while I get my feet underneath me at the new job.

"Like what?"

"Like you're Buddy the Elf and smiling is your favorite." She points at her cheeks, where they'd lift if she was smiling.

"Had a good day. That's all," I answer, taking a sip of a bubbly cocktail Shelbie is trying out. Sweet and fresh blood orange hits my tongue with prosecco fizz and a touch of rosemary. Separately, it doesn't look like these things should work, but together it's a slam dunk. The sip turns into a gulp, and before I can help myself, I've downed the entire glass.

Shelbie leans on the bar in front of me, eyes wide as she reaches for my empty glass. "I hope your good day had to do with you finally getting some basketball player dick."

I put my hand over her mouth while looking around to see if anyone is in ear shot. Luckily, it's just her and I around for her little outburst at the bar.

Under my breath, I hiss, "I told you—we're taking it slow." I stretch out my fingers, squeezing my hands in a fist and then extending them. My hands and wrists have continued to be oddly achy over the last few days.

"Yeah, yeah, I get it. You know I support that, but this is like a glacial pace. What are you waiting for?" She garnishes another bubbly cocktail before putting it in front of me.

The question slithers around me until it settles low in my belly. I'm definitely not a virgin but I've never really had a serious relationship—I've always been more of a 'have a free weekend, get on a dating app to have some fun' kind of person. Truly, I've never had the luxury of enough free time to put toward something other than immediate needs.

This feels like uncharted territory—like when you turn twenty-one so you can finally drink legally and it's your first night out. How much can I get away with? Can I handle it? Will I crash and burn?

Maybe I'm afraid of the emotional hangover?

"Use your words, Lia," Shelbie pushes, filling a pint with beer from the tap. "You're thinking awfully loud."

"It feels weird to have a main focus. Like, instead of filling my time with any way I could make some extra cash, I can focus on this job with the Jags. And Brooks is there. And it's just different," I admit.

She furrows her brow, leaning forward to ask, "Why the face? Those are all good things."

I sigh, letting my chin rest on my hands with my elbows on the bar. "It's complicated. It feels like this job and Brooks at the same time is a cruel trick. Like there's no way they can both be true."

Shelbie stops, shifting her weight to one leg. "Why not?"

"That's not how things turn out for me. That's just how it is." I throw my hands up and look down at the bar. The condensation from my glass has left a ring that I wipe away.

"My girl. You're being all glass half-empty when you're typically the opposite. It *is* possible for you to have nice things, and for fuck's sake, you deserve them." She lightly hits her hands on the bar, loudly enough for me to hear. "If you feel like these are good things, don't let them slip away because you were too scared to do something about it."

Oof. Punches landed. I'm not sure what to say, but luckily someone at the edge of the bar asks for Shelbie, which pulls her focus from me. The universe seems to know I need a second. I'm left alone in a room that's starting to crowd—the twinge of familiar loneliness at the edge—with Shelbie's words replaying in my head.

You deserve them.

I will myself to believe that. To try and think of all the reasons I deserve good things—even if they're surprising. Why is it so damn hard to not question it? I wish I was someone who could be handed a sparkler and not worry how it might set the small patch of hypothetical dead grass on fire.

Shelbie appears back in front of me and her lips soften from a thin line before she replies, "Lia. It's time. I can't believe you haven't crashed and burned yet. I know you're probably bargaining with the universe on how this happened, but instead of overthinking, you could try doing. Living. Enjoying life."

Living. When she puts it that way, there's a ball in my throat I try to swallow back. She never met my parents, but for some reason this sentiment reminds me of them. How they aren't living. How I am. How I get to.

For the first time, maybe ever, I feel lucky.

Chapter 24
Brooks

"Is this payback because I skipped the bar last week?"

Jalen laughs. "No! The wife is making dinner, and I want to spend time at home. Nothing more than that." He shuts the door of a car. "Why don't you ask Lia?"

"Maybe I will. Tell Steph I said hi." I end the call and put the phone on the side table as I sink into the couch.

Lia is working with Megan tonight. Since our schedule gets wild with travel and away games, sometimes they work nights, like tonight. I go through the list of people I typically hang out with and come up empty. Clay is working a private event at Oasis, Zack is gone for an away game, and my mom is still traveling with her girlfriends.

For a second I think about calling my dad, but I don't have it in me tonight. It's not that I'm disappointed with where we're at—to be honest, I'm thankful they want anything to do with me. But I'm tired, and sometimes it's a little like walking on eggshells. He and Zack invited me to a golf simulator next week, so we'll spend time together then.

Putting my head back on the couch, I take a few deep breaths. The silence hangs heavy in these rooms and it makes my stomach pinch. Some days, this doesn't feel like home. I think having a roommate could help, but I don't have it in me to ask and be turned down by anyone. Since I'm an NBA player, the list is short of who I'd be comfortable letting into my space.

Striking out for plans, I grab my phone as a text message come in.

Even if she didn't get a new phone, her old number didn't make the cut after the breakup. I didn't trust myself with it. She doesn't know that, though.

Rebecca never watched me play. If she came to a game, it was about what she was wearing and spending time with the WAGs. She viewed it as a chore until she found a way to make it work for her—something she'd always been good at.

I meant to text you sooner. She didn't.

I thought I'd hear from her when my season-ending injury was announced. Or when I had surgery.

But I didn't.

I'd be lying if I said it didn't sting—of course it fucking did. She'd been part of my life for a long time. Rebecca and I shared years together; we loved each other at one point, yet she couldn't even send a text message.

What is she doing reaching out now?

I scoff, even though I'm the only one to hear it, and close her messages. I'm not responding. Not tonight, at least. I don't even know what I'd say.

Instead, I open social media to waste some time. The first post I see is from the Jags—it's a series of photos of the team and the rescue dogs Lia brought in. The first few are of Jalen and some other teammates making Megan sweat by running the animals outside of the prepared area. Next is a picture of me and the English bulldog I sat with. I'm surprised when I see the smile on my face while I hold out a hand in front of his snout, giving him the space to warm up to me.

The last picture is Lia and the same dog. She has tears in her eyes as she's petting him, her hands touching his head and ears. Using my fingers to zoom in, I catalog every detail: the dog's tongue almost hanging out of his mouth, his eyes closed like he's the happiest he's been in who knows how long, and Lia's bright and captivating face.

The number to the shelter is in the caption of the post. *Smart*. Before I think too hard about it, I tap it and someone answers after the first ring.

"This is Brooks Pittman, and I'm wondering about a dog that was at the Jags event this week."

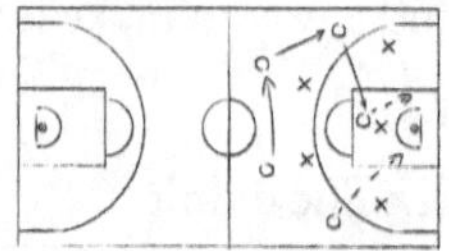

Surely I didn't see this in the realm of possibilities for tonight. I'm in the back room of the shelter, about to sign the final paperwork to bring Rocky home with me. The relief I felt when they said he was still here was like a drink of cool water on a hot summer day, and excitement bubbled in my chest.

I've never had a dog and barely know what I'm doing. But when I asked questions, the volunteers gave me everything I needed, as well as some recommendations for dog walkers and sitters for when I'm going to be traveling.

I was ridiculously nervous looking at the list—that's not something I knew was even a thing—that the volunteer brought out her own resume, showing me the athletes who she has dog sat for. I hired her on the spot for my next road trip.

"Alright, there's a small adoption fee of $150," she explains, pushing the paperwork in front of me with sticky notes where I need to sign.

Her excitement when I said I wanted to take Rocky home with me was something that will stick with me a while. She lit up with true and honest enthusiasm. It was in that moment that I knew I'd donate to the shelter, and there's no way it'd be the last one.

I sign the paperwork and bring out a checkbook—thankful I could even find it from when I moved. Since my financial adviser takes care of large purchases, there aren't many times when I need a check. I write one for the adoption fee, then another for $10,000. I hand them both to her and watch her eyes fill with tears when she sees the donation check.

"Are you sure? This isn't necessary, like, wow. Are you sure?" She looks at me with glassy eyes and I offer a nod.

"One hundred percent," I reinforce.

"Is this for anything specific?" She scrunches her eyebrows, almost like she's making sure she's taking in the number correctly.

"Use it for whatever you need." I put my hands up. "I know it must be hard to take in new animals. I'll want to arrange a monthly donation, if that's allowed?"

She quickly nods her head. "Yes. We can do whatever you need." She holds out a card, her hand shaking. "Here's my supervisor's email. You can contact her, and she'll start that process for you."

Before I can say anything else, the other volunteer swings the door open and brings Rocky out on a leash. Gone is the sleepy, scared dog I first met on the basketball court. It's almost like he knows his time is over here.

The volunteer drops the leash and I kneel. "Hey, Rocky! You want to go home?" The dog's ears perk up and then he sort of hops over to me—a mix between a run and a skip—closing the short distance. He puts his head right where my hands are. I pet him a few times and then he circles around, sitting between my legs and tipping his head to look at me.

"Look at that. He remembers you," they croon.

For fuck's sake. I'm about to cry in this shelter.

The volunteer text me a shopping list of his food preferences and the types of toys he's been drawn to. "There's a locally owned pet shop about five minutes from here. They're about to close, but I'll call them and let them know you're coming," she explains.

"You don't have to do that," I say, petting Rocky's sides

"Oh, it's not a problem. You have perfect timing, really. This way, no one will be trying to get pictures of you or freaking out. The store should be empty. Would you mind if we take your photo for the adoption wall at the front? If you're comfortable with that."

"Absolutely. You can post it to your socials in a few weeks if you want. I have some people I want to tell before they see it on social media."

Well, it's just one person, but still.

I stay kneeling, Rocky leaning into my hands on his rib cage, and the volunteers get to our level and take the photo. At first, I thought I was being impulsive. On the drive over, I kept doubting myself, the questions turning to knots in my stomach. But I was wrong.

Right now, I know this is one of the best decisions I've made in a long time.

Chapter 25
Lia

I HAVEN'T BEEN ABLE to take a full breath all morning. I woke up covered in sweat, knowing today is the day to try something new: flying.

I'm taking my first flight, joining the Jags for an away game. My new Jags social media account has been flooded with new followers, and it still barely makes any sense to me. We're using the trip as an opportunity to film a few "get ready with me" videos, which seem to be trending, and I'll be sharing things like taking my first flight and going to my first away game.

Megan and I are in her office, knocking out a few tasks before we go to the airport. She offered to ride together, knowing I'm freaking out a little bit. We love a supportive boss.

There's something she said that I can't stop thinking about. The other night, when we were digging into the details of recent posts, she casually shared, "You're much better than the first hire. Wish we would've hired you first... would've saved me a ton of stress."

I should've asked what happened as soon as it was brought up, but I didn't want to seem like I was gossiping. Megan is friendly and rarely gives off boss vibes. She's a great person to have in leadership—she makes you feel comfortable in a way that makes you confident.

I know if I don't ask, I'll never stop thinking about it. Before I can talk myself out of it, I spit it out. "What happened to the first hire? I probably should've asked when you first offered the position, but to be fair, I was too excited." I laugh, trying to soften the question. "But if it's not something you can share, that's okay too."

Megan pops her head up from her laptop. "Oh, it's no problem! It was a combination of things. One, she exaggerated her skills and what she could do. Two, she was dating a staff member who also happened to be married. Things got messy a few days in, and it was clear she wasn't a good fit."

It's like ice is cruising through my veins, sucking all the warmth from my body. My face, basically flushed with nerves all day, breaks out in a chilled sweat. I want to ask follow-up questions: What was the main reason? The skills or the relationship? Was it because he was married? It's like my mouth is a desert; plus, I don't want to draw attention to myself. I do my best to act like I'm having a normal reaction, just the right amount of shock, and not give away the alarm bells ringing in my mind.

"Ready to go?" She's bright and smiling as she shuts her laptop.

I nod because I don't trust myself to speak.

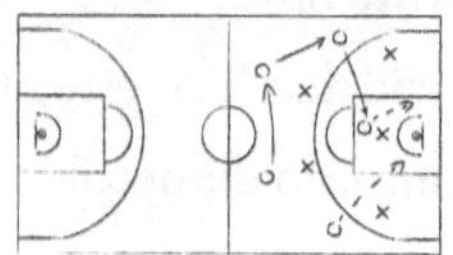

I am unwell. I thought when I made it to the plane and got in a seat, I'd start to relax. Instead, I have enough anxiety that my limbs feel as though they're filled with feathers and if I don't focus on breathing, it won't happen on its own.

I've never thought much about flying—airfare has never been in my budget. Now that I'm about to do it, I feel I've vastly underestimated the experience. Who was like, "Let's throw a bunch of fragile humans in this metal tube and try to catapult them through the sky to get somewhere else? Seems like a fucking racket."

Sitting in a window seat, in an empty row on the team plane, I catch Megan's eyes and wish she hadn't seen me like this: skin pale, dewy with nausea, and clasping my hands hard enough that you could use my knuckles as inspiration for your next paint color—I'd call it bone white.

"Lia, you look awful." Her face is etched with concern and surprise as she sits in the seat next to me. "I know it's scary, doing something new, but I promise this plane is safe." She puts a hand on my shoulder and then starts rubbing my back.

I whip my head around, too fast, and some of my hair gets stuck on the lip balm I aggressively put on while looking for anything to keep my brain off the impending doom setting up shop in my mind. I pull the hair from the slip and slide that is my lips and let my head fall forward. I try taking a few long breaths, but my lungs act like they're made of tight springs and I'm not strong enough to gain any leverage.

"I'd sit with you, but I have some things to get approved by the GM." She looks to the front of the plane but doesn't stop rubbing my back.

A voice cuts through, one that feels like aloe on a sunburn. "I'll sit with her."

Brooks.

"That's perfect." Megan squeezes my shoulder a final time before standing, moving to an empty seat behind me so Brooks can take her place.

I don't have it in me to look at him just yet. I feel him get settled, buckling his seatbelt while I try my best to catch my breath. When the air is barely there, the sounds of the overhead bins closing and people sinking into seats are muffled, almost like I'm underwater. I open my eyes, focusing on my cold and clammy hands while they open and close. Trying to match my breaths to something I can see is hard when you're trying to fade into the background. Luckily, I was one of the last people to get on the plane.

I lift my head as the safety demonstration starts, leaning hard against the headrest. I do my best to pay attention and find the closest safety exit. The lights dim and the plane starts to move. Rolling my shoulders back, I feel the start of boob sweat, which at this point simply tracks for this entire experience.

"You never told me you were afraid to fly." Brooks voice is low as I watch out the window.

Trying to keep my voice level, I reply, "I've never done it before. I didn't know." I catch a glance at him and he's wearing a turtleneck. It's mauve. The man is killing a fucking mauve sweater as I try to not pass out sitting up or think about my tendency to sweat when I'm nervous. How is that even fair?!

Brooks nods in understanding, his eyes light brown and almost glowing, reminding me of looking through the trees in the fall.

This fucking guy. It's actually inconsiderate for him to look this gorgeous when I feel this way. I roll my eyes even though he can't see—that's just for me.

"Want to see a secret?" he asks, reaching for his phone. My face must give me away, the rule follower that I am, because he adds, "Don't worry, it's on airplane mode." He unlocks his phone and shows me a picture.

It's Rocky, the bulldog from the shelter. He's sitting on a fluffy blanket with his tongue hanging out of his mouth, almost like he's smiling.

Wait.

I know that couch.

I reach for his phone and pull it closer to my eyes, pinching to zoom in and confirm my suspicion.

"Why is this dog at your house?" I demand to know.

Brooks smirks, catching my eyes with his and answering, "Because I adopted him."

"I don't follow. Not sure if there's not enough oxygen going to my brain, but what do you mean?"

He laughs and swipes, showing me another picture—this one is of Rocky sitting with a stuffed elephant. It looks like a chew toy, but the bulldog is snuggling it, using it as a spot to rest his head.

"I saw the Jags post on my feed and called the shelter to see if he was still available. Obviously he was, so I went and picked him up. I hired one of the volunteers to watch him while I'm gone." Brooks looks at the photo and continues, "My house is too quiet. Too much space. I think he's the perfect addition."

I think he's onto something when I catch his expression as he flips through some more pictures of Rocky. Tears pool in my eyes. I made an actual difference with my event. It makes me feel optimistic and light, but it's short-lived. The plane picks up speed and I fear we're going to take off soon.

"Well, twenty-six is a long life for some, right?" The joke falls out of my mouth before I have a chance to stop it.

Brooks reaches for my hand under the armrest between us. When his fingers intertwine with mine, it's like I can almost take a breath. I close my eyes and sit razor straight, my muscles feeling like they've all flexed at once.

"You're making it to at least twenty-seven." His voice matches the joke.

I know it's risky, us touching like this while Megan's words from earlier run through my head. My eyes scan the seats around us and notice everyone is in their own little world. No one looks the least bit bothered. Surely no one is paying attention to the two of us, which makes me feel the tiniest bit better.

Not enough, though. My heart pounds quickly enough that I push my head into the headrest, a little afraid I could pass out. The fear of the unknown wins and I squeeze Brooks' hand as the plane takes off, feeling like my stomach gets left behind on a tarmac in New Jersey.

Chapter 26
Brooks

THE GAME IS TIED at the half and we're warming up before the third quarter starts. I've spent the last few minutes trying to find where Lia is sitting. I scan the seats behind the bench until I find her, seeing fans from the other team talking to her. At first, a knot of uncertainty pulls in my chest, but then it's clear they're excited to see her—further confirmed when I see her take a selfie with the couple.

I get up a couple shots and watch as they all fall through the net. That's kind of the vibe for tonight—I'm making everything. Nights like this are rare but fuck do they feel good. It's like, no matter what, I'm not going to miss. Not sure if there's a basketball god out there, but it's hard to say there *isn't* one when I have games like this.

With a double-double under my belt in the first half—eighteen points and ten rebounds—I'm happily anxious to get the third quarter going.

Jalen dribbles next to me and quietly comments, "Seems like everyone wants a piece of Lia." He nods in the direction of her seat, where she's standing and taking more photos with more fans. At least this time, it's a mixture of traveling Jags fans and the opposing team. "You would show off like this when she's here." He winks and dribbles towards the basket, hiding a fadeaway jumper.

"I'm not showing off. Just having a good night." I hit another shot from behind the three-point line. I reach down and rub my fingers across the tape around my knee. The fabric wraps to the front of my leg. Maybe I'm checking that it's still there? It's not something I'm actively thinking about, but feeling the tape under the tips of my fingers is almost soothing.

"Bro, I'd prefer you show off. If this is you holding back, let these fucks have it in the second half." Jalen laughs and gets right in my face.

The announcer's voice fills the arena, directing everyone's attention to the Jumbotron. "We were challenged by the Jersey Jaguars to DO IT FOR THE DOGS!" A few pictures from our event and social media show on the screen. Everyone 'awes' in unison then laughs when a video of Jalen being chased by a puppy starts to play.

"What the fuck?" he laughs at himself.

The announcer returns and says, "We're donating $50,000 to these local three shelters. There's a QR code on the screen—everyone who donates will be entered to win floor seat tickets at a game of your choosing." The crowd erupts, clapping at the donation and incentive, and it feels like everyone gets their phones out.

This is the moment I choose to look at Lia. *She* did this. Her hands are on her cheeks, watching in awe while the Jags staff hypes her up. Megan gives her a squeeze around the shoulders, and someone gives her a high five. But then her eyes find me—even from here, I can see the crimson taking over her cheeks.

I put the basketball between the crook of my elbow, holding it to my side and freeing up both hands. I clap for her, and the look she wears makes me want to finish this fucking game. It also makes me want to run over and kiss her, but I know that's not allowed.

Fuck. It makes me want to do it more.

"That *almost* makes me feel bad for wanting to beat them," Jalen grumbles as we walk towards the bench. The buzzer finally sounds, letting us all know it's game time.

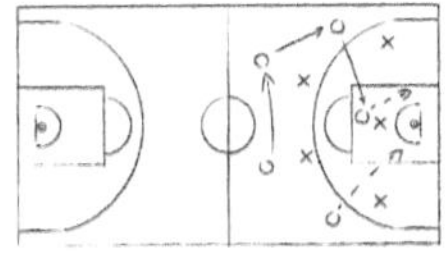

I did not, in fact, feel bad for beating them, *or* for having one of the best games of my entire existence. I ended up with a triple double—forty-three points, thirteen rebounds, and ten assists—which is solid, but I'm more excited about the six three-pointers I hit in the second half. I walk to the podium, ready for the press conference, and the Jags media clap while I sit down.

Usually, I'd laugh it off and fall into the golden boy graces, but not tonight.

"Is that all you got? I have a game like *that*, and we get some lukewarm clapping from the corners?" Laughs fill the room and then mostly everyone joins in the applause. The Jags reporters stand, getting even louder.

I pull the microphone closer, sinking into the praise. Tonight, it feels like I deserve it. My skin buzzes, the way it does when I'm on a shooting streak. It feels fucking good. Some might try to shift the conversation or end the interview early, but not me—give me every fucking question you have.

A hand goes up, and the reporter's voice fills the room. "Brooks, the future for you and the Jags is looking bright. How does it feel to be in this position, especially after a major injury?"

Pulling the microphone close again, my eyes catch my stat line. "Honestly? It's a bit unreal. I didn't expect to be playing like this. Coming back to the game is something I wanted so badly, but usually the universe doesn't give a damn what you want. I hoped to come back and play like this, but I didn't expect it." I sit forward, tapping my fingers on the table.

"What do you think has made the difference?"

"Coaching staff. Trainers. My teammates."

Lia. Lia fucking Stone. I think it over and over again, but don't say it aloud.

"Your title odds keep climbing each week, it feels like. That's gotta feel good, right?" the reporter asks, and laughs fill the edge of the room.

I emphatically nod my head. "Yes, it feels great. Feels like some other words I wish I could say but can't without getting fined, so we'll leave it there."

Back to the locker room, what I think about is Lia. She's the difference: the thing I didn't see coming, someone I don't want to be without. My whole life, I've dreamed of winning an NBA championship. I still want that so fucking badly, but now it might not be only me on a podium with a trophy—someone else could be there with me.

When I'm showered and ready to go hang with the team, my phone buzzes.

Chris

are you kidding me?

what a game!!!

I grin at my phone, stopping in my tracks. This is the cherry on top of one hell of a night. This almost makes it feel more full—complete. While I won't be able to look back and remember any games where my dad yelled my name over the crowd or urged me to get more aggressive, I'll remember this, and hope for more experiences like tonight.

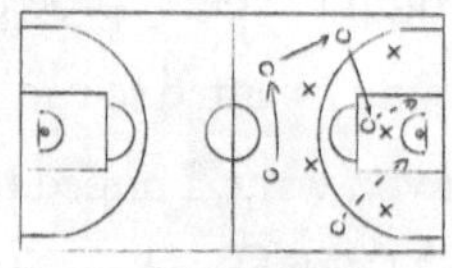

The entire Jags organization is posted up at the hotel restaurant, which is reserved for our post-game team dinner. I'm at a table with a few teammates, Jalen included, and my eyes keep going for the door, searching for a certain blonde media staff member.

The house sitter sends a text, causing my phone to buzz. I open it to find a picture of Rocky lying in the middle of my king-size bed. When I adopted him, I asked if they had a dog bed recommendation, since they made a few comments about how they didn't think he'd want to sleep with me. A lightness pulls at me when I look at the photo—he's clearly comfortable.

"Wait, whose dog is that?!" Jalen grabs my phone and zooms in, his nose close to the screen.

I don't get to surprise Jalen often, so I soak in the next few seconds. "Mine."

His head dramatically falls forward, like it's going to hit the table, and his eyes are wider than the coasters our drinks sit on. "What do you mean, *yours?*"

"He's mine. I adopted him."

Jalen slaps the table with both hands and lets out a full laugh, one that anyone on our team would know is his. "Y'all better get your checkbooks out. This guy went and adopted a dog!" He takes my phone and shows my teammates.

"And made a donation," I add as I shove him.

My eyes find the entrance as Lia walks in with Megan, a few other staffers trailing behind. She tosses her head back, clapping her hands at something Megan says. I try not to stare, breaking up my glances while they slip into a booth.

Jalen roll his eyes. "Of course you did."

"Do it for the dogs," Jamison, our center, laughs. "That was pretty cool what Lia did. Smart, too." He shifts and tries to get his phone out of his pocket, which isn't easy for someone who is almost seven feet tall.

The table nods and I work on holding back a massive grin. I'm so fucking proud of her. My teammates calling Lia smart? Fuck yeah. They're right, too.

As I'm about to put my phone away, it buzzes.

Unknown

good win ;)

Rebecca. Still haven't saved her number. Definitely haven't responded or told anyone about her messages. I almost blabbed to Jalen, but honestly, I didn't want to get into it. I'm not sure there's even anything to get into. Her texts don't get much of a reaction—I'm not worried about missing out or anxious about leaving her on read, and there's no part of me wondering "what if" when I think about her.

Nothing like the way I felt when I saw Lia in the stands, or when I basically felt her walk in. It's like there's something we share; something that lets me know when she's close or missing when she's not.

There's no feeling of dread, like 'what is she trying to get from me?' It's a gross question but one that had hit me like a truck in college. As soon as I played a few good games, the buzz started to grow and all bets were off. Girls would wait for me outside my classes and guys would wait outside my dorm. Everyone wanted something and I barely had enough for myself.

It's gotten better, considering I play professionally, and my teammates deal with the same sort of thing—it's nice to not experience it alone. And while I may be a known name in the NBA, there are players much better—and more scandalous—than me.

I've never questioned Lia's motives. Not once. The woman I happened to meet by fucking accident, who I watched verbally burn a man who put his words where they didn't belong, feels like the first string of something good in a while.

"Think much harder and smoke might come out of those big ass ears," Jalen jokes, waving his hand in front of my face. "What's up?" he asks.

"Nothing; just zoned out," I lie as I hear Lia's laugh from across the room.

Jalen slinks back into the booth, shaking his head. "Doesn't seem like nothing."

My eyes must've given me away.

Chapter 27
Lia

IT'S HARD TO SECRETLY date a professional athlete you're constantly in close proximity to. I wanted to run up to him after the game, put my arms around him, feel his hands on my waist, and kiss him. His lips. Move down his neck. The blush hits my cheeks, and I hold back the desire to fan myself.

This man makes me physically fucking hot.

We're wrapping up dinner and I've kept count of how many looks I can steal, doing my best to make them sporadic and carefully spaced. I know I'm taking this a bit seriously, but I kind of like the game. Except when I caught him looking at me and I swear I was a few seconds from melting into a puddle.

I pull my credit card out, waiting for the bill, but Megan stops me. "This is a work trip," she reminds me. "You don't pay for anything like this. Not tonight. Not ever. You want room service or anything from the snack bar or cafe? Bill it to your room and the Jags will takes care of it."

Wow. That's generous.

"Is there some sort of limit?" I can't help asking for more details.

Megan holds back a laugh, "No, Lia. There's no limit. Just don't be an asshole, and I'm sure you'll be fine. I'm not worried."

I hate that my brain immediately goes to my grocery budget. If I had a short cash month, this is one of the areas that would suffer. I once went a whole month eating only ramen noodles and peanut butter sandwiches—I couldn't even get jelly. I count the number of away games

I'm scheduled to attend over the next six weeks and can't help but think of these in terms of days I won't have to pay for food.

Before I get too emotional thinking of the extra cash I've sort of stumbled on, my group gets up and begins walking to the elevator. It takes everything in me not to steal one more look at Brooks.

Everyone says their goodbyes as soon as the elevator dings. We're all staying on the same floor, but it's clear our time together is over. Once I'm in my own room, I shut the door, push my back against it, and slide down until I hit the floor.

I take a moment to appreciate where I am. I've never stayed in a luxury hotel, while also practically having floor seats to watch my favorite NBA team add a notch to their win column, and have it cost me zero dollars.

A smile hits my lips and I can't help but laugh. I didn't see this coming, and I'm still waiting for Megan to tell me there's been a mistake or for some weird bill to show up that I forgot about. For now, I need to try and soak this in. I take a picture and send it to Wes.

Wes

wow, rub it in why don't you

i had peanut butter on saltines

Me

don't act like that's not your favorite snack

psh still stings when you're posted up in a 5 star hotel

also, did brooks get bit by a radioactive spider or something

Laughing at Wes' response, I step into the bathroom and turn on the shower, the smell of fresh eucalyptus slowly fills the space. It makes sense, considering the fresh eucalyptus sprigs hanging near the shower head. When I take my clothes off, I brace for the chill of the bathroom tile, but it never comes. *Heated floors*. My shoulders fall farther from my ears, the stress melting away. I make a mental note to find out if there's such a thing as DIY heated floors for my little bathroom because this is amazing.

When I step into the shower, hot water hits my skin with pressure you'd only dream about. Steam envelopes me as I stand face first, letting the water rinse me from head to toe. The complimentary shampoo, conditioner, and body wash are a brand I've only ever used a sample of—I could never afford it. When I rub the shampoo together in my hands, the suds are soft, and the scent of rosemary and peppermint mixes with the eucalyptus.

I don't know if I slept wrong again, or if it's the stress from flying, but my body is oddly sore. It's like my limbs are heavier than they should be and some of my joints are slow and rough. I take in deep, slow breaths and roll my head from side to side, letting the warm air stretch my lungs while welcoming the spark of the peppermint. Back home, I never allow myself long showers for fear of what will happen to my water bill. Tonight, all bets are off. I let the water run over my skin, flushed with the heat until my fingers are wrinkled.

When I'm in my pajamas, I put my phone on do not disturb, pull the heavy duvet from the bed, and fall in. I pull the blanket up, letting my hands fall to my sides, and groan. The sheets, the weight of the down comforter, the pillows—all of it is incredible. I put my hands over my mouth as I let out a squeal and kick my feet.

I reach for my Kindle and open a fantasy series I've been dying to start. Part of me thought I'd start it on the plane, but instead, I gripped the armrest and wondered what it'd be like if we crashed about a hundred times. It wasn't productive and my fingers are feeling it.

I don't know how long it's been, but a knock at the door scares me. Maybe it's someone from the hotel? Or Megan needs something? I'm out of the bed and practically running to the door. My hand has pulled it open an inch before I remember that women who don't check the peepholes at hotels usually end up on a true crime podcast.

Taking the risk, I open the door all the way.

It's not the hotel. Or Megan.

It's Brooks.

Chapter 28
Brooks

As soon as my teammates wanted to go out to the bar, I knew I was staying in. I kept checking the time on my phone, doing the math for how long it'd been since Lia had left.

The elevator doors open and I know where I'm going—it's not my room. I stand in front of Lia's door—which was information I had to finesse the front desk staff to get—and look around. There's no one. The hallway is completely empty.

For now.

I knock on the door, matching the thudding of my heartbeat.

Lia opens the door and her eyes settle onto mine, a smirk pulling on one side of her lips. She's wearing gray pajamas, a matching set with a lace tank top and tiny shorts, which draws attention to her legs—the ones I dream about kissing up and down. Her blonde hair is damp and wavy.

"What are you doing here?" she asks softly.

"Had to see you. Wasn't an option." The answer comes out quickly, and I kind of wish my mouth had held onto the words a second longer.

"Not an option? Dramatic much?" she laughs, tilting her head.

I nod in agreement and say, "No. I spent the team dinner thinking about you. About how we were on the same floor."

She tries not to smile as she steps closer to me, leaning against the door frame. Lia goes to speak, but the ding of the elevator has us looking to the doors.

Jalen walks out, taking two or three steps before looking up from his phone.

Caught.

It's like time is frozen for a few seconds, or however long it actually takes for Jalen to look between us, smile and step back, pushing the button for the elevator. The doors open and he mutters, "Tsk, tsk, tsk. Thought you were going to bed, Brooks." He emphasizes 'bed' with a twinge of 'disappointed dad' and a side of 'friend giving you shit.' Jalen crosses his arms and grins while the door shuts.

"Well, fuck," Lia groans, covering her eyes with her arm.

"Don't worry about it. He already knew. He's just being Jalen." I try to reassure her but don't know if this is the time to tell her I told our secret.

"That could've been anyone," she protests. Her eyes dart up and down the hallway, looking for others.

I let out a sigh, glancing up at the ceiling while shifting my weight. "You're right. I should go," I practically whisper.

I don't even turn my body all the way before Lia grabs a handful of my shirt and pulls me to her.

"Get in here," she orders, her nose scrunched and eyes fucking sparkling.

The door shuts behind me and she's still holding my shirt.

"You were unreal tonight," Lia laughs, looking at her feet before settling her gaze on me. I can almost see her relax, bit by bit, until she lets go of my shirt and her hands fall to her sides.

"Me? You're the one who has NBA teams donating to local animal shelters."

Lia's lips pull into a real smile, the type that makes her glow. Before I can say anything else, her arms wrap around my neck and our lips meet.

Maybe it's more like a crash, because there's something behind this. This kiss. This moment. This fucking woman.

My hands find her waist, her hips pushing into me as I move until I'm grabbing her ass through these tiny, perfect shorts. She smirks against me and I squeeze, grabbing a handful of her soft skin in my hands.

I walk us further into the room. Her legs hit the bed and she stops, offering me a wicked grin before reaching for the bottom of her tank top and lifting it up and over her head.

Lia watches as I take her in before she falls back onto the mattress. Her hair splays all around her, those tempting blonde locks a mess on the white of the comforter. A hand reaches up to her breasts and she squeezes a nipple, rolling it back and forth between her fingers.

"Fuck. Do you know how hot that is?" My voice is raspy as I put a knee on each side of her legs. Once I'm straddling her, I hover my body right above hers before our lips connect. I lick the seam of her lips and when she opens, I taste her, bringing my dick to full attention.

I'm right next to her—right here—but it doesn't seem close enough. I need to touch more. Taste more.

More.

My lips find the nipple she isn't touching and I flick my tongue, feeling Lia respond underneath me. She arches her lower back, pushing up and away from the mattress while she moans.

Fucking perfect.

I let my tongue dance on the top of her tits, covering as much of her skin as I can. My hand lightly presses on her stomach, moving down until I'm touching her through her shorts.

"Wait. Too many clothes," Lia pants as she props herself up on her elbows.

I stand and step away from the bed, grabbing my shirt and lifting it up and over. Next, I unbutton my jeans and pull them down, stepping out until I'm only in my briefs with my cock straining against the fabric.

"All this. It's cruel. Like, it's unfair how hot you are," Lia murmurs while taking me in, and I'd be lying if I said I didn't love it. Not *what* she said, but the *way* she said it, because it sounds like how I imagine talking about her.

She sits up, tucking her feet under her ass before putting the weight forward on her arms. Now on all fours, Lia looks at me and starts to crawl.

I bite my lip and try to memorize every single fucking detail. Her messy blonde hair thrown over her shoulder, her eyes looking up at me like that, the swell of her pink lips. I take a mental photo—a series of them, really. Lia is crawling to me and it's something I'll remember, and go back to for personal use, for a long time.

She's in front of me, reaching for the front of my briefs. I help to pull them down. The bead of precum gives me away, just in case it wasn't clear how hot she fucking is. She smiles as she reaches for the base of my shaft, her thumb brushing the head. Lia leans forward, putting the head on her lips before slowly opening her mouth.

Her tongue swirls on my most sensitive part as her hands move on me in slow strokes. She pulls me out of her mouth with a pop of her lips, and I eagerly laugh, putting my hands on my hips. I don't want to get too aggressive, and I feel like I barely trust myself.

She glances up at me, her lips resting on the tip of my cock as her hands release my shaft. I'm missing the pressure until her hands find my balls. She cups them and I moan, "Fuck. That feels so good."

Lia takes me in her mouth, sucking and turning her head, still using a hand to balance herself on the bed. I start moving my hips further into her, trying to get more, and she gladly takes me. When she gags, I reach for her face and bend down to kiss her.

"If you keep going, you're going to be disappointed," I groan as I bite her lower lip.

"I owe you. For the pool," Lia replies matter-of-factly.

She thinks she owes me? What in the actual fuck?

I put my finger under her chin and lift, my eyes searching her face for the sign of a joke or a laugh. When I don't find one, I sternly state, "Let's make something clear—we don't keep score. You don't owe me anything." I push a hard kiss to her mouth before she can respond. I break it and finish my thought. "As if having you in my pool, the way I did, wasn't for me? I'm not sure what kind of men you've been with, but I don't think we're the same."

Lia lets out a breath, trying to tip her head down, but I won't let her.

"Got it?" I ask sternly.

"Got it," she answers, raw honesty on the edge of her quiet voice.

She sits back on her heels, pushing her bottom lip up against her teeth. I grab her waist, lift, and lightly toss her on the bed. It must catch her off guard because she lets out a yelp before moving her hair away from her eyes.

"As much as I love that wicked mouth of yours, the first time we do this, I want to come inside you," I admit.

She nods as her chest rises and falls quickly, like she's trying to catch her breath.

I look between us and ask, "Is this okay?"

Lia's voice is breathy and full when she says, "Yes."

Without hesitation, I reach into my jeans, which are strewn on the floor, to get the condom I put in my pocket and set it on the bedside table—just in case.

"Now, let me see you, baby."

Chapter 29
Lia

MY MOUTH IS WATERING while watching Brooks. His forearm flexes and ticks as he strokes himself. His dick looks heavy and full in his hands, and I can't believe I had him in my mouth a minute ago. I'd never been excited about doing that with other partners, but there's something about him, something that makes me want all of him.

His voice is on a loop in my head: *let me see you, baby.* I listen to it over and over as I reach down and remove my tiny pajama shorts. A fleeting nervous thought tries to take shape, but my eagerness kills it before it becomes anything. I'm bare for him, and when he sees me, there's a weight between us—who will make the first move? The tension hangs heavily on my bones, on my lips that were just around him, and it makes my skin sensitive to almost every touch and breath.

I wait for Brooks to hover over me, his chest broad and muscles flexed, but instead he pulls my legs to get me to the edge of the bed. He kneels, his hair falling into his face and his eyes lock on one of my most sensitive places as he licks his lips. I moan, my orgasm inching closer and closer, simply by having him this close while looking at me like that.

"Let's be clear. I'm going to eat this perfect pussy because I want to, not because you had my dick in your mouth. Sometimes we can trade, but there's no score to keep. Do you understand?"

Each word he says rubs me the right way and I don't know if I've ever been this close without someone else touching me.

"I'm not going to keep going until you say so," he reveals.

"I understand." My words are quick and rough like gravel.

Brooks smirks at me, hovering right over my center. When I look down, I can't help but moan and lift my hips. The man is ridiculously hot and seeing his face between my legs, watching me like this, has me squirming.

He moves closer and lightly blows before kissing my skin. Brooks drags his tongue along the inside of my thigh but stops before he meets my center. Teasing, he does the same thing on the other leg, and my body responds by trying to angle my hips in a way to gives me what I want. He won't do it. Not yet at least.

His hands, massive and strong, start at my knees and run up my thighs until his fingers rest on my lower belly. His mouth is completely off me, just for a second, before he licks from my entrance up to my clit. Slow. Intentional. Full.

"Oh fuck," I whine when he finally touches my clit with his tongue. It circles and flicks as he uses a single finger to enter me. Brooks backs his mouth away but pumps in and out before adding another. He hooks his fingers, and the building pleasure has the room closing in.

My hands find his hair and I tug, needing his mouth. I tilt my hips to find the right position, his lips sucking my clit before his tongue hits exactly how I need it, all while his fingers continue to work me. He presses on my lower belly with his other hand, and it makes the pressure much more intense.

He changes it up and licks me down to his fingers and back up again. Ending on the right spot, I arch my back, so close to my orgasm. Brooks must know I'm close because he picks up the pace, his hands and mouth turning me into a puddle.

I pull his hair and shallow breaths hit my chest.

Suddenly he's gone. It's only a second or two, then he's rolling the condom down his length.

"Still okay?" he confirms, pausing with his dick outside my entrance.

"Yes!" I practically yell as I reach and dig my nails into his back.

I've barely finished answering before he's nudging inside, stretching me. Filling me up. He pumps in and out slowly, letting me get used to him.

"You're fucking soaked," he moans before biting my ear lobe.

Brooks keeps his pace slow, feeling me out, but it's not enough. I was so close to rolling through my climax with his mouth on me and now this is such a tease.

"More. I need more," I basically beg, a hand scratching at his chest before reaching up and pulling on his shoulder.

Brooks gets the message, thrusting into me faster and harder, not holding back. My hands find his hair and I pull, maybe a touch too hard, but he isn't fazed. His mouth finds my neck and bites down to my collarbone.

My lips find his mouth. I'm *this* close. He holds his weight with one arm and reaches down, touching my clit as he pumps into me.

Fuck. This is a game changer.

His mouth. His fingers. Him inside me. It's the perfect combination and hits me hard. I cry out and he covers my mouth with his hand, which makes things even hotter. I can't even describe it. There are no words in my brain, only stars and fireworks.

Brooks keeps fucking me while I squeeze and come on his dick. I'm at the bottom of my climax when he reaches his. I watch as his head tips back, his hips going a touch faster while his hand still covers my mouth.

He slows to a gentle rock, removing his hand and holds himself up. His breathing is heavy and loud. His mouth finds mine and he kisses me. Like, *really* kisses me. My arms loop around his neck and I don't want him to ever stop touching me.

When he rolls to his back, Brooks pants, "That... that was amazing. You're amazing." He turns to me, grabs my hand, and pulls my wrist to his mouth for a soft kiss.

I'm never coming back from this. There's no way. My brain struggles to compute what just happened, but there's one thing I know—we raised the stakes. That's not something you can have once or twice. It's something I'm going to need. Frequently.

"Let's get cleaned up and then we can go to bed."

Of course I want him to stay. Fuck, I want to do *that* again. But it's like a jolt back to reality—we're staying on the same floor as the rest of his team. The last thing I need is someone seeing him walk out of my room.

Brooks stands and reaches for my hand. "Don't worry," he assures me with a wicked grin. "I'll set an alarm and get back to my room early, before anyone will be awake and getting ready for the flight back."

"Are you sure? I don't want to be a pain. If it's just easier, you can go back to your room."

He stops and squeezes my hand, pulling me close to him. "Yes, I'm fucking sure, Lia. I'm staying here," he replies, like this isn't something up for debate.

I take his hand and follow him into the bathroom. He starts the water then comes back to me, placing his hands on the side of my face and slowly kissing me.

It's sweet.

It's like he's telling me a secret.

It's everything.

Chapter 30
Brooks

A KNOCK ON THE door is the one true way to get Rocky up and away from wherever he's decided to take his latest nap.

I open the door to find Zack, carrying a gift bag.

"I know we're fairly new to the whole brother thing, but you do know that it's not my birthday, right?" I question.

"I'm the king of birthdays," he quips, shrugging his shoulders. "Of course I know that. This is for Rocky!" Zack sinks down, putting his hand out to a tap-dancing English Bulldog.

By the time I shut and lock the door, Zack is already lying on the floor in my living room, letting the dog lick his face. I swear, Zack can match any sort of dog energy. He pulls out a few dog toys before holding up a small Cosmos jersey.

"Wait. What is that?" I laugh as Zack gets on his knees, still holding it up.

His eyes go wide as he rolls them, right into a laugh. "Obviously this is my jersey, but dog sized!" Rocky smells the fabric and wiggles in excitement. Zack puts it on him and it's fucking awesome.

"Will you take our picture?" Zack asks as he holds Rocky beside him, repping #34 and Cosmos blue.

Grabbing his phone, I take a few pictures and know these will blow up on social media. I can't help but grab my own phone to text Lia.

Me

listen rocky has his own cosmos jersey

zack brought it over

Lia

pics or it didn't happen

I'll get you one

"Uh oh. Who are you texting?" Zack practically sings, slinking into the couch.

Looking up from my phone, I try to play it off like it's no big deal. "No one."

His chin tilts down as he stares at me. "Fuck you. I refuse to accept that answer." He crosses his arms and leans back. "Spill."

The thing about Zack is he makes you feel like you should tell him everything. I wrestle with sharing about Lia, but the protocol for keeping secrets roars. "I shouldn't," I protest, sitting on the loveseat across the room.

"Maybe you should... it looks like you're sweating bullets," Zack observes as he leans forward. I wipe the sweat from my forehead—shit, he's not wrong.

Before I can launch into any of it, he interrupts me. "I'm a vault. I can keep a secret," he promises, pretending to zip his lips.

I hesitate for a moment, then decide to give him something. "I met this woman a few nights before my first game this year—"

"There's no way you got her pregnant," Zack interrupts, leaning forward on his elbows.

I scoff. "What?! No. It's not like that. It's—"

"She's stalking you? Is that why you locked the door?" He turns to look at the entryway.

"Normal people lock their doors. Especially athletes who don't want random visitors. But no, she's not stalking me." I shake my head and run my hands through my hair, nervousness creeping in.

Zack nods his head. "Is she married? Does the guy know? Is he threatening you?" Concern deepens the lines on his forehead, and if I didn't know him, I'd think he was on something.

I shake my head and let it fall forward. "What is actually wrong with you? No. None of that. If you'd let me tell you, we could quit this weird back and forth."

To my surprise, he doesn't say anything else and sits back, his foot tapping on the floor.

"I met her a few days before the game. It wasn't planned. Sort of just happened. We hit it off. And then a few days later, she got a job offer with the Jags."

"That's who you were texting?"

I sigh out a breath. "Yes. I was texting Lia."

"And you look like that because...you and Lia... are secretly dating? You can't get enough of her? But it's probably frowned upon?" Zack unravels the web in front of me. He jumps up, clapping his hands. "We've got a forbidden romance on our hands!" He leans over, offering a high five.

I hesitantly hit my hand to his. "Why are you acting like this is fun? Also, who the fuck says forbidden romance?"

He gives me a long look down his nose. "Don't act like you don't know what I'm talking about. You and I both know you read romance books."

I pause, locking my eyes on his while trying to keep my face blank. "Who told you that?"

"You did. Just now. Other than that, I heard Riley and Emilie gushing about some book with bats and fairies and one of them let it slip. They didn't know I was listening."

Damn. I didn't think either of them would willingly tell Zack. It's a guilty pleasure that could be much worse. Who knew that books could be something to help pull you from of a depressive episode? Not me, until my therapist recommended trying something new to keep my mind busy. If Zack went upstairs, he'd find that entire series on my bookshelf and quite a few more like it.

"Listen, no shade. You can do whatever you want, but don't act like you have no idea what a forbidden romance is." He grins as he sits, reaching down and petting Rocky.

"Fine. Yes, we're keeping it a secret. Some could call it forbidden."

"Well, do you have any skeletons in closets? Perhaps a sex tape you thought was private? Or sexting photos?" Zack's eyebrows raise as he runs through the questions.

"You and I are very different people. No sex tapes, and I don't think I'm cool enough to sext."

He lifts his hands in surrender. "There's no way you have zero skeletons. Think hard."

"My ex has been texting me." I shift on the couch, my words quick and messy. "I haven't texted her back or anything. But I haven't told Lia."

"Are you talking about Rebecca? She didn't even come see you when you were recovering. Why is she texting you now?"

I shrug my shoulders, letting my hands fall to my sides. "I don't know. She wants to get together but I'm not going to do that."

Zack's blonde hair flops in front of his eyes as he dramatically listens. "Sure, sure. Well, why are you keeping it from Lia?"

The million-dollar question and one I don't have an answer for. Well, I have an answer, but it's shit. *I don't know.*

"It sounds stupid, but I don't know. Part of me thought she'd leave me alone once I didn't respond. It's just... this thing with me and Lia, it's new and I don't want to seem like I have all this baggage and shit."

"Right. You already have a surprise family. I get it," he jokes, and it makes me feel better. "If I'm remembering correctly, isn't this the ex who quite literally didn't give a single fuck and cheated on you, for like... a while?"

"Yeah, that's the one." I think back to the night Riley and Zack took me to a bar, where I had too many beers and told them the entire Rebecca saga. They both blocked her from social media that night, a small showing of solidarity, but at the time it felt like the most loyal of things.

"Hate to break it to you, but I don't think she's the kind to take a hint. You should tell her."

"Right. I know. But still... I don't have the balls to bring it up. Why am I like this?" I scrub my face with my hands.

Zack claps his hands, making me jump and causing Rocky to bark and run to the door. "Hey! None of that. There's nothing wrong with you," he protests. "I get it. You finally have something good, and you don't want to ruin it. Believe me, I've been there." He laughs to himself and looks at the floor for a few seconds. "Someone should learn from my mistakes. Don't let any of this come out and surprise her... that is not what you want. Can confirm."

He's right. I absolutely don't want to make Lia feel like I have anything to hide. Immediately, I'm putting myself in her shoes and wondering how it'd feel if the roles were reversed. My stomach rolls. This would fucking sting. No doubt.

"You're right. I know you're right. I don't know why I've been avoiding this. Now it seems like a bigger deal than it should."

"Well, we can't go back, only forward. Talk to her about it. Look at that—I gave advice to my little brother." The grin stretching across

Zack's lip is contagious. Ultimately, he's the most unbothered person I've ever met, and I wish I could steal some of it—bottle it up for when I spiral.

I smile and nod before putting this topic to rest and moving on. "Wait, do you seriously not lock your doors?"

Chapter 31
Lia

"I FEEL LIKE YOU bribed me with margs and queso," Shelbie accuses, taking a fresh tortilla chip from the bag and covering it with cheese.

"I don't know what you mean." I feign innocence while turning the volume up, as the second quarter is about to start.

Shelbie looks at the TV then back to me. "You just wanted someone to come over and watch the game with you." She gestures to the TV with her margarita before pulling the salt-rimmed glass to her lips. "You know what, doesn't even matter. What's the deal with this food? It's fucking incredible."

"All thanks to Brooks. He took me here after a game and now I'm dreaming of it at least once a week." I take a chip through the salsa before popping it in my mouth.

"Good dick and a food rec? You should keep this one."

I roll my eyes and can't help but laugh at her—she has such a way with words.

"Just watch—you're going to end up marrying this guy. Only you would meet a random ass professional athlete who turns out to be the kind of man you could actually end up with."

I take a long drink of my own margarita, letting the salt meet the shining sour of the lime before it balances out with the tequila. Her words hit me like below zero windchill when you finally open the door to brave the winter cold.

The kind of man you could actually end up with.

I've been trying to catch myself from falling too deep. The truth is that being stuck in our bubble, existing within the secret only we know, isn't what real life is really like. I've been so wrapped up in the job, the slight slowdown of life, and Brooks. If there's one thing that scares me most, it's the hope. The hope this thing between us is real, even outside the veil of away games and luxury hotels. The hope it's more than the allure of sneaking around. Keeping a secret.

Part of me thinks Shelbie is right; that even after everything my brain tells me is wrong with this situation, there's still a chance. This isn't your typical type of hope—it's the massive kind that wraps around you like a never-ending blanket, fills a room, and takes up the space that's been empty and lonely in your ribcage.

"Quit with the overthinking. You're going to ruin the food buzz." Shelbie pushes my shoulders and has me smiling. Everyone should have the type of friend who knows you enough to sense the spiral as it's happening. "You know you don't have to marry him. It was a joke," she insists.

"I know. All of it feels... big."

"I want to make a dick joke right now, but I'm not going to. That's how much I know you need to talk."

I laugh and shake my head. "It's like I expected this to be short lived. The way I could think about the future is like the second before you drop at peak of a rollercoaster. It's hard to explain."

"No, I think I get it. It's like you didn't let yourself believe it, but then you did. It's more than you thought."

Nodding my head in agreement, I sit back and catch a glimpse of the TV. The Jags are up by five and they show Brooks resting on the bench.

"It feels too good. If it feels this way when everything is going well, what will it feel like if I lose it?" My voice cracks and I clear my throat.

Shelbie's head tilts, taking me in as her brows furrow. "What if you don't lose it? What if it's something that works out? Something you keep?"

The lightness blooming in my chest is met with tears in my eyes. *What if I can keep it?* What if Brooks isn't a blip, but something long term? Fuck, I want that. And it terrifies me.

"I know sometimes it feels like shit is too good to be true, but at some point, things swing the other way. Unless it's someone telling you cauliflower is way better than pizza crust or chicken wings... that will never be true."

I start to laugh but Shelbie stops me. "Buffalo cauliflower is too good to be true. I said what I said and will die on this hill." She crosses her arms and puts her nose in the air.

Shelbie wouldn't be who she is without a delicate balance between the heavy and the hilarious. Maybe she's right; maybe this *is* the type of good thing I can really have. Shelbie gets up to refill her drink and I focus on the game. The Jags are still up, and I watch Jalen delivers a perfect pass to Brooks. He dribbles past a defender, pulling the ball back to dunk it when an arm comes in, trying to swipe the ball away or block the shot. Brooks gets hit while he's in the air and he lands awkwardly, sort of on his shoulder.

When he doesn't pop up right away, I'm standing in front of the TV, trying to decipher what's going on. The training staff meet him on the court as Jalen kneels next to him. It's hard to watch as Brooks' face twists in pain, the arm he landed on limp by his side. The broadcast goes to commercial break—an injury timeout—and I'm pacing back and forth.

Shelbie says nothing as she sits back down on the couch. My hands scrub my face before pushing through my hair and ending at the base of my neck. I pull at my skin and pace in front of the TV, a mountain of nervousness building in my belly. *Brooks.* Is it his arm? His collarbone? Is something broken? How long is this recovery? The questions stack onto one another and when they get to be too heavy, it's like they explode into pure chaos.

"Why don't you sit. You have a full marg over here." Shelbie pats the space next to her.

I take her suggestion and sit. Reaching for my glass, I start to tremble. Shelbie reaches for my hand, holding it tight in hers. "Take a breath and then take a drink. Tequila is perfect for this situation."

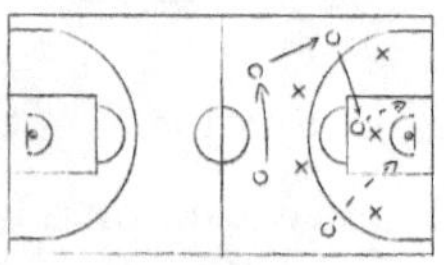

"Nothing is broken. It's a stinger," Brooks insists, his face filling my phone screen.

I finally let out a breath and the relief is like a drink of cool of water on a scalding hot day. A stinger is an injury to nerves in the neck and varies in severity. Some can be remedied with a few days of rest, while some may need months to heal.

"The burning has already stopped. Seems like it's mild." His voice is quiet as he sits in his bed, propped up on pillows with an ice pack taped to his shoulder.

Mild. Nothing is broken. All of these are good things. "How do you feel?" I ask as I rub my hand on the duvet cover, holding my phone with the other.

"I mean, I feel okay. My hand keeps cramping and my arm feels... heavy? I don't know, it's weird." He tries to lightly move his neck from side to side, probably itching to stretch the pain away. "I've never had one, but they seem fairly common." He lets his head lean back and hit the headboard.

"Did they give you anything to take?"

"Anti-inflammatories and a Xanax. I asked for something to take the edge off so I could sleep tonight."

I nod my head—this all makes sense. The urge to be there with him in that bed, making him comfortable and relaxed, is strong.

"I wish I was there with you." I let the words out before overthinking has me keeping them in.

"Yeah, me too. I'm not that much fun tonight, though."

"I don't need you to be fun. I just wish I was there to help you feel better. If that sounds stupid—"

"No, it sounds nice. Supportive. I know I'd feel better if you were here."

The words warm my skin, the blood rushing to my cheeks as I fight the urge to smile like an idiot. That doesn't feel like it fits the mood.

"Let's talk about something else. I'm all injury detailed out." Brooks' eyes look heavy as he slowly blinks.

"Thanksgiving is in a few days. Any plans?"

Honestly, I sort of forgot the holiday was this week until Shelbie reminded me. When my parents were alive, they'd do the whole full dinner thing, but when it was with my aunt and uncle, they never had the capacity to do anything more than order a pizza from the single shop that would stay open for a few hours that day. Now, Wes and I try to get together and eat pizza. If my aunt and uncle invited me, I'd go back and eat with them, but they seem too tired to do much of anything—that's how it's always been.

Brooks looks up, like he's trying to remember something. "Yeah, my mom should be back from her trip. We'll do something small, only the two of us."

"That sounds nice. Where is she coming from?"

"She's been in Hawaii for a few weeks with my aunt. It seems like one of her favorite places she's visited this year."

I let out a sigh. "Hawaii seems like a dream. I can't even imagine." I think about what it'd be like to be someone who traveled regularly. Maybe it's not a good idea, considering the thought of getting on the plane for the next away game may give me hives just thinking about it.

"You and your mom? That sounds perfect," I say, finishing my thought.

Brooks nods and doesn't ask me about my plans. I'm kind of glad I don't have to explain the lore of the delivered pepperoni pizza. Whenever I tell that story, people look at me with the "you poor thing" mask—one I wish I'd never see again in my life.

"I'm exhausted. I'm going to get some sleep," he says, rubbing his eyes with his good arm.

"Text me when you land and let me know if you need anything, ok?"

"You got it. Good night, Lia." Then the phone goes blank.

I put my phone on the bedside table and pull the blanket up to my cheeks. I'm not tired; adrenaline is still cruising through my veins. Talking to Brooks and hearing him tell me how he's feeling did ease my worry. Seeing him in one piece, in a hotel room and not a hospital bed, was the best I could have hoped for.

Something pulls at me, snagging the relief I should feel. Ruining the smoothness.

We hadn't talked about it, but part of me thought he might have asked me to get together for Thanksgiving. If he were going to his dad's house, I know that wouldn't make sense and wouldn't expect that invite. But knowing he's going to be at his place with his mom, I would have thought maybe he'd want me to meet her. Maybe it's too soon. Maybe he doesn't have the mental space to take on anything else.

Who knows.

It's unfair for me to feel bad about something I didn't bring up.

But I feel it anyway.

Chapter 32
Brooks

"WHAT DO YOU MEAN you're not coming home for Thanksgiving?"

"Brooks, darling, it's not by choice. There's a tropical storm and the entire airport is grounded," my mom's sweet voice answers. Even over the phone, I can see her sigh as she looks at me with her deep brown eyes. It's the same look that usually has her touching my cheek with her finger.

It seems ridiculous to be upset, but I'm pissed. Pissed at the weather, the airport, and the fact that my mom won't be here for a low-key Thanksgiving.

"I know. I was looking forward to it. That's all."

She tilts her head and smiles at me, the way she has my entire life. "Why don't you call Chris?" Mom suggests. "I'm sure they're doing something for the holiday. No need to hang out alone."

I know my dad is cooking—I turned down that invite because I wanted to spend time with my mom.

"Yeah, don't worry about me," I reply. "I'll figure something out. Let me know any updates with the flight, okay?"

We exchange *I love you's* and I hang up. Shortly after that, a message comes in.

Clayton

I've not been able to connect with Clayton since the first night when I met Lia at Oasis. It's not very surprising; we typically hang out much more during the off-season. We text and try to stay connected, but a lot of messages lead to a dead end because we're both on to the next thing. That's life, I guess? I could text him back and let him know I'm on my way. The glimmer of plans fade quickly. I can't do it today. I feel like everything is wrong—my body hurts and my brain is slow and hazy. Stringing words and thoughts with other people seems like an impossible fucking task.

Being alone is the only thing I can fathom. If my mom isn't going to make it home, there's no one else I want to see. I text him back and say my mom is coming over, the lie easily falling off my fingers. Once the message goes through, I turn my phone off. I can't do it today.

I slowly climb the stairs to my bedroom, Rocky following behind. First, I pull the shades down and the blackout curtains over the window, removing all the light. When I crawl into bed, Rocky follows, curling up at my feet. He doesn't care that it's noon and neither do I. I want to do nothing. Feel nothing.

The quiet of the room pricks at my brain, fueling the anxiety and panic. Everything about this seems fucking wrong. I've never had to deal with injuries before; I thought after the ACL injury, I'd have some sort of points that could get used up before my next one. Seriously—I've been through this recently, I didn't expect something else so soon.

An accident. A fluke. Nothing anyone planned. It wasn't a dirty play.

I'm aware I'm feeling sorry for myself over an injury that shouldn't take me out more than a few games. Some would say I'm lucky, but I don't believe that for a fucking minute. I feel like I could crash out. Burn from the inside out. The flames are almost unmanageable—fueled by fear and doubt. I stare at the ceiling, my eyes adjusting to the dark as I let the feeling I've been running from catch up to me.

Its claws are sharp and smart, searching for the old wounds—the ones still pink and scarred. I feel them push into my skin, reach into my ribs, and bring a chill that makes my lungs hard to stretch. My breathing is shallow, but I don't fight it. I've learned I'm no match for the claws. Better to try and coexist instead of pushing it out. Today, I'm simply not strong enough. Maybe I never have been?

When my hand cramps, a slight pinch from the stinger injury, I'm only reminded of how my body is betraying me. It used to be better than this. Do I not train hard enough? Is this what my future is going to be? The shadow of my knee injury is barely behind me and more ailments are piling on top. How much until my body simply combusts? Fucking explodes into particles and nothing. Like I never existed.

The blades from the ceiling fan are the only thing that keeps me feeling like I'm not floating away. They're reliable. They have a purpose. The switch turns them on and they do what they're meant to. It's like I'm losing my switch on the court, the injuries like an electrical problem. My chest feels full of bricks, leaving barely any room for my lungs. The heaviness sits on my already tired muscles and it's the last thing I can take. A tear spills and falls onto my pillowcase. I don't wipe it away; lifting my arm feels impossible and I don't need to fail at another single fucking thing.

My circle of people fills my head. Lia. Jalen. Zack. Riley. Clayton. My dad. I could call any of them and they'd try to help. The claws are smart, dangling the hope in front of me before pulling it just out of my reach. I know I won't call anyone or let them know I need something. Depression isn't something I can explain with words. Even if I thought I could, it's as though the claws move to my throat and there are no words.

I use all my strength to grab a sleeping pill from my bedside table. It's a leftover prescription from when I was constantly up late battling anxiety. It's a cheap fix but it's the only thing I can think to do. I swallow the pill, trying to lean into the heaviness of all of it like a blanket keeping me in place, and wait for the sleep to hit me.

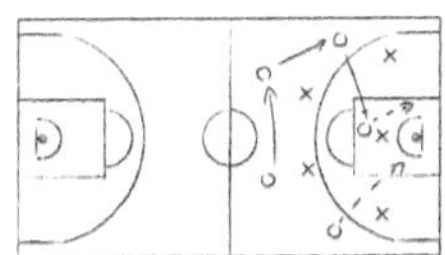

After a solid seventeen hours of sleep, the claws aren't as big as they were yesterday. I turn my phone on, bracing for messages and notifications. There's an email from the restaurant I had ordered Thanksgiving dinner from, back when I thought it would be me and my mom. It should be here in a few hours.

I open my messages to see my most recent texts.

Lia

> happy thanksgiving! hope you have the best time with your mom

Me

> thanks. happy thanksgiving to you too

I should ask what her plans are, how she'll spend today. But I don't have it in me. The claws might be smaller, but it takes all the energy I have to keep them that way.

I send a quick email to the restaurant, asking them to leave the food at the door, and fall back into bed.

Chapter 33
Lia

"Wait, you already prepped all this content?" Megan asks as she sits next to me, pointing at the to-do list with most things marked as completed.

I look from my laptop to her. "Yup. I'm going to finish getting content for a day in the life, because those views are insane."

"I told you. People love it. You're a breath of fresh air in a space which needs it." She smiles while she pulls up her phone, opening my social media account—the one for the Jags—and shows me the most recent view total.

It blows my mind. I truly thought this would fizzle so fast; that people wouldn't care if Brooks wasn't in the picture. It was an idea that wouldn't pan out and I'd go back to focusing on the main social channels. Well, joke's on me. I'm the clown. I'm hitting influencer status and it's not a thing I planned for.

"You have some PR waiting for you at the front."

"I'm sorry. I didn't apply for anything like that. I'm sure it's annoying—"

Megan starts to laugh before putting a hand on my arm. "Lia. Chill out. You think we're bothered by you being so successful that companies want to send you free stuff? As long as you do your brand research and don't turn the entire channel into an unboxing video, I could care less. Let good things happen."

Let good things happen.

Well, shit.

"Brooks is ready when you are," a trainer calls as he pops his head in the office.

It's our first time filming since his injury—and the first time I'll see him face to face. We've been FaceTiming before bed but neither of us have made plans to see each other. I get the feeling he's needed some space. Dealing with an injury can't be easy and the last thing I want to do is be a burden. That sounds dramatic, but I don't want to make anything any harder for him.

I practically skip to the training room. The plan was to film some rehab exercises towards the end of the session.

Before I walk in, I stop for a second, smoothing out the fabric of my wide-leg pants. I love the purple—an obvious nod to the team. My heart beats quickly as I try to take a deep breath; like it's trying to tell me *Lia your secret man is on the other side of the door in all his hunky athlete glory.*

When I see Brooks sitting on a training table, he turns and smirks at me. In my head, I run up to him, wrap my arms around his neck and kiss him. The kind of messy kiss where you haven't seen someone in a while, and they're surprised and they might laugh into it. A kiss where he dips you back and you push your hips into him. In real life, I wave and walk up to him—how fucking boring.

The ice pack is gone from his shoulder and he's doing some mobility exercises, testing the range of movement.

"Heard you were ready for me?" I beam at Brooks. But when his eyes look at my mouth, I want to strip in the training room and straddle this man on the table where he sits. Not appropriate, and maybe a little more athletic than necessary, but I can't help it.

"Is it too warm in here? You look hot, Lia." The trainer checks the thermostat. He'll find the temperature is completely fine.

"I'm fine," I insist, fanning my face. "I just raced Megan from our office. Gotta get that heart rate up, you know?"

The poor man smiles at me because what the fuck else would he do? I told him I ran here, like I'm a middle school boy. Classic. It's worse when I look at Brooks and he's trying not to laugh.

"I won. So, yay me!" I put one hand up in a celebratory wave but I'm dying inside. Why am I being so cringy? Another reason you shouldn't date someone you work with—you might do dumb shit, like pretending you're racing colleagues in the hallway, and wind up dealing with the repercussions. What if this guy starts telling people I like to race, and then I have to start *actually* racing people in the hallway? Ah, god, this sucks.

"Way to go!" The trainer tries to match my excitement but makes it worse. "Brooks, keep going through the stretching circuit for ten more minutes. Come to the court when you're ready."

As soon as the trainer leaves, Brooks' laughes escape his mouth. "Are you okay?"

I groan loudly. "Don't worry about me. How are you?"

"Excited to practice. Definitely needed the laugh from whatever that was." He points to me before standing and doing a variation of an arm circle with both arms. "You ready for me to record? Or do you need a few more minutes?"

I watch his Adam's apple bob as he swallows before answering, "Ready." His voice cracks and he immediately looks away. Brooks turns from me and shakes out both of his hands.

He doesn't say it, but I can feel it: he's scared. It's like the second the trainer left, he let his mask fall a little bit—enough for me to see what's really going on.

Taking a step closer, I ask, "Brooks... What can I do?"

His body doesn't stop moving and he doesn't turn back to me. "You're doing it. Just be here. Let's do what we always do." He shakes it out and looks at me. The seconds stretch and I swear I can *feel* the moment he puts the mask back on. His shoulders roll down and back, and he nods, indicating he's ready for me.

I grab my phone and get ready to record. Back to work.

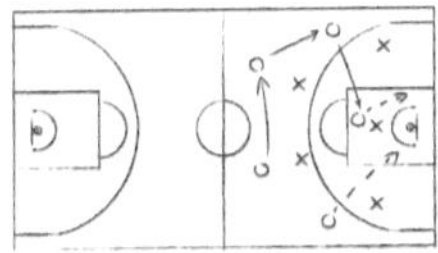

There's no way I was leaving Brooks on his own tonight. Maybe he and I are more alike than I thought. We both seem to have a difficult time asking for help or leaning on others. Seeing him today, in person, let me see the pieces I couldn't through the phone. The ones he tried to keep from everyone, but he showed me a part of.

After he looked at me like that, I knew I needed to do something for him. My idea may be wild and completely off-base, but I want to make him feel like he matters. Like he's worth it. Like this injury isn't a permanent mark that makes him less of what he was. The recent injury, the old injury, it doesn't matter—it's true no matter which way you look at it.

It's late, but we were texting, so I know he's still awake.

As I was getting dressed, a wave of confidence hit me in my apartment. I walked out feeling like I was on top of the world—so sure in my decisions. Now, I'm sending Brooks a message and kind of losing my grip.

Me

hey, i'm outside. you ready for a visitor?

Instead of texting him back, I walk to the door and lightly knock, the early December air licking at my bare legs. The door swings open and Brooks is standing there in all his fucking glory. He's wearing a dark green T-shirt and basketball shorts, and when I see his head, I let out a gasp. The man is wearing a backwards hat. He grins, much brighter than earlier, and I know this was the right move.

When he reaches for my hand, pulling me to him and closing the door before putting his lips quickly on mine, I start to melt. I'm about to reveal the surprise when Rocky pads over to us. It's the first time I've seen him since the shelter event, unless you count pictures and videos. I swear he's actually smiling as I dip down to pet him. I scratch behind his ears, taking in all his wrinkles and squished nose. He's perfect.

"Rocky, it's good to see you again," I coo.

He sits down, rolls to the side and lets me pet his belly—his legs sticking out in bliss.

"What's the special occasion?" Brooks asks.

I stand, grab a handful of his shirt, and pull his lips to mine. "I feel like you're in need of a pick-me-up. That's where I come into play."

He raises a curious eyebrow. "Ah, okay. What did you have in mind?"

Slowly, I breathe in, willing my hands to steady as I reach for the zipper at the top of my winter coat. I pull it down, revealing the surprise underneath.

Chapter 34
Brooks

"Fuck. Are you serious?" I stare at Lia, who is standing in my living room wearing only my jersey. Her legs are bare, long, and I bet as smooth as I remember. Her nipples show through the jersey, meaning she's braless.

I rub my jaw as my eyes roam over her, the purple of the Jags jersey a contrast to her pale skin. "Are you wearing anything under that?" I choke out.

She offers me a devilish smirk, reaches for my hand, and pulls us toward the kitchen. "Why don't you find out?"

Lia stops once she reaches the kitchen island. She puts her hands on the ledge and hoists herself up before scooting back. Slowly, and one at a time, she brings her knees to her chest, resting her heels on the counter. Lia's fingers dance across her kneecaps as she flips her hair to the side.

She presses them open, just an inch, before closing them. My mouth waters and I'm licking my lips, taking her in.

"I want you to tell me what you want," she teases, keeping her legs shut. A sliver of her ass peeks around her bent legs, and the words go straight to my cock. "Take control."

Pushing my bottom lip up against my teeth, I cross my arms and answer, "Spread those legs for me like a good girl."

Lia soaks in the praise, tipping her head back with a wide fucking smile before snapping her eyes back up to mine. She splits her legs, slowly giving me what I want. When she's open for me, completely bare, in nothing but my jersey, my knees almost fucking wobble.

"Did you like driving like this? My jersey the only thing between you and the seat?" I step forward, not touching her quite yet. She leans into my words, and I can almost see them wrap around her.

She tips her chin to her chest and looks up at me through thick, dark lashes. "Loved. It." She pops the 't' as the air rushes between us, and her eyes are magnets to mine.

Lia leans back a little on her forearms and elbows as I let my fingertips touch the skin above her ankle. My hands glide up the sides of each of her legs before reaching behind her knees. I cup my hands behind and pull her legs a little further apart. Her muscles stretch, giving way and showing her flexibility.

"Were you making a mess in the car? Thinking of me. Touching you?" I put a kiss on the inside of her thigh and then nip it.

Lia sucks in a breath before she lets out a moan, her eyes rolling back and her head falling with it. "I'm definitely making a mess now."

My fingers move from the inside of her thigh, across soft skin and strong muscle, and find her entrance. I swipe her wetness until it coats my fingers, and my cock aches.

"Touch yourself," I rumble while unbuttoning my pants. Taking them off, I strain against the fabric of my briefs and can see a dot of wetness seeping through. I pull my briefs down and stroke my cock, as slowly as Lia draws circles on her clit.

She uses two fingers and picks up the pace while she watches me stroke my shaft, my dick heavy and full in my hand. Lia bites her lip, letting out a whimper which sends a shock to my balls.

I move closer, the head of my dick almost touching the hand she uses to tease her center. I let it rub against the back of her hand, only for a second, and she nibbles on her own lip, stopping like I've burned her.

"You like when I tease you like this?" I ask huskily.

"Yes." The word rushes out, loud and confident.

"Let's switch. You touch me and I'll touch you." I let my dick stand on its own and wait for her to reach for it.

When her hands grab me, squeezing, the pressure is perfect. I take my ring and pinky finger and slide them through her entrance, while my pointer finger lightly touches her clit. Pump and touch. She watches my hands like she's hypnotized. Her chest shudders with each bump from my finger against her bundle of nerves.

Lia lifts my cock as she twists her hand, letting her thumb touch the bead of precum—or what's left of it. Her other hand holds her up, like the fucking queen she is. Watching her touch herself, hearing the moans, and feeling her fingers around me is next level. It's almost too much but somehow it feels like just enough.

My stomach clenches and I'm closer than I want to be. I want this to last forever. I do know I'm not about to come in her hand, not when she showed up like this.

I pull my hand from her and dip my mouth to hers. Our lips meet and it's searing—our bodies screaming for more. She bites my lower lip and I nip her back.

I grab my dick and nudge her entrance, watching her move in response. Her chest shudders, and her eyes focus on me like I have the answer to every question she could possibly ask. I can see her pulse thrumming in her neck.

"Are you sure about this?" I ask as I tease her, desperate to enter her bare.

She nods before the words fall out of her mouth. "Yes. I have an IUD."

I pull Lia off the counter so her feet are touching the floor and then turn her. Quick. Her ass touches my dick, the jersey bunching up around her hips as I bend her over.

It's like a fucking fantasy. That ass on display. The contrast of the purple jersey. My number. But seeing my name on her? I'm never going to recover.

Inch by inch, I give her more, stretching her with each thrust.

"You feel so good," she moans, her blonde hair falling in front of her face as she turns back to look at me.

I push into her faster, holding the front of her thighs for leverage. The feel of her around me, the sounds she makes—it's fucking intoxicating.

My climax is close and I can tell Lia's isn't far behind.

"Touch yourself for me, baby. I want you to come with me." I get the words out and they sound more like a growl than I intended.

She listens and I watch her shoulder dip while her hand reaches down. The second her fingers find her clit, shallow breaths race from her chest, her face turning so her cheek rests on the cool counter. I plunge into her, ferocious, hungry, needing her. When she clenches around me, it's only a few seconds until I'm falling apart right after her.

Her shocks have me spilling into her. I don't stop until she's putty beneath me. I reach for her, pull her off the counter and turn her towards me. My forehead falls into Lia's shoulder, and it's just us, sharing breaths. I kiss the column of her neck and feel her head lean into mine.

This must be what heaven feels like.

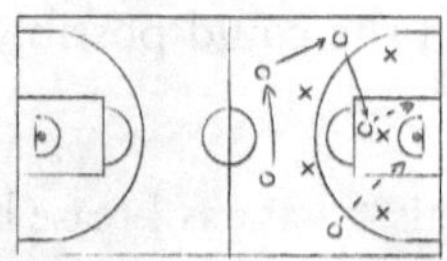

After we took a shower, each of us spent and wanting sleep, I was about ready to beg her to stay. Luckily, I didn't have to. Lia sleepily crawled into my bed, wearing one of my Jags T-shirts and a pair of panties she kept in her coat pocket. Like she planned to stay. Which I love.

With a palm on my bare chest, she's turned into me, and I didn't envision my night going this well. Lia is a fucking queen. Coming over here like that, knowing I needed her, even though I didn't ask. I couldn't bring myself to do it, no matter how much I knew she'd made me feel better. But she already knew.

She breathes against me, which makes me feel lighter than I have in the last week—from the injury to the depressive episode and a lonely holiday, to facing the reality of my body not being invincible. She made a guess at what I needed, and she was right.

It was *her*.

Tonight, I wanted to tell her about Rebecca. We were getting ready for bed and the words were right on the tip of my tongue. But it seems like the last week has been nothing but darkness and barbs that got me when I least expected them. I didn't want to ruin the lightness of Lia and our evening with something that probably doesn't even matter. I haven't heard from Rebecca—maybe she took the hint? There's no need to make something harder for no reason.

There's a string of doubt that tangles itself in my brain, but when I watch Lia's eyelids flutter with sleep, I know tonight isn't the night.

Chapter 35
Lia

"You didn't need to come," Wes argues, his eyes darting around before settling on mine. "I just saw you on Thanksgiving."

I shift my weight on one foot, taking in my little—but much taller—younger brother. He's wearing a dress shirt, light blue to match the color of his eyes, and khaki pants. There's something about him that still feels young, but he's almost a legal adult, which doesn't seem real. It feels like he was crawling into my bed, recovering from a nightmare, not that long ago.

"Stop. I'm so proud of you! There weren't that many athletes up there today." I look around the school auditorium, which is filled with families and friends.

The high school is celebrating any athlete with a GPA of 3.8 or higher. My aunt and uncle couldn't make it, and there was no way I would leave Wes with no one cheering him on. No matter how badly I slept last night, nothing was going to keep me from this. My skin has been itchy when I try to go to sleep, no matter what I put on it. I think I'll have to try Benadryl or something tonight.

Ugh. I wish my doctor's appointment wasn't so far away.

He rolls his eyes. "Isn't there a home game? Shouldn't you be working?"

Ah, there's something he got from me—the worrying about everyone else before taking the space for yourself.

"I rearranged my schedule and am going in later. Only thing I'm missing is the catered food, but since you and I have a lunch date, I'll be fine." I bump into him before reaching up and pulling him in for a hug.

I hold him longer than either of us anticipate. Wes squeezes me before asking, "Wait, is something wrong? Are you sick? That's why you came today?"

Pushing myself away, I gasp, "No! Why would you think that?!"

Wes shrugs his shoulders, tilting his head and replying, "All I know is you trading any time away from the Jags arena, to be anywhere else, is cause for concern."

I scoff at the joke and lightly push his chest, which he then turns into a dramatic stumble backwards, his hand covering where my fingers barely touched him.

"You're just jealous you haven't been to a game yet," I scoff.

His eyes flash with confusion. "You're right. What the hell is up with that?" He shifts from trying to be funny back to the dramatics.

This is the best part about Wes. He's always been extremely likeable and easy-going. While he may try to perpetually put others first, which is something I'm still trying to grow out of, he's always had a good head on his shoulders. Typically, he gravitates towards people like him and stays out of trouble. He gets it, even when someone his age shouldn't have to.

Maybe it was the tragedy that changed us both down to our bones, and we lost a lot of the bickering that siblings are almost programed to do. It's not that we never fought or annoyed each other again, but it was always short-lived. We were always so eager to get back to our baseline that no fight really lingered.

"Let's look at the home game schedule at lunch and pick a game. Sound good?"

"Yes. Especially now that Brooks is back. He's starting tonight, right?"

Brooks. It's like I watch him slam into the court on repeat. It hurts in a way that I almost lose my breath. I try not to think about him that night on FaceTime. The fear in his eyes. I don't know if it would've been worse or better if I had made the trip for that away game.

"I think so. I watched him practice yesterday and he looked solid," I reply. He played with a hesitancy he's probably familiar with. It was probably worse when he was coming back from the ACL injury, and part of me is glad I didn't get the job until after. Him playing like that, beating himself up, questioning everything? It hurts me.

"That injury looked way worse when it happened," Wes adds. "Glad he was out for only a few games."

I nod in agreement, afraid to open my mouth and give myself away. We walk towards the exit and I wonder if I should tell Wes about Brooks and me. We're not big on keeping secrets, mostly because we know each other too well. There's a solid chance he'll come to the game, watch me with Brooks, and figure it out on his own.

That might be the other reason I haven't offered Wes a complimentary ticket, but who can really say? Maybe I'm afraid to see him watching Brooks and I together. I mean, he's a teenager—maybe I'm giving him too much credit?

Wes stares at me curiously. "I'm not trying to be weird, but what's going on with your eyelids?"

My reflection from this morning roars back. Red bumps appeared again at the corner of my eyes. I didn't remember seeing them the night before while I was doing my skincare routine.

I try to brush away his concern. "Ah, don't worry about it. Just allergies."

I have no idea what it really is, but I'm still waiting to get in to see a dermatologist. If there's something that is complete bullshit, it would be healthcare in America. Even if I had the money to pay out of pocket for an appointment, everyone I've called is booking six months out. My name is supposedly on a few cancellation lists, but I'm not holding my breath.

"You had the perfect opportunity to say you were allergic to me and you didn't even take it," Wes jokes, shaking his head as we get to my car.

I let out a laugh, almost too loudly, and playfully push Wes in response.

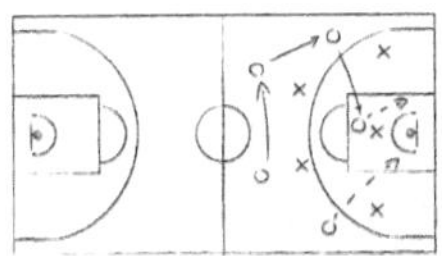

There's something spectacular about a good thrift store find. I walk through the arena with my head held a bit higher—yes, it's game day, but I'm also wearing the most perfect purple blazer. It's one of those pieces that's bold enough to work in the best of ways.

I thought the idea of home games would lose its luster, but that's far from the truth. My heart races enough for me to notice and a smile is permanently on my face, sort of aching my cheeks.

I walk courtside and can practically feel Brooks before I see him. It's as if there's a string between us which snaps into place when we're in the same vicinity. He's dribbling up and down the court, warming up for a key matchup in the conference. The Jags are third in their conference while the opposing team is first, but only two games separate them.

Tonight is a prime-time game—it'll be aired nationally, which means some of my favorite commentators will be working. I pick up the pace, eager to get in the booth to watch everyone get ready for tonight.

For a prime-time game, we seem a little light on staff. Entrances and places which usually have three to four security or building staff seem to have only one tonight. Maybe they're wrapping up a meeting or had an incident?

Before going to the booth, I stop by the staff hospitality suite to grab a Dr. Pepper and a snack. Lunch with Wes was so much fun, but naturally we talked for way too long and I had to rush to get here. I wanted to have time to stop and get something, or see if any catered food was left, something easy to grab for later, but I ran out of time. It won't be the first or last time I have chips for dinner.

I'm opening a bag of Doritos when Megan stops me. "Lia, I'm so glad you're here," she says hurriedly. Once she gets closer, it's clear something is wrong. A sheen of sweat glistens on her forehead and upper lip, and it showcases how pale she is.

"What's wrong?" I lean back, trying to put as much space between us as possible.

Megan groans and puts a hand to her mouth. She takes a second, lifting her eyes up to the lights like she's trying not to throw up.

"Not contagious," she barely gets out before taking a deep breath. Once she steadies herself, she continues. "The catered food. Bad. Half the staff has food poisoning."

"What about the players?!" I look out to the court and see what looks like a full team going through warmups.

She slowly shakes her head. "No, they had a different caterer. Thank god."

As Megan seems to get it together, standing tall and moving her hand from her mouth, the sound of someone else throwing up in a trash is much closer than I wish it was.

"Oh no," she slumps, her face even whiter than before as she rushes into the connected media booth.

I follow to see one of the commentators—someone I'd do unspeakable things to meet and pick their brain about the craft—casually throwing up. This is a nightmare. I feel like my feet are superglued in place.

"So, as you can see, we're down a body. I haven't eaten anything since we've been here, but we can't have only one person calling this game. I called the studio and confirmed there's no one they know of who made the trip that can step in. Do you have any backups in the building?" Blake, the commentator and an ex-NBA player, asks while acting like his colleague isn't currently throwing up four feet away from him.

Megan puts the back of her hand to her forehead, pacing a few steps back and forth. "No, I don't think so," she groans.

"No coaches who can spare the night off?" Blake persists. "Anyone on your staff who has a decently pleasant voice and can help fill the silence by going back and forth?"

There's a flame of nervousness in my stomach. It grows with each second Megan doesn't offer a suggestion. I look at the clock; there's only twenty minutes until coverage starts—there's not a lot of time.

I take a deep breath, doing my best to keep my voice level and mustering as much confidence as I can.

"I can do it."

Blake's eyes go wide for a second as he rocks back on his heels, arms crossing in front of his chest.

"Are you sure?" It's not condescending or dismissive, but he's giving me a second to reconsider.

The basketball part of my brain, one filled with a bunch of random filed away facts and tidbits, lights up and my mouth hurries to keep up. "I'm sure. We're looking at an Eastern Conference matchup between two honest title contenders—neither has won one yet. The away team is on a five-game win streak, but the Jags have the best winning percentage on their home court. The real test will be the points in the paint and offensive rebounds."

The words spill easily from my mouth, and Blake's lips pull into a smile the longer I rant. "Plus, I thought you should've won defensive player of the year in 2014. Honestly, it's a crime you *didn't* win… I mean, how often is there a 7'3" center who has an average of 6.1 blocks per game?"

His eyes sparkle as I rattle off the stat I don't even remember holding on to. I let out a long breath; my head feels full of feathers as my skin buzzes with energy.

"She can totally do this. I know she's familiar with the tech side of the booth. Plus, our fans love her," Megan assures Blake, her hand still touching her stomach while her other sits not far from her mouth.

"What's your name?" He smiles and steps closer to me, reaching his hand out for a handshake. It's like everything is happening in slow motion.

I put my hand in his, happy my Doritos are tucked under the other arm. "Lia. Lia Stone."

"Alright, Lia. We've got about fifteen minutes to get your notes in order. Let's do this."

He sits down at the booth, and when he gestures to the empty seat and headset next to him, I swear I almost pass out.

Chapter 36
Brooks

Tonight's game is sold out and I can feel it. My dad and Mack are in attendance, which flips my stomach. It's a good thing; I'm thankful they care enough to spend time at a rowdy NBA stadium, especially knowing they get so worked up about watching Zack play in person that they rarely attend games.

Nervous energy flows through my blood, making my ears itch and heart race. I keep moving my arm, stretching my shoulder before feeling for the tape I know is on my knee. Tonight, the tape soothes me. It's fucking bizarre to be thinking of something other than my knee, to worry about a different injury, but it's kind of a nice break. Without another collision, I shouldn't have to worry about the nerve issue reappearing, but I still wait for the burn.

I'm fucking ready for tonight. I've been cleared to play for days, but my trainer wanted me to sit out an extra game as a precaution. Again, I'm fucking lucky to have people here who care about me.

The stakes are raised with each fan on their feet, decked out in team colors. The NBA season feels long some weeks, like we'll never get to the end of the eighty-two games. Tonight, it feels like we're on the brink of the postseason; in reality, I hear the station lead in and I can't help but bounce on my feet. Jags fans are going wild. There's a collective gasp for air building into a roar. Taking in the crowd, I look up to find people are pointing to the Jumbotron.

Lia. Wearing a headset. Next to an NBA hall of famer who became a commentator for one of the major networks.

I'm standing with my team when Coach asks, "Wait. Is that...?"

"Our girl, Lia? Sure as hell looks like it," Jalen cheers, bumping my hip with his as he says our girl.

"Ooh. I wonder if someone ate the fish," Coach wonders. When we all look at him like he's speaking another language, he continues, "Apparently, half the staff got food poisoning. I didn't want to say anything because some of us get queasy..."

Everyone looks to Jalen, who shrugs. "I can't help it." He shakes his hands like he's trying to get something off him.

"Damn. You know what, though? She knows her shit. She was basically grilling me the other night about a pick and roll play," Jamison adds, stretching his neck from side to side.

Having your friends and teammates refer to your girlfriend, even a secret girlfriend, as sports smart is top fucking tier. It makes me want to do anything to play my best for them. It also makes me want to devour Lia.

I'd be lying if I said I hadn't thought about her showing up at my place. In nothing but a jersey. Her making a mess on my counter. Those thoughts pop in at the most inopportune times... like right now. It's been a week since that night and I'm itching to spend another with her.

Looking up at the Jumbotron and hearing the Jags fans clap for Lia, I feel full. It's almost like my chest felt hollow, like there was too much room—for what, I wasn't quite sure. That's different now. It was meant for someone who wanted to know me *for me*. The room was for these big-ass feelings I can barely compute in my brain, but they feel right in my chest.

Holy shit. Lia is sitting in the booth, which is closest to the thing she's wanted to do for her whole life. She's wearing a Jags purple blazer, and

I can see her flushed cheeks. I don't know what the hell happened but I'm almost salivating for the details. Right now, I'm so fucking excited for her. I wear a grin like it's part of my uniform. We both deserve good things tonight.

The lights shift in the arena as the players make their way to the court.

Jalen reaches out to slap my hand. Clapping my back, he says, "You better do something tonight. Can you imagine Lia having to publicly talk about your shitty game in the booth?" He breaks into a laugh at his own joke, eyes squinting and hands on his knees.

"You're really not that funny." I get into position, wiping my hands on the front of my jersey, and wait for the tip.

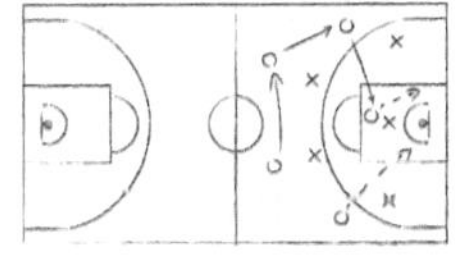

The game is over and I *definitely* gave Lia something to say. We won, 112-108, and I scored the most points I've ever scored in a game: 50. I'm in the 50-piece club and the night couldn't get better. The buzzer sounded a few seconds ago and my teammates crowd me, jumping before bowing in front of me.

Jalen runs up and puts a crown on my head, something I've only seen brought out one other time—last season when another Jags player scored 50 points. It only makes the guys more hyped. I can't help the smile that's plastered on my face as someone claps my back.

Pulling me in for a hug, Coach says, "Fucking proud of you. What a comeback." He pats me a few times and grins before he's stopped by an on-court reporter. I don't know if I've ever been this happy. It's not a championship, or a game with major implications, but winning a close one at home and being a key contributor is the fucking best.

The guys carry the energy all the way into the locker room, where they play music and dance in our space. I get in the middle of the circle, some loud rap song rattling my bones in the best way, and someone sprays me with champagne. Definitely overkill, and a little reckless because I don't have goggles on, but so fucking fun.

When someone comes and gets me for the press conference, I decide to go as is—crown, champagne-soaked jersey and all.

The press laughs as I settle into the seat. I know the crown is over the top, but I don't fucking care. It's rare to do what I did tonight, and I want to remember it. Forever.

I scan the room and look for my favorite reporters—or that's at least how I make it seem. Honestly, I'm looking for a gorgeous woman in a purple blazer. The one who can make my heart race or stop beating, depending on the interaction.

Lia stands in the corner with no other media staff to be found. I wonder if they are all sick, and she's the last one standing. I don't have to look long to see, or feel, that she's glowing.

The first reporter jumps in. "Brooks, you seemed like you were on another level. Guess the knee is holding up? And the stinger is gone?"

I wonder if there will ever be a game when people won't ask about the knee. For now, I don't want it to kill my vibe, so I answer, "Sure is—enough to at least keep this crown on my head." My joke is well received, the room content with happy laughter. "I've been feeling good. The stinger was a completely different type of injury, and I can't say enough good things about the training staff here. For the knee, it seems like I'm back to normal, maybe even better than before? I don't know... tonight was unreal."

"How do you feel mentally? Any doubt when you're going out to play?"

I take a deep, slow breath in, hold for a moment, and sigh it out before continuing. "I feel good. Some days I'm more mentally hesitant than others, if that's a good way to put it. All I can do is trust my trainers and my body. And hope I don't take any other hard falls." I watch as heads bob and nod along with understanding. "Recovery has tested me in more ways than I thought. But right now, my life is the best it's ever been." I choose that moment to quickly look at Lia, long enough to see her perfect red lips smiling at me.

Another reporter, someone local and close to the team, raises her hand. When the microphone is brought to her, she asks, "Do you know anything about Lia Stone being in the booth tonight? I know you guys are close, based on social media and her work with the team. I was surprised to see her in there."

I nod, guessing the reporter doesn't know the person in question is in the room. "I don't have all the details, but yeah, I guess Lia was in the booth. I'm not exactly sure what happened, but there is no one better to fill in. She's smarter than some of the guys on my team... especially Jalen." I make a joke, one Jalen will never let me forget, but it's what we do to each other. "I'm sure she was great. I can't wait to hear what she said when I scored that fiftieth point."

My cheeks flush as I think about what tonight means, and luckily they're still crimson with excitement and adrenaline. I'll be able to watch this game back and hear what my girl thought while she was in the booth, doing something she's dreamed of her whole life.

Fuck.

As a reporter puts their hand up, Blake runs up to the table and grabs the microphone. "Lia was a blast tonight. She stepped in when we were in a pinch, and there aren't many people who could do what she did, the way she did it. I hope to do it again. Let's give her some love."

Blake points to where Lia is standing, and everyone's attention follows. She stands by herself and lifts her hand in a tiny wave. When everyone realizes she's in there, they follow Blake and start to clap. People standing near her offer their hands for a handshake, and I know they're telling her good job and congratulations.

From here, I can see her raised eyebrows and wide eyes—she didn't expect this kind of recognition, which makes it even more special.

Next thing I know, a reporter is standing. Then another. And another. All the women in the room rise and give Lia a standing ovation. When I see the flashes, I'm so fucking thankful someone is taking pictures of this moment.

Not a single man stands, but they do clap for the women in the room. They've probably had to do more than their male counterparts to even enter the conversation or be considered for jobs like this. I can't imagine the journey was easy and there's still a long way to go, but fuck, I'm proud of this.

Blake yells from the corner, "Who run the world?"

And the entire room shouts back, in unison, "Girls!"

Lia wipes away a tear just as my own eyes get glassy.

Chapter 37
Lia

I'M SWEATY ENOUGH TO believe tonight really happened. If this were a dream, I would be a glowing goddess, minus the sweat.

Tonight. Really. Happened. I sat in a booth and helped call a game. Like, I actually contributed. Blake took the lead, mostly giving me space to reinforce what he was talking about. There was a moment while I was watching the game where I tried telling myself I was back in my apartment, doing it only for me. I've practiced a lot—an embarrassing amount, if I'm being honest—so I started doing what I always do.

Blake lit up when I took the lead on a play call. His eyes were like actual sparklers; like I was his protégé and not like we'd just met. He did everything in his power to make me feel comfortable and would coach me or give a heads up on what was coming next during commercial breaks.

It was fucking terrifying, no matter how much I loved it, but this was an experience I'd never trade. I should send a thank you note to wherever the bad food came from—I couldn't have done this without them.

I'm waiting outside the locker room, trying to catch up on my text messages. Megan must've made it home and turned the game on because I have a few messages from her. Unfortunately, some of them are hard to read, riddled with typos, but she gets a pass considering the whole food poisoning situation.

Mostly, they're from Wes. He tried FaceTiming me during the game, maybe to see if what he saw was really happening. I can't wait to call him back and tell him everything.

Some of the team's family members and close friends come up to me, introducing themselves and shaking my hand. The excitement from my night must've spread.

The first player to see me is Jalen. I can't help but be reminded how he's one of the people in on our secret. How could I forget—he sort of caught us at the hotel.

"Lia! I told Coach the only film I'm watching is the version with your commentary." He pulls me into a side hug—it's not surprising that he's a hugger. "I heard you were awesome."

I try not to be embarrassed and say, "I'm not so sure about that, but I appreciate it."

He winks at me before tipping his head to the locker room. "Brooks is finishing up. He'll be out in a minute."

A few players who I've only exchanged a few words with congratulate me while finding their families to head home. I've always loved watching athletes with their significant others and friends; it always feels so wholesome.

Brooks walks out of the locker room, still wearing the crown, and people clap for him. I know this night is significant for him. He was absolutely amazing. This man played like his contract depended on it, and it looks like the Jags got the better end of the deal. This is the type of game that moves you up the ranks—one that has coaches and other teams preparing specifically for you.

When he sees me, he starts to clap. His eyes, bright and like honey, lock on mine. I do everything in my power not to melt right here and now.

And then he does something I don't see coming—he wraps me in a hug. It's quick, something you'd expect between friends, but the way my body leans into his is undeniable. It's like a missing piece of me has been returned.

"I'm so proud of you," he murmurs, the words falling over me like the warmest blanket. "This must've been one hell of a night. I can't wait to hear about it."

I nod, quickly scanning the people around us. Everyone seems to be in their own world, which bodes well for our conversation.

"Me? You were incredible. An instant Jags classic."

"Good. That means lots of people will listen to you call the game for years to come."

I place my hands on my belly. "Okay, that sort of makes me want to throw up."

I smirk as he playfully shoves my shoulders. In this moment, I want to kiss him. I wish we weren't at the arena, but somewhere we could be just the two of us. Pretending to be only his friend isn't always easy.

"Brooks!" someone yells.

Before I can see who it is, a woman runs up, stepping between us like I don't exist. She wraps herself around him until all I see is dark and curly hair in front of me. The hallway starts closing in; my peripheral vision is nothing but darkness, and the only thing I can focus on is this woman all over Brooks.

She finally lets go of him, only to kiss him on the cheek.

"Baby, you were so good tonight!" she cries, loud enough for everyone to hear. I step back with each letter that comes out of her mouth, needing space, more room. When she looks at me, she offers a pathetic wave.

Thanks to Shelbie, I know exactly who this is.

Rebecca.

Ex-girlfriend Rebecca.

The only woman Brooks has ever been known to publicly date. The only ex he told me about. She's here, right in front of me. Calling him baby. Coming to his game. Hugging him like that. He doesn't do any-thing. Doesn't push her away. Just looks at her.

My mouth feels like sandpaper. I can't say anything. Even if we weren't secretly dating, I'd never want to be the person who airs their drama in front of others. Even if I were that kind of person, there are no words. Tears form behind my eyes, and I know they're seconds from falling down my cheeks—probably following the same path of my happy tears from earlier. What a fucking turn of events. I don't have it in me to cry in front of these people—in front of *her*. Slowly, I turn and start walking to the office. I count my steps, doing anything to focus on the task ahead of me.

I allow myself a single look back when I'm almost all the way down the hallway, about to turn.

They're still standing there. Talking. When Rebecca hugs him again, it's like a knife being twisted in my gut. I turn back before I can see if he hugs her back. I can't take it.

Lia, you're a fucking idiot.

I round the corner and basically jog to the office, grabbing my coat and bag. I need to get to my car. My apartment. I need to leave.

With each step I take, it's like I'm stepping on my own chest. The pressure is almost too much; I find it hard to breathe. Trying to channel the yogi in me, I attempt to gather enough air to stretch my lungs.

I'm unsuccessful.

I'm in my car. Keys in the ignition. Driving towards my apartment. It's completely silent besides the muffled sounds of my shallow breaths. When I hit a red light, my head falls forward to rest on the steering wheel and I cry.

The tears rush out, my breath following. Internally, I berate myself. Why would she be at the game? Brooks told me he hasn't talked to her in over a year. He didn't even have her phone number.

The breaths aren't there.

But the panic is.

Her running up to him like that doesn't track with what he told me. The way she called him 'baby,' overly sweet like too much aspartame, the aftertaste so strong it's disgusting.

The light turns green, and I feel better the farther I get from the arena. Away from the place where I had a dream come true only to be knocked down. Stepped on. Salt poured in the wound.

My teeth grind, obeying the clench in my jaw. I try to relax, to move my head and shoulders, but it's like my body is frozen. There's no room. Nowhere to go.

I focus on the road, looking for the next landmark to reach until I'm pulling into my apartment complex. Then I watch my feet as I walk to my unit. One step at a time.

The relief is so close I can taste it as I put my key in the lock. But when the door swings open, there's a sound of something that doesn't belong.

Water.

Running water.

The floor glistens with a puddle of water. Slowly, I look through my apartment to find the culprit. There is water pouring in through the ceiling, right over my bed.

No. No. No.

This isn't happening.

I run, the water splashing across my feet as I look up. The ceiling looks like a water balloon with water coming off the edge, like the balloon isn't tied right or contained. I run to the bathroom for towels and freeze when I need to decide between a clean or dirty towel. It doesn't matter. This is a full-on disaster. I grab all my towels, leaving a single clean one in case, and put them on the floor. I walk to where my bed is but it's like putting a Band-Aid on a bullet wound. The towels are soaked and useless in seconds.

I don't know what to do.

Standing near my bed, I put my hands on the comforter, only to feel the amount of water my mattress is holding. I can tell the mattress, and all my bedding, are completely soaked through. When I put my weight on it, I can hear the water squishing out and sputtering out to the floor.

Fuck.

This is bad.

The ceiling squeaks, and as I look up, it completely collapses in front of me.

Chapter 38
Brooks

"WHAT ARE YOU DOING here?" I hiss at the person I absolutely didn't expect to see. My jaw is clenched and my teeth grind together.

"What do you mean? I've been texting you." She steps closer to me and my reaction is to lean back, needing more space between us. I step back when the lean isn't enough.

"Surprise!" Rebecca cheers, her hands posing above her head.

I shake my head and snap, "This is a fucking horrible surprise."

I look down the hallway to see Lia leaving. I want to run after her, but I will not cause a scene. Rebecca is not fucking worth it. I don't want anyone leaking this interaction, causing tonight to be all about this bullshit drama. No fucking way. Not for Lia and not for me.

"I haven't texted you back. How did you even get back here?" I look for the security guards who typically man this area and only find one. I bet staffing is thin at this position tonight and Rebecca found a way to use it for her advantage. Typical.

"What? You're not happy to see me?" She puts a finger to my chest and looks up at me, almost like she's about to lean in and kiss me.

I walk away from the nearby friends and family, not wanting anyone to overhear any of this. "Rebecca. No. Not particularly. The last time I talked to you was when you packed your shit to go back to the man you were having an affair with. Do you remember that?" I whisper sharply.

She rolls her eyes, agitation rolling off her skin. "Why can't you forgive and forget? It was a mistake. I said I was sorry."

Despite everything we went through, she still sounds like she couldn't give a fuck. Part of me thought we might connect later in life, not as friends but as people passing, and I'd be able to look at her and know she's changed. Today is not that day. I don't know if that will ever happen.

"You said it. You never meant it. Not then and not now."

"We just need to sit down. Hash it out. I think—"

"No. I really don't care what you think. I'm uninterested in the next part of that sentence." I scrub my face with my hands, willing myself to be in a different interaction. "You showed up here and snuck back to the players' area like it was nothing. Like it was owed to you. Doesn't that seem off?"

An issue with Rebecca is she knows exactly what to do to get what she wants. She did it when we were together and she's doing it now. I want so badly to scream that there's someone else. Someone who left so fast. Someone I wanted to chase after. Someone who didn't deserve this. I'm sure Lia has too many questions about a woman I haven't willingly seen in years.

Rebecca sighs out a huff, her eyes on mine, and there are no old feelings creeping to the front of line. The only thing she makes me feel is anger and disappointment.

I try to make her hear me. "Listen, you showing up here like this? I don't want you to do it again. This isn't how this works. You don't get to decide this. Just because you're ready and assume I want to see you, even if I've never texted you back."

"I just want five minutes." She sounds borderline sad but it's not enough.

I put my hand up, literally wanting her to stop. "You don't get five minutes. I have nothing else for you. Please don't text. Don't call. There's nothing left for you to chase."

"Brooks." She steps closer and I immediately move backward, as if her hands could burn me.

"No. You've had your chances. I was never enough. The only difference now is I know *you* were never enough for *me*." I laugh because it's so clear. How didn't I see this before? "I wish you nothing but good things."

I turn and walk to the exit. When Rebecca doesn't call after me, the relief starts to creep through my bones, permeating to the blood coursing through my veins. I pull out my phone and call Lia, but she doesn't answer. I try one more time with the same result.

Fuck. There's no way I can let this go tonight.

Within minutes, I'm in my car and driving straight to Lia's apartment.

I hate thinking about how Lia's feelings were hurt tonight. It's like getting the wind knocked out of me while trying to catch my breath. I didn't think there was any harm in keeping Rebecca's texts to myself—I literally never engaged—but maybe that was wrong?

I go over the whole situation and the key points shine in my brain, like, "Hey, asshole. Don't forget about this!" And I do feel like an asshole. There's no part of me that ever thought Rebecca would show up like this, or that she'd sneak through the lack of security guards to get to me.

I kick my own ass until I'm pulling in front of Lia's apartment. From here I see her door is cracked open and my heart clenches in my chest. That isn't right. She would never leave it open.

Jogging to it, I knock before calling out, "Lia? You in there?" No one answers so I push it open cautiously and look around.

Water. Everywhere. Her apartment is flooded.

I see Lia standing near her bed with her arms crossed.

"Hey. It's Brooks." I announce myself one more time because I don't want to scare her.

Once I'm in her room, I look up at what Lia's fixated on. The ceiling broke open and water is still coming down. Debris covers her bed. Fuck.

I lightly touch the side of her arm, standing in front of her. "Are you okay?"

Her eyes gut me. Rimmed with red, they're a stark contrast to her pale skin. When she doesn't say anything, I grip her tightly and move her away from the bed. There's still a chance that more, or even the rest, of the ceiling could collapse, and we shouldn't be standing here if it does.

Tears run down her face, mixed with water from the flooding, and this hurts me.

"Lia, did you call anyone? Are you hurt?"

As I ask, firefighters come in and immediately start assessing the situation. They only take a few looks around before turning to us. "Whose apartment is this?" one of the men asks.

"Mine," Lia croaks out. It's another haymaker to the body that almost brings me to my knees.

"We need to get you out of here. I can give you a minute to grab a bag of some things you need. We're running out of time."

Lia doesn't move. She stares at the firefighter, who then looks to me.

I turn and face her. "Lia, you need to pack a bag," I repeat.

She doesn't say anything but moves to the bathroom, collecting a few things. When she emerges with a bag, her next stop is a laundry basket on the couch—it looks like clean laundry needing to be folded. I watch her grab whatever she can from the basket.

Lia sets the bag she packed, her work bag, and purse on the kitchen counter.

Someone walks in, and it appears to be the landlord.

"Fuck. This is bad," he whines with no tact at all. "We turned the water off to the building." He looks at Lia as one of the firefighters gets out of the way, in time for her twinkly lights to fall with part of the ceiling near the hole. "Lia, you obviously can't stay here. I can call you once we get this situated, but that might be a few days. Do you have somewhere you can stay?" the landlord asks.

She doesn't say anything.

"Yes," I jump in. "She can stay with me."

Lia's head whips to me so fast, her eyebrows scrunched in confusion. The water stops coming through the ceiling, but another piece falls.

"Okay, time to go," a firefighter insists as he directs everyone outside. I grab one of Lia's bags while she takes the others. Once we're outside, the firefighters and the landlord dive into a deep conversation about what to do. They leave Lia and I standing outside her door.

"Let's go to my place," I suggest, tipping my head to where my car is parked.

"No." It's the first time she's spoken to me.

"What do you mean 'no'?"

"I don't need your help. You can go," she answers flatly, her face blank and still turned toward the door. Her arms are crossed and her shoulders are by her ears.

I sigh heavily. "Lia, let me explain. Tonight was not what it looked like. And if you think I'm fucking leaving you out here, you're wrong."

"Does Rebecca know you're inviting me back to your place?" This time when Lia turns to me, she shivers, the early December cold taking advantage of her wet skin.

"Rebecca is nothing. I promise, I'll explain everything." I try to make her hear me, but I know she's probably in emotional overload. "You're freezing, soaking wet, and I'm not leaving you here."

Lia uses her trembling hand to tuck her hair behind her ears. I want to wrap my arms around her, but I know that isn't what she needs. Or wants.

I shift my approach. "You're shaking. You don't need to drive like this. Let's go back to my place and at least make a plan. I'll take you anywhere you want tomorrow." I'm pleading because I need to get her somewhere safe.

She looks at me, and her eyes have gone completely dull—none of that emerald sparkle I'm used to can be seen. She doesn't say anything but starts walking to my car.

Fuck. I'll take it.

Chapter 39
Lia

THE ONLY THING THAT brings any sort of relief is when we open the door to Brooks' place and Rocky greets us. He wiggles his nub of a tail when he sees me.

"I think he remembers you," Brooks says.

I can't respond. There are so many things I want to say but I simply don't have it in me.

I squat and put my hands, which are practically numb with cold, behind Rocky's ears. I pet him, the warmth feeling heavenly on my still shaking fingers.

Brooks locks the door behind us, sets the alarm, and grabs my bags. "I'll show you the guest room," he murmurs.

Reluctantly, I pull myself from Rocky and follow Brooks. I hate that I need his help. I feel like I don't fit here, or with him. The only reason I didn't call Shelbie is because I'm so drained, I wouldn't be able to give her any of the details she'd ask for. I'm absolutely tapped out.

My legs carry me up the stairs and into the guest bedroom. Brooks sets my bags on the floor and opens a door.

"There's a full bathroom right here. You should have everything you need but let me know if you don't." Brooks grabs a couple towels from the cabinet and places them on the counter. His eyes don't find mine as he steps around me, shutting the bathroom door behind him.

I turn the water on and strip down. My body shakes as I lose the layers, and I can't tell if I'm in shock or truly that cold. The shower has body wash and luxury shampoo and conditioner. It doesn't matter—all I want is the hot water.

Steam starts to fill the room as I step into the shower, letting the almost too hot water hit my body. I lower myself to the shower floor, pull my knees to my chest, and let my head fall forward. The steam surrounds me as I try to pull in a slow breath, the type that fills my chest and expands my lungs.

It takes a few tries but I'm finally able to do it. I focus on my breathing, recognizing my heart rate as I flex and stretch my fingers. My joints ache from the stress of tonight—some of it good and unexpected, but most of it not. After a few minutes of hot water and catching my breath, my brain fog lifts a little.

My apartment. The place I've poured my soul into and made my own. The first place that felt like home since my parents. Wrecked. The things I've worked long hours for, sacrificed sleep and time with friends and family—all ruined. I start thinking of what I've lost just in my bedroom alone, and the number hits me hard.

Brooks. Standing there with someone else like that. Maybe he preferred we kept this a secret because he had other plans? Before the thought is complete, I'm already doubting it. I don't know the whole story, or any of it really, but I don't believe that's the kind of man he is.

It still hurts. Being in the dark, choking on the doubt of the two of us. What does this mean? What happened tonight?

What happens next?

I stand to wash my hair and scrub my skin. The water soothes me until it starts to run cool. When I get out and wrap the towel around me, I realize I don't have any dry clothes to put on in here. In the guest bedroom, I see a few of Brooks' things folded at the end of the bed, presumably for me to wear. Pulling on a pair of basketball shorts and a hoodie, I wrap my hair in a towel.

In the bathroom, I find the cream for my skin. I still have rough patches I can't get to go away, and they're sensitive from being in the hot water for too long. I also put moisturizer on my face, considering I wore ceiling water before drying it out with tears and a shower that probably lasted twenty minutes too long.

I take my hair down and shake it out, towel-drying the ends before putting it in a French braid. My arms ache from holding them this way, my joints and muscles screaming in exhaustion.

I'm as put together as I can handle when I step into the hallway, looking for signs of Brooks. I don't see him but Rocky is waiting for me at the bottom of the stairs. He starts to wiggle and tap his feet as I slowly take the stairs. I don't smile, but I do feel a lightness in my chest.

I walk to the living room, and Rocky follows as I sit on the floor with my back resting against the couch. My legs straddle out in a V and Rocky gets comfortable, sitting between my legs. My arms wrap around him and move to pet him. He lolls his head to the side while I rest my head on his back. The rhythm of his breathing continues to calm me down. It's like he knew I needed something.

We sit like that for a few minutes until Brooks comes in.

"There you are," he says. "He must seriously like you because I just put food in his bowl, and he abandoned it. Definitely a first." Brooks sits on the couch across from us, elbows resting on his knees as his hands rub together. "I'm guessing you didn't eat. I ordered some food, and it should be here any minute."

My stomach rumbles at the mention of food. I haven't eaten since lunch with Wes. I didn't even get to finish my Doritos—there was no way I was going to have orange fingers in the presence of an NBA great like Blake.

"We can talk about as much or as little as you want, but I need to say a few things," Brooks states. "One, you can stay here for as long as you need. There's the guest bedroom and tons of space. Two, the thing with Rebecca was *not* what it looked like. And three, whenever you want, I'd like to hear about you and Blake tonight."

The mention of Blake makes it feel like everything happened days ago, but it was literally today. It's only been a few hours since I was riding the high of my dreams coming true and not sucking at it—or at least, that's what it felt like in the moment. Now, I'm not so sure.

Brooks' phone dings and he stands to go to the door. He comes back with bags of food and walks to the kitchen. I follow him, with Rocky following me, and sit at the bar. There are a few containers of soup, salsa and queso, chicken tenders, and a few sandwiches. Definitely all from different places.

"I tried to think of what comfort food you might want." Brooks puts out silverware and a glass of water, then sits next to me, putting a few things on a plate. I pour soup into a bowl and grab a spoon.

We eat in silence, except for the crunch of Rocky eating his own food. Each bite of food makes me feel more like a person and not something floating through space. I'm not sure how much I have left in me, but I'm thankful Brooks thought of this and didn't leave me alone, like I probably made it seem like I wanted.

Maybe I thought I did. But I really don't.

After I've eaten a bit of everything, I lean back in my bar stool, looking at the clock. I watch the minutes go by before I finally grab the remaining courage I have to say, "Okay. I want to hear about Rebecca."

My words hang in the kitchen and a pit opens in my stomach. I'm terrified for what could come next.

Chapter 40
Brooks

THE SECOND LIA GIVES me the go-ahead, I spill my guts about anything remotely relevant to the Rebecca situation. Diving deep into the archives, it's sort of like word vomit. I tell her about our relationship, the terrible breakup, and the lack of contact until recently. Anything Rebecca touched that has to do with me makes its way into the conversation.

Lia doesn't ask any questions. She watches and listens, sometimes nodding, but not giving me more than that.

"I didn't invite her. Didn't know she was coming to the game tonight. Here, take my phone. Look at the texts. Log in to my social media if you want. You'll see her messages, but you'll never see me respond. I swear I didn't." I slide the phone toward her on the counter.

"Brooks, that isn't necessary. I believe you. You've never given me a reason not to." Her voice is level and calm but doesn't give me much of anything besides that.

I let out a breath, one I've been holding in with a vice grip. Part of me was worried she'd hear this part and I'd still be fucked. Like she wouldn't believe me or give me a chance to get it in front of her. Like she'd beg me to take her somewhere else tomorrow.

Fuck. She still might do that. I can't let my mind get too far ahead.

She flexes her hands open and close. "I don't understand why you wouldn't tell me when it happened," she admits.

"Honestly, I didn't think there was anything to tell. Like, I didn't reach out and don't even have her number saved in my phone. I thought if I didn't respond, she'd get the hint and move on. I have zero reservations about cutting her off or leaving her behind."

Lia nods her head in understanding. She reaches for my phone, sliding it back to me.

"I almost told you the night you showed up, but everything was going so well," I admit. "I didn't want her to have any part in ruining it." I look at my fingers as I rub my hands together, my knuckles turning white.

"Brooks, if she's nothing, she can't ruin this."

I nod because she's right. I know she is. Guilt creeps in because I'm supposed to be comforting her, but it feels like she's taking care of me all over again.

"I trust you," Lia says, her words soft and intentional.

The words warm me from the inside out.

"That might make me the most gullible and naïve person, but it's true. I trust you," she reinforces.

Well, that makes me feel *less* good.

I stand to the side of where she's sitting, turning the barstool so she's facing me. "You can trust me. I promise nothing is going on with her or anyone else," I insist.

She rolls her shoulders down and back. "Has she always been this bold?" I feel the trace of a joke sitting behind her words.

My fingers go through my hair before letting my hands hit my neck and sort of hang there. "I'm not sure if it's boldness or her ability to make situations work for her. That's how it's always been. It feels good when you're part of whatever situation she needs to work, but that tide can turn fast." The pain of how Rebecca treated me rises; it's quick, but I'm able to push it down.

Lia nods, trying to understand. "I know what you mean. I've met people like that."

"I want to be clear with this next part. The only person I want is you. Ever since that first night, it's been you." My words get quieter as I go on.

She tilts her head, eyes like emerald velvet locked on mine.

"You're sure?"

And instead of answering with my words, I tilt her chin to mine and press a soft kiss to her mouth. She doesn't push me away or resist; instead, she kisses me back. It's the first time across the entire night I've felt like things are going to be okay.

"I've never been more sure of anything," I promise, my forehead pressing to hers.

Lia's lips pull enough to go from a pressed line to at least the start of a smile. I wrap my arms around her and she hugs me back. Rubbing small circles on her back, I kiss her temple.

"I'm sorry about your apartment."

"Thanks. I don't have the capacity to go there," she admits through a yawn.

"Let's get you to bed," I suggest, reaching for her hand. She trails behind me as we walk up the stairs. Rocky follows, the jingle of his collar letting us know where he is. I stop in front of the guest room and swing the door open, but Lia pulls on me.

"If it's okay, I'd rather sleep in your bed. With you," she shyly requests.

Something in my heart flutters as I respond. "That's more than okay. As long as you don't mind Rocky. He sort of sleeps in my bed."

"Sounds perfect," Lia says as we walk to my room.

As we get situated under the covers, I make a promise to myself—one I'll share with her when the time is right. I'll never do anything that has her doubting us, if I can help it.

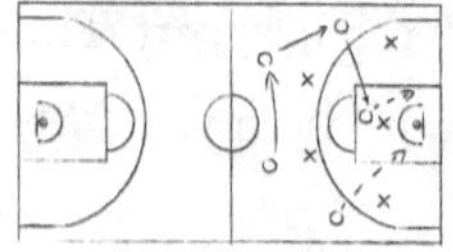

How does it feel like there's barely any room in this king-size bed? Rocky sleeps at my feet on top of the blankets, and Lia is curled into me. The culprit is the sixty-five pound English bulldog who gets too hot to be under the covers, but him lying on top makes it almost impossible to move.

I look over at Lia, watching her chest rise and fall with her slow breaths. She sleeps with her hands curled under her chin.

Fuck. I'm so grateful this morning. Grateful she let me help her. Grateful I could get all the shit with Rebecca cleared up. Grateful she's in this bed with me.

Her phone buzzes a few times on the bedside table, waking her up. Her arm falls to the side, reaching for it.

"Shit," she groans at whatever is on her phone.

"What's wrong?"

Lia wipes the sleep from her eyes with one hand, holding her phone in the other. "I'm supposed to go to breakfast with my brother. I completely forgot. Plus, I don't even have my car. But it's alright. I saw him yesterday. He'll live if I cancel," she sighs.

"I can take you to breakfast. That's no big deal."

"It's all the way across town," she protests while looking at me.

I turn and face the woman who refuses to let anyone do anything for her and place my hand behind the nape of her neck. When I pull her mouth to mine, she kisses me back and I can feel the trace of a smile.

I break the kiss. "Let me help you. Please quit making this so hard." I kiss her forehead before pushing the covers off me as much as Rocky's position allows and swing my legs out of bed. I reach up and stretch my arms over my head.

"You could come with me?" Lia offers quietly. "Like... stay for breakfast. We go to this hole in the wall back home. Our table is always tucked in the back."

She wants me to meet her brother. One of her favorite people. My heart swells at the thought.

Her words run together as she continues, "It's probably too risky, right? Not worth it. I can take an Uber." She gets out of bed and starts to walk past me.

I lightly grab her arm and spin her to me, pressing my mouth on hers. This seems to be the only effective method I have to make her stop and listen.

"Lia, I'd love to go with you. This, right here," I point between the two of us, "is an example of you making things hard." I press another kiss on her mouth before walking to my bathroom.

I smile as I brush my teeth; it feels like we're taking a step out of the Rebecca woods. I know other things may come up, but I was completely honest and transparent. With nothing to hide and everything to prove to Lia, I'll take on the challenge any day.

Starting with breakfast.

Chapter 41
Lia

I DIDN'T SEE THIS coming. Really, that could be said for the entire previous twenty-four hours. Food poisoning. The game. Rebecca. Flooded apartment. Brooks taking care of me. And now, my secret boyfriend is meeting my brother.

Even when I asked Brooks if we could drive in silence, my brain needing the quiet, all he did was smile, grab my hand, and kiss the inside of my wrist. What is that? It's so sweet, when I tell Shelbie about it, she might literally gag.

I'm fucking nervous about my apartment. I haven't heard from the landlord yet, but I'm sure they're still figuring it all out. I have renters' insurance, but it was the cheapest plan I could find and knew it was more of a formality than anything else. You never think you're going to need something like this until it happens. This is going to sting financially.

Maybe there's more I can do for the Jags? I already manage my Jags account and the teams, and sometimes it's tough to get everything done, but I've always found a way to make it work. Or maybe I could do more yoga classes during the week?

I can't even think about losing that space. I left a piece of myself in those walls with every project; through all the sweat and tears of trying to do all I could to have something I was proud of. Tears cloud my vision as I look outside the window, trying to tame my emotions. It's not that I don't want to feel them but now is not an ideal time. Doing my best, I barter with my brain. *Listen, we can cry until there is nothing left but that needs to be later—not before breakfast with Wes and Brooks. Sound good?*

I look over at Brooks, who smiles as he drives the thirty-eight minutes for diner food. He holds my hand, resting the other on the steering wheel, and I try to get a handle on everything between us. He was honest when it counted, and I could feel the nervousness roll off him as he walked me through the entire Rebecca saga. He kept stumbling over his words, talking too fast and needing to stop and take full breaths.

I don't ever want to be a partner who feels the need to check someone's phone or social media, but him offering it—almost begging me to look—screams volumes. I do trust him. What he's shared about her, and the way she showed up uninvited but like she belonged, kind of tracks.

Brooks parks the car and looks over at me. "How much do you want to tell Wes? Like, are we hanging out for a work thing, or do you want to let him in on the secret?" he asks sweetly.

There he is, thinking of everything again, because my mind didn't even get this far. I take a few seconds to contemplate and when Brooks squeezes my hand, I know the answer.

"Let's let him in. It's always been Wes and me. He can handle this."

The grin Brooks wears has my stomach flipping. Good god. He only lets go of my hand to get out of the car and walk over to my side.

We walk in and to my relief, no one cares. I don't know if they don't recognize Brooks or what, but I'm thankful. Wes sees the two of us and his eyes go wide. I texted him on the way here and told him I had a surprise for him.

The first thing Wes does is wrap me in a hug, one that soothes me to my core. Being in his presence is almost like having a security blanket. He knows my apartment flooded but we didn't get into the details. He rocks me back and forth for a second until I push away because I know he's itching to be introduced.

"Brooks, this is my baby brother, Wes."

Brooks reaches for a handshake and Wes grabs it, but slowly, like he's in a trance.

"Good to meet you. Thanks for letting me crash your breakfast," Brooks says to a hundred-watt-smile-wearing Wes.

"Anytime. Brooks Pittman. You can come to breakfast. Whenever you want."

I laugh at Wes being starstruck, and I'm excited to spend time with my two favorite men. Brooks slides into the booth, I sit next to him, and my brother sits across from us.

"Lia, I heard you were on TV last night," Julie, our regular waitress who we adore, says as she drops off orange juice for Wes and coffee for me.

"Yes. Wild circumstances, but it was a blast." I know she's not a sports fan, but she's been a fan of ours ever since we started coming in here when I was a teenager.

She gets Brooks' drink order and drops off menus.

"Lia, we'll get to you, but I have to start with Brooks." Wes turns his attention from me. "First question of many. Sorry in advance. But how does it feel to have a basketball in your hand and just will it to go in, every time you touch it, and score fifty points? Like you did last night?" Wes beams at the two of us, and when Brooks smiles back, I'm practically a puddle on the floor.

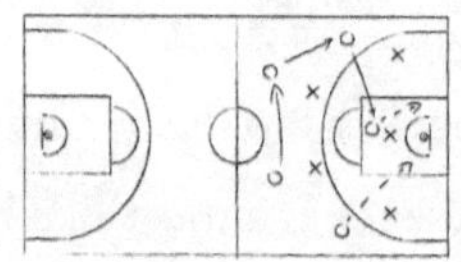

We've been done with breakfast for a while and I know we're going to need to leave a big tip, considering we've taken Julie's table for longer than planned.

"Do you have any college plans yet?" Brooks asks Wes.

He shakes his head. "Not yet. It's going to depend on if I can get an offer."

"Well, I'd love to watch you play. Lia and I could come to a game. If you're anything like I've heard, I'd love to get you connected with my alma mater. I also have some friends on the team who are still connected to their schools."

Wes' mouth hangs open as his chin dips, almost touching his chest. "That would be... like... so fucking cool." I laugh because hearing my brother swear like that is still funny to me.

"Wait, you and Lia? Like?" Wes asks the question I was waiting for.

"Listen, it's a secret," I stress, "but we're dating. We started hanging out before I got the job with the Jags."

Wes playfully smacks his hands on the table before immediately crossing his arms. His lips press together in a thin line before he responds, "Cool, cool. I can keep a secret. That's no problem. I thought you and me were closer than that, but hell, what do I know?"

"It was me. We kept it between us until now. You're the first person we've told." Brooks jumps in, telling a little white lie but making Wes feel special.

Brooks has that way with people.

My dad would've killed for this moment. The wish for my life to be different than it is hits me for a brief second. Wes and I have done a lot of life's milestones just the two of us, or with my aunt and uncle if they could swing it, and I'm thankful. But every once in a while, I think about how much my parents would love to be here to witness this.

I'm not sure what the afterlife is like, but I hope my dad gets the memo or knows this is happening, because I know he'd love it.

Chapter 42
Brooks

"Three months? You're kidding," Lia screeches from the other room. She's on the phone with her landlord and I don't think it's going well. "Oh, I'm sorry, at *least* three months." Sarcasm drips from her voice as they go back and forth.

I pretend like I can't hear her and put away the groceries I had delivered. It's not that I don't ever keep food in the house, but it depends on my game schedule. Plus, I usually only plan for myself.

Lia joins me in the kitchen, her shadow Rocky following close behind.

"So, once we left yesterday, more of the ceiling fell in," she cries. "Everything in my bedroom is a loss. All my clothes. Bed. Books. All of it."

"That is awful. Do they know what happened?"

Her eyes water as she slips into a barstool. "Apparently, the unit above me started running a bath and forgot about it. Like, left the apartment for the weekend."

"Wow. That's not what I expected you to say."

Lia shrugs. "They think it will be at least three months until it's fixed."

I meant what I said when I brought her here—she can stay. I have nothing but space. Now, seeing if she *wants* to stay is a completely different question.

She rambles on. "I can't afford a hotel. I texted Shelbie about staying with her, but she already has a roommate in a one-bedroom apartment.

Someone already sleeps on the couch. There's no room at my aunt and uncle's place. I don't want to disrupt Wes either."

Leaning on the counter in front of her, I say, "I know your immediate answer is going to be no, or you can't, but let me offer." I pause, and she raises an eyebrow. "You can stay here. There's clearly enough room. Plus, we're going to be traveling together for away games. If you don't want to, I understand, but if you're trying to convince yourself that you don't deserve this or you don't want to be a burden... Lia, let me help you."

"Don't you think it's fast?" Her question is quiet while she picks her head up. "Do I move in and sleep in your room? The guest room?"

I shrug my shoulders and answer, "It's up to you. I mean, it's not like we're saying you'll stay here forever. Or maybe you could? I don't know. I'm just saying, I have the means to help you through this. If you're comfortable, I'm comfortable."

"What I'm too much for you?" she asks meekly. "I don't want this to ruin this. I know I'm a lot and sometimes I do annoying things, and I've never really lived with someone like this and—"

I put a finger over her mouth and let out a laugh. "Lia, I've never felt you're too much. Honestly, I can't get enough of you. Maybe this is a good thing? We won't know unless we try."

She looks at me then gets off the stool, kneeling to pet Rocky.

"Okay," she agrees after a quiet moment. "But only if you know you're not locked in. If we try and it doesn't work, that's okay. I know I just went down my shortlist of options and they all feel like a 'no,' but I'd make something work."

I walk over and press my mouth to hers. We've been through a lot in the last twenty-four hours, and this feels like we're making a turn. My fingers move up her back and into her hair, which became curly once she took her braids out. When Lia circles her arms around my neck, I murmur, "Okay. I can do that."

She smiles and kisses me again. Rocky interrupts when he gets on his hind legs, putting his paws on our legs and looking for attention.

"Now, I have an idea for clothes," I suggest, pulling my phone out and making a call.

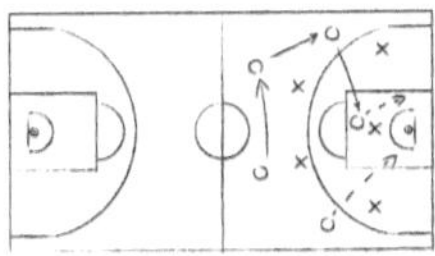

"Wait, can you get into the arena whenever you want?" Lia asks as I hold the door open after punching in my code.

I can't help but smirk at the awe in her voice. "Maybe? I've never tried when really no one is here... seems like someone is always doing something."

"What are we doing here?"

I so badly want to reach for her hand and walk with her through the halls, but I can't risk it. I usually always see someone from the coaching or training staff on random days when I come in to work out. Instead, we walk side by side until we end up in front of a set of doors I know are unlocked—the ones I called about. It always helps to have some inside connections, like random equipment managers who don't mind helping you out on an off day.

"Are you ready?" I ask, catching her eyes bright and looking around. She has no idea where we are.

"Maybe? I don't even know what we we're doing." Lia's voice is hushed, like she's trying not to get caught.

I swing open the door, turn the lights on, and step in. "This is where all the extra teamwear goes after each seasonal drop. There's stuff from the last few years, some that's never been sold. You, my little Jags fiend, are welcome to take anything you need. I also anticipate there will be lots of items in your size because you're not exactly a big and bulky NBA player or coach."

Her jaw drops. "This isn't real," she insists. "Did you have to pay to get me in here? There's no way all of this is up for grabs."

"I promise it is. Only thing I did was call in a favor to get this room unlocked. Really, anyone from the organization can come in here and take what's left. We're not breaking the rules," I reassure her.

Lia's mouth hangs open as her eyes move from shelf to shelf, bouncing from sweatshirts to tank tops to shoes. She moves closer, checking sizes and holding items up to herself. She turns back to me, and I can see the exhaustion lining her face as she says, "Thank you. For this. For all of it."

"Can't think of anyone more worth it," I reply.

And it's the truth.

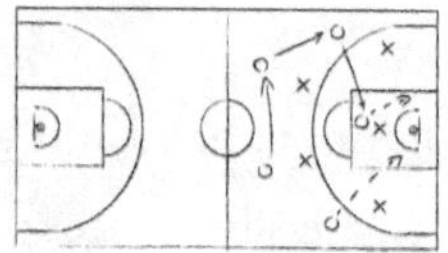

"Is this what you feel like when you watch game film? Because this makes me want to throw up, cover my face, then run far away from all of it." Lia puts her hands in front of her eyes, dramatically peeking at me through them.

We're on the couch, Rocky snoring between us, and watching the game back. "At first, when I got drafted to the NBA. Then it felt like everyone was keeping track of every single mistake I made; like the fans thought I was a bust. Lia, this is pretty fucking incredible," I gush. "You sound like you belong in that booth."

"Belong? Bold statement." Lia scoffs and brushes away my compliment.

"For a bold woman who fucking deserves it. I wanted to ask—how was Blake?"

She stops and gives me a long look. "He was amazing. I had to keep telling myself I wasn't sitting next to an all-time great. But he gave me pointers during commercial breaks and did nothing but encourage me."

My chest warms at the thought. I've only met him once in passing but I'm glad he was so supportive. Lia turns back to the TV, watching as the first quarter wraps ends.

"My voice was quiet and a bit shaky at the beginning. Plus, I kept bringing up random stats from the front of my brain. It didn't necessarily flow." She rattles off the things she doesn't like about watching or listening to herself.

I reach a hand over the sleeping dog and squeeze her thigh. "Yes, you sounded the smallest, littlest, barely noticeable kind of nervous at the beginning. Sort of like it was the first time you did it on one of the biggest stages." I give her thigh a shake. "Give yourself some credit."

Lia lets out a slow breath, leaning back on the cushions. "Fine. This is me giving myself credit." Her smile is weak but at least it's there.

"How many people do you think would do what you did? Put themselves out there like that? Not many," I remind her.

"I guess you're right. It did feel encouraging that Megan vouched for me."

"I have a feeling people are going to keep doing that. You're fucking worth it."

"That's the second time you've said that tonight." She turns her body to face me, leaning her head on the couch.

I love that she picks up on it. "You're right. Because I want you to believe it."

She reaches for my hand that's still resting on her leg and turns it over. Lia puts her hand in mine, squeezes once, and pushes play on the TV, ready for the next quarter.

Chapter 43
Lia

I WALK PAST THE hallway leading to the court, hearing bouncing basketballs and squeaking shoes. It's perfect. There's a lightness, an excitement to get back here, back to a routine. Apparently, everyone has recovered from the food poisoning that made its way through the staff.

I walk into Megan's office, which is how we always start our week, and am caught off guard by the sight of our general manager sitting across from her.

"Oh, I'm sorry. I'll come back later," I stammer and almost stumble as I stop, like the floor of her office is lava.

She stands quickly. "No, no. We both want to meet with you."

Why? Panic sprints through my veins and I immediately start to sweat.

Megan smiles warmly. "Have you met Trent Jones?"

No. Why would I have met Trent Jones, the youngest general manager in the NBA? As I'm being sarcastic in a place only I can hear, he stands.

"Lia, it's great to meet you," he exclaims. "Trent Jones. Take a seat."

Fuck. They know about me and Brooks. It's over. I'm about to get fired. I sit down and wait for the worst to come.

"First, I want to say thank you," Trent begins. "The way you stepped in the other night to help with the game was incredible. I've never heard anything like it. Neither have any of my owner friends."

Huh... what a weird way to start letting someone go.

"Not only did you step in, but you were good. I asked Megan to pull your job application so I could see your previous job history, but there's nothing on here that indicates you've done this professionally. So, why don't you tell me about that?" he asks.

This isn't where I saw this going. I take a deep breath before replying, "I've been obsessed with basketball, specifically the Jags, since I was a kid. When I noticed there were jobs in this area, I started practicing. It's embarrassing, but I'd turn on a game, mute it, and call it like I was in the booth."

Trent looks at Megan, clapping his hands and rubbing them together. "That. That right there is incredible. You're passionate. You love the game," he emphasizes.

"Yes, sir," I say.

Trent laughs. "Please, don't call me sir. It makes me feel like I'm eighty years old."

Megan jumps in. "She's been amazing with the social media accounts she's taken over."

"I know that. My owners also called about the dog campaign you got underway. Do you know that over fifteen NBA teams have made donations?" he shares with us. "You've made a real difference."

Maybe I'm *not* getting fired?

"Thank you," I reply. "I appreciate the kind words. Learning from Megan has been an amazing experience. I love it here." I shrug my shoulders and set my hands in my lap, my knuckles bone white from squeezing them together.

"Second," Trent continues, "because you were so good, I wanted to see if you'd be open to other opportunities during games. Maybe some on-court interviews between commercial breaks or quarters. Or even including that as part of your home game wrap up?"

"You mean letting me on the court to talk to Jags players after? I'd love it."

"Not only Jags players. Any players, really. As long as we let everyone know our protocol, all the teams will be cool with it."

My mouth hangs open. I don't know what to say. How to react.

Megan saves me. "Lia, you'd be great. It's so refreshing to meet another woman like you; someone who loves the game and talks about it with such enthusiasm. We think it's a great move to include highlighting women in sports."

A tear falls down my cheek and I don't move to wipe it away. Megan and Trent see it, smile, and somehow I find a tissue in my hand. I dab my eyes and then fan them, trying to keep the rest of my tears at bay.

Sighing out a breath, I ask, "Are you being serious?" My voice is squeaky with emotion, but I don't care.

"Yes. I want to keep you with the Jags as long as we can," Trent proclaims. "People like you are rare. Those who jump in and do whatever it takes."

Wow. More tears fall because I can't believe it. I've always been proud of my work ethic but to hear someone else—someone like Megan or Trent—call it out this way is next level.

"Yes. One hundred percent yes."

Megan stands and walks over to me, standing with her arms out for a hug. I stand and hug her back. Trent reaches for a handshake, which I take and maybe squeeze his hand too hard but I'm so excited.

"Amazing. We'll figure out how to compensate you for games where you're doing work like this, but for now, these are for you." Trent reaches back and hands me a massive bouquet of purple and white flowers. There's a thank you note attached, and it's signed by all the coaches and leadership.

"Thank you. I appreciate it," I repeat, tipping my nose to the flowers and smelling the sweetness.

"I'll be in touch," Trent assures me while waving to the both of us.

Megan and I stare at each other for long seconds until we're sure Trent is gone.

"Holy shit," I mutter.

Megan takes a long breath, blowing it out and replying, "Holy shit is right."

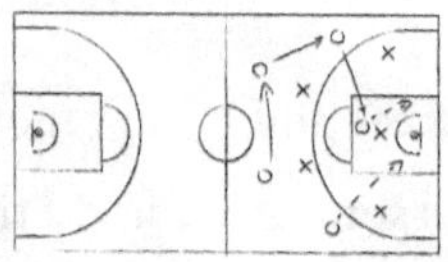

"I can't believe Trent just showed up in Megan's office. You've had a day," Brooks exclaims while pouring me a glass of white wine.

I put the glass to my lips and take a tiny slip. I'm careful when I put the wine glass back on the island, as it feels delicate and expensive. It'd be true Lia fashion if I man-handled the beautiful stem wear and smashed it, like I'm some sort of cave man, unable to manage nice things.

"What do you need?"

This is one of Brooks' questions he's asked more than once. Most of the time, I don't have the guts to ask for anything.

This time, I grab my Kindle from my bag and answer, "I want to get cozy and read a book."

He smiles and starts towards the stairs. "I have the perfect spot for you."

We walk in silence; the only sound is the jingling of Rocky's collar as he follows. He typically wants to be where one of us is. Brooks stands in front of a door I've not opened. Yes, I've been staying here, but I definitely didn't want to snoop. Well, I wanted to, but I held back. Brooks opens the door and steps inside, leaving space for me to follow.

It's a library. A full ass library. Floor to ceiling bookshelves cover an entire wall, and anything that isn't filled with books is filled with puzzles.

There's an oversized chair and a couch in the corner, a mini sitting area, and a table where a partially done puzzle sits.

"Brooks Pittman, you've been holding out on me. Tell me everything," I squeal as I immediately move the shelves, looking at what kind of books he has.

He scoffs, running a hand through his dark strands. "After my surgery, I sort of got obsessed with reading and puzzles. Like, it was the only thing I wanted to do when I wasn't at rehab. When I moved in, these bookshelves were already here, and I decided to keep them."

I know my mouth is hanging open, but I can't believe it. The books are all sorts of genres, like he reads mostly anything. When my eyes hit a box set of a popular fantasy series, the very same one I'm reading on my Kindle, I shriek. "Wait, tell me you read this? I just started the second book!"

He nods, his cheeks a little flushed. "Yes. I read all five of those books in six days. I could barely stop to eat or shower. It was a dark time."

I gasp in excitement. "Stop it right now. You mean I can gush to you about these and you're going to know what I'm talking about?" Am I dreaming? This is way too close to a man written by a woman to be real. An NBA player who loves to read?

Brooks' hands are in his pocket as he steps forward. "Yes. I'd love it if you did. Mostly, I need to know your Tamlin feelings as you get through that next one." He taps on the book spine.

I throw him a side-eye because he clearly knows something I don't. Wow. This is a dream I didn't know I had.

"Brooks! You read romantasy!"

"Want to trade secrets?" he asks and I'm nodding my head yes before he even finishes his sentence.

Brooks steps closer to me until our noses are almost touching. I breathe him in, and he smells like pine and citrus on top of the book smell. It's heavenly.

"I also have a Kindle. That's where my"—he fakes looking around for anyone else, even though it's just the two of us—"romance books are."

I cover a squeal with my hand and remind my knees to hold me up.

"This isn't a joke. You're for real?" I'm scanning his face and body language for the hint I'm being pranked.

He grins. "For real. It was so easy to binge; I could not get enough of it."

My head shakes in surprise. "Do you still read romance?"

"Sometimes, especially when I travel for away games." He smiles wider as he lets me in on this secret. "I've learned a lot from these books."

Brooks puts his hands on my waist and backs me to the door frame, the wood gently hitting the middle of my back. He puts one arm above me as his other hand touches my face, pushing through my hair before tucking a piece behind me ear.

"Like, the door lean? I know *all* about it." He moves slowly, his nose brushing mine before our lips meet. His tongue sweeps against my bottom lip and I let him in. My hips press into him, and I reach one arm up and around the hand he's holding above me. I grab his wrist and he moans into my mouth.

"I owe you a secret," I whisper against his lips. His eyes burn into me, and I swear I can see flames licking on the edge of the caramel brown. "I've never, in my entire life, been more turned on than I am right now." I kiss him again, feeling his lips pull up in a grin against mine.

"Well, we should do something about that," he murmurs before his lips are back on mine.

Yes, we should.

Chapter 44
Brooks

YOU NEVER KNOW WHAT you're in for when it comes to a therapy session. Some feel like a casual chat with a friend, while others are the equivalent of staring at pieces of a puzzle that never seem to fit together—like they're not even from the same box.

My foot taps as I settle into the leather chair, my usual spot, as Jen sits across from me. With the season in full swing, our visits are sporadic and typically virtual. Today, all the stars aligned to bring me in person for my session.

"We haven't talked since your shoulder injury," she starts. "How are you feeling?"

"Today I feel good. It's not something that should have long lasting issues, not like the knee, so it seems to be trending in the right direction."

Jen pauses—the thing she's so good at. Before asking another question, she always gives me the room to keep going.

"At first, it was terrifying," I continue. "Like, being on the court, having everyone run over to me. It brought up a lot of what the knee injury felt like."

"How did you cope with that? I know that time was difficult. You put in a lot of work, mentally and physically, to get back where you wanted to be."

I go back to my bedroom, to the moment before I took the sleeping pill and needed a break from everything. Even being a few days removed,

I could look back and know it wasn't all that helpful, but sometimes you have to fucking feel.

Rubbing my hands together, I admit, "The first couple days were bad. It was Thanksgiving and my mom was supposed to come to my place, but she had travel delays that kept her from coming home. That sort of set me off, or over—however you want to view it."

Jen nods, her face completely neutral. "Tell me about the last part. Setting you off."

Something I respect about Jen is that she doesn't judge me or ask me questions which make me feel like I didn't do the right thing.

My knuckles strain against my skin, turning white. "I don't know if you'd call it a depressive episode or what the term is, but I felt like I flew back. Almost to how bad it was when I was trying to get through the knee injury. The thought of doing anything was fucking overwhelming. I turned my phone off. I didn't want to text anyone or see another notification. Basically, I spent two days in bed, one of those being Thanksgiving."

"What happened after that?" Jen asks.

Part of me is grateful she doesn't want to dwell on this. Saying it out loud kind of makes me feel like a fucking loser. Like I can't handle basic emotions. But that's probably not true.

"I did some at home rehab with the training staff and then I went back to practice. I felt better."

"What does better look like?"

"Like I could get up and do something. It wasn't that I really wanted to, but it was something I felt was possible. Like I wasn't a complete dark cloud but almost like a light gray."

"And how do you feel today?"

"Good." I let the smile spread on my lips and watch Jen smile back at me.

She sets down her pen and looks at me. "Brooks, I've never seen you smile like that. Why do you think you're feeling this good? Sometimes with therapy, people think we should only focus on the dark, but that isn't true. It's important to examine and understand all the light."

Well... here goes nothing. It's not that Jen doesn't know about Lia, but we've not talked about her a lot. Mostly because there were lots of other things to cover and it didn't feel like the right time. I guess that's what happens when you find out you have secret siblings and a parent later in life.

"Do you want the long or short version?" I joke with her.

She looks at her watch and replies with, "Long version. Always. We've got time."

I tell her everything. About how I met Lia that first night and for the first time felt like something was finally right. About how she ended up working for the Jags. About the secret. About Rebecca. About Lia staying with me.

"Brooks Pittman," Jen gushes, "I fear you've been holding out on me. Which is fine, but know that here, everything is safe. You don't need to carry all this alone. Let me have some of it... even if it's for only a few minutes."

I let out a sigh and sit back.

"There's a lot to unpack, but let's start with what I think is the most important." My stomach flips at her words, even though I knew this part would come next. "First, it sounds like Lia is a lovely person. Hearing you talk about how important it is for you to help her when she needs it is a sign of a solid relationship. Also, it shows real maturity to own your misstep when it came to Rebecca. Accountability is hard but it's important."

"It's like part of me was too afraid to bring it up. Like I didn't want to ruin anything," I admit.

Jen nods. "I get it. Especially in a scenario like yours where you're trying to keep this under the radar. But you know the power of honesty."

"I do. I know. Fuck, I know." My head falls into my hands.

"Brooks," she prompts, waiting for me to pick my head up and look at her. "You can't beat yourself up about things that are resolved. What's the point in that? The lesson here is you move forward, being as open as possible."

She's right. The words hit me and it's like a piece of the heavy I've been wearing lifts.

"Something you need to consider is the pull of your profession and things you can't control," Jen adds. "Injuries are pretty common, and you're never promised a certain amount of time. While you can't determine what injuries are waiting for you, I think it's important to catalog things you have outside of that. Besides basketball, who or what else makes you happy? Those are some of the things you can control."

My brain starts making a list. My family. Lia. Rocky.

"Athletes are a different type of person. It's like your whole life is typically devoted to a sport that is impossible to serve you forever," Jen reminds me. "Even for people who still work in their sport, whether that's coaching or working for a team, it's not the same as being an athlete. You've done amazing things when it comes to basketball, but you'll do even greater things outside of it. Does that make sense?"

"Yes, but I'm sweating thinking about it." The honest reaction comes quickly, and I wipe away the sweat that smatters my brows with the back of my hand.

Jen chuckles and replies, "A fine reaction." She closes her notebook, meaning our time together is almost up. "I have a few things for you to consider before our next session. First, it may be beneficial for you to keep a short journal for your mood. Depression isn't a line, and it isn't the same for everyone. I know you've never wanted to get on an anti-depressant or anxiety med, but a low dose is something we may want to consider. Maybe during the off-season? But the first step is trying to understand how you're feeling."

The suggestion for a medical approach doesn't turn me off as much as it did the first few times we discussed it. I've never needed some sort of regular med, and at first it felt like a cop out, like I wasn't trying hard enough. Now I'm wondering what it'd be like to try something like that.

"Next, be open with Lia," Jen continues. "With the good and bad. It sounds like she's taken care of herself and those close to her for a long time. It might be hard for her to let you do things for her, like helping her with a place to stay. Keep the conversation going."

She's right. To be fair, she's usually right. I nod. "Yes. Thank you, Doc."

"And lastly, go Jags. Y'all are on fire lately."

Chapter 45

Lia

"Tell me again how you got concert tickets to something that's been sold out for months?" Shelbie asks as she grabs our giant pretzel.

We're in the food court at the only nearby mall worth going to. Since most of my clothes are Jags teamwear that was leftover and close to my size, or stuff I can work in, I decided it was time to shop.

Especially because I'm about to be in elite company and I want to feel good.

"Brooks' brother, Zack. He plays for the Cosmos and is best friends with Tripp Owens, who is Willow's fiancé. Plus, Zack is marrying Emilie, and she's worked with Willow the last few years." I explain the connection, trying to make sure I get it right.

"Do you have seats or how does that work?"

Cutting into the pretzel, I dip it in the spicy queso, steam rolling off the cheese. "No, we'll all be in a suite. A few of Brooks' teammates are coming too. And then we're all going out to Oasis after."

Shelbie raises an eyebrow. "Wait, what do you mean?"

"After each concert, Willow rents out a local spot and the crew, friends and family go out. Brooks suggested Oasis and Willow loved it. So that's the plan." I share this like I'm not nervous.

Shelbie looks up at me over a forkful of pretzel, calling my bluff. "You're freaking out."

I groan. "Yes. I'm freaking out."

"Makes sense. You've been obsessed with Willow ever since I've known you. That must be wild." She looks to me and asks, "Any news on the apartment?"

"I got an email that they were able to save all my kitchen stuff and the living room couch, but almost everything else is a loss."

"I can't believe that happened. But look, you get to play house with your hottie NBA player." Shelbie shimmies her shoulders. "Question—the pictures of Rocky on Brooks' socials... is that you or him?"

A chuckle falls out of my mouth. "All him. He's never had a dog and has totally fallen in the dog dad hole."

Brooks is always looking out for Rocky. It has gotten to the point where he's started making homemade dog treats and exploring a natural diet for him. He orders tons of toys, trying to find the one that Rocky likes best, and donating the rest to the shelter. He really loves him, and it makes me so happy that my event brought them together.

"And we're not playing house," I protest. "I needed somewhere to stay. He has the room."

Shelbie rolls her eyes. "Okay, it's been three weeks. How many times have you slept somewhere other than his bed?"

I smile before putting a too-big bite in my mouth. The answer is zero, but she already knows that. This is a rhetorical question.

Shelbie scans my face and asks, "Hey, what's that on your neck?"

My fingers find the rough patch, right under my ear and creeping onto my neck.

I look from her to the table. "Same sort of dry skin. I finally found a doctor who will see me, but the waitlist is eight months long."

"Wait, so you have to wait that long to even see a doctor? That's fucking ridiculous," she exclaims.

"I know. I'm still using the mediocre insurance, but I'll be eligible for the Jags plan in January. Maybe I'll be able to find someone then?"

What I don't tell her is that I'm also dealing with significant joint pain. Maybe it's stress or maybe it's related to whatever's going on with my skin? I don't know. Every time I Google it, I think I'm dying so I try to leave it be. It has to be something to do with stress—life has been wild. This isn't the first time I've had pain like this; it seems to pop up whenever I forget to sleep, or eat, or fall into a routine where I'm doing too much.

"I didn't mean to call it out," Shelbie apologizes. "That wasn't cool of me."

How does she know these things? I've been agonizing over these small spots in the mirror. A lot of the dry spots are on my back, but occasionally, one shows up where it's harder to hide. I'm not one to typically be self-conscious about my body, but whatever this is makes me uncomfortable. I think it's mostly because I don't know what it is. I certainly don't want people thinking I've got some sort of contagious skin disease or something.

"It's alright," I assure her. "No worries."

I close the book on this conversation with a little white lie.

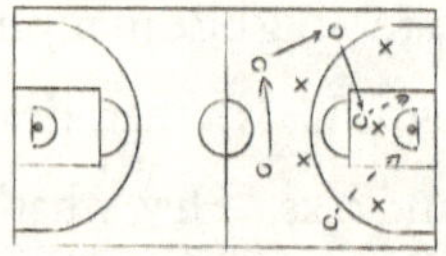

We're in the VIP suite as the concert is about to start. People keep coming in and it's weird because I know them, but I don't know them. Like, I don't live under a rock, so when Tripp Owens comes in, I do my best not to fan girl. Basketball is my favorite sport, but I still fit in football when I have the time. I know he's a Super Bowl Champion and MVP who plays for the Upstate Cosmos alongside Zack—Brooks' brother. Tripp is also dating Willow, and while I'm not one to be in the know about athletes'

love lives or gossip, the way all of that played out was too good to not devour every scrap of information.

Zack Andersen, who I've not met yet, skips into the suite and darts for us. He swallows Brooks in a hug, even though Zack is slightly shorter.

"Where's your better half?" Brooks asks once Zack finally lets him go.

His smile is contagious and bright. "She's backstage with Willow," he explains. "They have some new openers tonight so she's making sure everything is all good." His attention turns to me and he sticks out his hand. "I'm Zack, and I think you're the reason I now have a quarterly donation arranged for one of the local animal shelters. What a great idea!"

I give him my hand and he shakes it. "Lia. Nice to meet you," I reply. "And thanks. I'm glad it got a little bit of traction."

"Well, dogs like Rocky are hard to pass up helping them out, right?" He claps Brooks on the back.

"Right."

"Hey, I'm Tripp. Thanks for coming out tonight." Tripp waves as he stands next to Zack.

"Lia. And thank you for having me. I'm kind of trying not to freak out, in all honesty."

Tripp shrugs and replies, "It's been years of me being with Willow and I still lose my shit every once in a while. I get it." The way he talks about her makes me so fucking happy. He's always seemed like her biggest fan, and now it's like I feel it.

A couple walks in, people I don't know, and find Tripp.

"Let me introduce you to Ivy and Holland," Tripp says. "They run this amazing lodge out in Washington area. We met through a charity event but kind of hit it off."

Ivy beams at all of us as she holds on to Holland's hand. "When I can get this guy to leave the woods, we're typically in a big city, getting my fill." Holland says nothing but smiles and kisses the top of her head.

Ivy leaves to get drinks from the bar and the guys settle into catching up, sharing sports updates. I would love to jump in but don't want to overstep. Plus, Jalen arrives and finds his way over to me.

"Miss Stone! You on content duty tonight?" he teases, tapping my glass of wine with his beer.

"No content tonight. Just hanging out," I reply as level as possible. I know he knows about me and Brooks. He nods and quietly adds, "You know, you're really good for him." The words catch me off guard and I take a sip of wine to hide my reaction. "He struggles more than people know, but since you, he's been happy and more like himself. He reminds me of me when I met Steph."

I know enough about Jalen to realize he's talking about his wife.

"Well, that makes me feel good. Honestly." I put a hand to my chest. "Plus, thank you for keeping this to yourself. Or I think you have—" My words get ahead of my brain because I actually have no idea if Jalen told anyone or not.

He laughs. "Your secret is safe with me. Brooks is the kind of person who will be part of my life, no matter where our paths wind. Even if we end up on rival teams or anything like that, he's still my best friend, and I'll do what I can for him."

Just then, Brooks comes over and starts chatting with Jalen. Even though they see each other all the time, I swear they could talk for hours.

The lights start to dim in the arena, and I know we're only a few minutes from the start of the concert. I take a picture and send it to Wes.

Wes

lowkey jealous

why are you so cool

Me

lucky for you it's probably genetic

tell brooks i said hey

or don't if you think that's stupid

i'll tell him, he'll love it

Excitement crawls all over me, flushing my skin and making me antsy. I look over and when I see Zack and Tripp hitting hands, doing some sort of handshake and getting hyped for the concert, I can't help but smile. This is what true support looks like.

"They're great, right?" Brooks asks, sliding next to me.

"Yes. Have to say, your description of Zack being a golden retriever puppy couldn't be more spot on." I lean my head over to see Zack whistling and jumping.

Brooks reaches around my hip, squeezes me, then lets his body settle in next to mine.

"I'm glad you're here with me," he whispers before placing a quick kiss on my cheek.

My first reaction isn't to run from the affection. Instead, I want to give in. I look around, and when everyone seems to be doing their own thing, I put my hand on the side of his face and turn him to me. I lean in for a kiss. It's slow but quick. The feel of his lips on mine, full and soft, makes me feel like we can do almost anything.

"Me too," I admit as he smiles at me; the same smile that could, and has, brought me to my knees.

I never would've guessed this kind of evening could ever be an option for me. It's exciting but also puts things into perspective. Things never go the way you think they will—whether that's good or bad. I let my hip push into Brooks' side and the look he gives me has everything snapping into place

How I've never felt this way.

How thankful I am.

How easy this is.

How I'm starting to fall in love with him.

Or, maybe, I'm already there.

Chapter 46
Brooks

Watching Lia meet Willow is one of my favorite interactions to date.

"I love you. I mean, I don't love you. I don't know you. It's your music. All of it. I love it. Big fan. Sorry. Like, for making it weird or annoying or—" Her words run over each other and Willow gets her to stop talking by wrapping Lia in a hug.

I've met Willow a few other times, mostly in the Cosmos suite, and she's one of the nicest people. It's refreshing for someone like her—who has won every award and is one of the most successful artists of our time—to be so genuine and kind.

Lia looks at me, mouthing "OH MY GOD" as Willow hugs her and I can't help but smile at my girl. Her excitement makes this all worth it. She's not someone who thinks she's owed something, and it makes all the difference.

We're standing at the bar getting drinks. Willow and Tripp rented out Oasis for after the concert. It's all friends, family, and concert staff letting loose and having some fun. Willow is going on a break after tonight, so it's a little more laid back than a typical afterparty.

Willow invites Lia back to the table with her and Emilie. I nod, encouraging Lia to go as I wait for my drink.

"Hey Siri, play 'U Got It Bad' by Usher," Clayton shouts playfully into his phone.

"That's how you repay me? I suggest your bar for a once-in-a-lifetime dinner, and you're busting my balls?" I shout. He reaches out for a high five and I give him one, laughing him off.

"Oh, come on. I'm just kidding. Well… I mean, I'm not, but we can pretend if that makes you feel better." He shakes a drink and winks at me. "But this is pretty cool. Thanks for telling Zack about this place. Also, he likes the peanut butter whisky drink."

I scrunch my face in disgust. "That doesn't surprise me."

"So…you're head over heels with the woman you saved from that dickhead? How did that happen?"

It's not even worth arguing with him; plus, he isn't wrong. "It's a long story, and one that isn't public."

Clayton presses his lips together and stares pointedly at me.

"Text me what nights you're free and we can go out for a drink. I'll tell you what I can," I suggest. A line starts to form at the b ar and Clayton is already pulling away from me, about to start taking orders.

He grins and says, "You got it. Thanks again for coming in, man. Good to see you."

I walk back to the table and sit next to Zack, who is arguing with Tripp about some trick play in the Cosmos playbook. Lia sits with Willow and Emilie, laughing, pink-cheeked and fucking gorgeous.

Looking out the window, I see fat snowflakes falling. It's as if Lia knows what I'm thinking, because her eyes find mine and I mouth, "pool night" while pointing to the window. She turns, sees the flurries, and mouths, "yes."

Tonight has been fun, but I'm excited to get home. I've got plans with my girl.

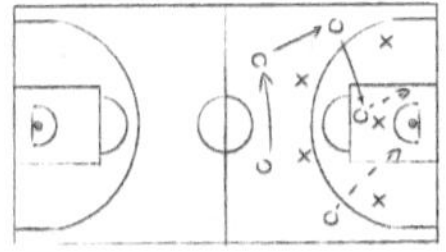

The first snow of the season falls heavy and thick, quickly accumulating. The roads were slippery enough to drive slower than normal. We get back home and I use the app to pull the pool cover off—it's one of the things I thought I'd never use in the house.

Home.

Lia makes this place feel like a home. It's the way she likes to sit down and plan meals for the nights we'll be together. Or how she smiles getting blankets out from the dryer, immediately finding me to wrap us up while it's still warm.

And that is fucking scary. This whole arrangement is supposed to be temporary. Soon, her apartment will be finished, and she'll go back living there and it will only be me and Rocky. I swear, his butt wags more when she walks in the door than I do—the dog will be crushed.

My therapy session highlights replay in my brain. I can't necessarily control this whole situation, but I can be open. I can do that. I can tell her.

Fuck. Why do I feel like I'm at the top of a rollercoaster about to drop?

Lia comes down wrapped in a towel, her hair in a messy bun. Her eyes gleam when she says, "Well, I still don't have a bathing suit."

"Oh, what a shame," I reply sarcastically. "How will I ever recover?"

She gives me a quick kiss while she walks past me. The towel is wrapped up, covering her chest, but when she's in front of me, I can see her back is red—broken out in a rash, or hives, or something.

"Babe, your back," I exclaim. "What's wrong?"

Her hand reaches back, touching the top of her shoulder. All it does is enhance the contrast between the skin on her hand and the agitation on her back. I step closer, putting my hands lightly on it, the bumps rough under my fingers.

"Oh, it's not a big deal," Lia says over her shoulder.

I hook my fingers at the top of her towel and pull it away, only to find the rash is covering her full back.

"Lia, it's your whole back—"

"I know. I have a doctor's appointment scheduled." She tries to brush me off again and keeps walking toward the patio door.

Reaching for her hand, I stop her and turn her around to face me, her cheeks flushed pink. "Hey, where are you going?" I ask gently.

"I don't want to talk about it," she protests. "I know it's gross, but I know it's not contagious, so there's nothing to worry about it."

She thinks it's gross. That it bothers me. That couldn't be farther from the truth.

"When is your appointment?"

Her eyes look to the floor, then the ceiling as she says, "Ummm, I'm on a waitlist for cancellation. But I have one in July."

"July? As in like... almost eight months from now?" I ask, feeling my brows press into my forehead.

Lia sighs. "It's the best I can do."

"You *are* aware that you work for an organization who has doctors on staff? And if they can't help you, they most likely know someone else who can?"

She shifts her weight, crossing her arms tighter across her chest. "I'm not asking for any favors. I don't need to bother anyone with this. It's not like I'm a player. I've got this under control."

"You're part of the team," I stress. "And under control? You have something going on that looks like it fucking hurts, and it's taking over most of your back. Will it be your entire body by the time you get to see the doctor?"

"Why do you sound mad? This doesn't impact you in any way shape or form," she snaps while walking past me, headed for the stairs.

I follow her. "You know what? I am mad. And this does impact me."

Surprised by my answer, Lia turns from a few stairs up and snaps back, "Do tell."

It feels like she's challenging me. "I'm mad that you'd rather hurt and suffer over taking help that I, or someone else, can offer. Yes, that makes me mad. And this," I point between the two of us, "does impact me. You are part of my life. I care about you. I want you to be both happy and fucking healthy."

I'm afraid she's going to run upstairs, pack a bag, and leave, but I can't let this go.

"If you're pissed at me for wanting to take care of you? Go ahead. Be annoyed enough that you don't let me help you. But that doesn't mean I'm going to quit trying. I guess I'll spend the rest of forever trying to do what I can. Give you everything you deserve. There's a lot I'm willing to do to keep you, for as long as I can, why can't you understand that?"

My voice dwindles and sounds softer than I planned.

Lia's eyes widen. "Forever?" she asks, stepping down the stairs and getting closer to me.

"Or however long you let me have you," I admit, putting my hands on her hips as she stands in front of me. "I think of things that could happen in the future, and you're there. You're always there."

She's silent, but steps down onto a stair closer to me. The air between us is charged, heavy and full. Like it's full of the secrets we've been keeping—together and on our own.

"You mean it?" Lia asks softly. "Even though I'm a lot... with flooded apartments and random illnesses and—"

I put a finger to her lips. "You can tell me that you're a lot all you want... but you still feel like the right amount for me." Something crackles in the air; I can feel it rush over my skin. Something is coming.

Moving my finger from her lips, I wait for her to argue, to push back. Instead, she leans in and places her mouth against mine. I wrap my arms around her lower back and lift her from the stairs. When she's flush against me, her hands move from the towel to my neck, pulling us closer together.

Lia breaks our kiss and her eyes, shining like pieces of sunlight through the trees, make me want to spill my guts. Anything she wants to know? It's hers.

"Brooks, I'm going to say something to you. You don't have to respond. But..." Lia takes a deep breath before sighing and saying, "I'm in love with you."

The air breaks. *There it is.* I can't help the smirk that spreads over my lips.

"I tell you I want you forever, and you don't think I love you?" I look away before catching her eyes. "Of course I love you," I insist.

She falls into me, letting me hold her for what feels like the first real time. There's no part of her holding back.

"I've got you," I say as I carry her upstairs.

I feel lighter, finally telling her my secret—how I love her the way I do. And how I plan to keep doing it.

Chapter 47
Lia

I'm in a private training room after everyone has gone home for the day. Brooks told me he had a shift in his conditioning schedule, but I know it's so he can stick around in case I need him.

It's been three days since I told Brooks I love him. Three days since he told me he loves me back. Three days since we started trading even more secrets. I don't expect this won't continue to have challenging moments, but all we can do is take it day by day.

Today, I'm seeing a team doctor and I'm a ball of energy. Nervous to potentially get answers, but anxious about what it could mean. Brooks was right; there's no way waiting until July was going to work.

When the doctor introduces himself, he's kind and welcoming, picking up on my anxiety. I take off my top and show him my back, keeping my bralette on.

"Are you having any other symptoms? Any pain?"

"Sometimes my hands and wrists are really sore," I admit. "Like I did a weird exercise using muscles I haven't used before." I put my hands out and he feels through each knuckle and does some range of motion stretching.

"How bad does this hurt? Or itch?" The doctor stands in front of me and waits for a response.

I think back to all the nights I've struggled to sleep, all the burning from lotions and creams meant to help with the dryness. My brain kept trying to convince me it could be worse, but I never took the time to think about how awful it truly was.

"Depends," I answer. "I've had trouble sleeping some nights and burning with lotion, things like that."

He sighs and then is behind me again, looking closely at my skin. "Where else have you had redness or areas like this?" He asks this while delicately touching the skin on my back. "My eyelids, scalp, and sometimes on my elbows. It's never been as bad as it currently is on my back."

He nods and I'm surprised with how he's listening to me. I feel like most doctors I see are trying to get me in and out as quick as possible. Maybe having a connection to team doctors is a true perk I didn't know I needed.

"Everything here seems sensitive skin friendly, so that's great," he says while reviewing the list of products I use on a regular basis.

He looks at some other spots on my neck, my lash line, and then asks me to put my shirt back on.

"As a reminder, I'm the first step for you figuring this out. But I think this is severe plaque psoriasis. The spots on your back aren't presenting the way tried and true psoriasis does, but if we don't treat it, it might. With your other symptoms, I'd want to rule out psoriatic arthritis. Both are autoimmune conditions. Are you familiar with that term?" His voice is kind and soft.

I swallow harshly. "Ugh, yeah. The body attacks healthy parts of itself, right?"

"Pretty much. Autoimmune conditions range from asymptomatic to severe, and no patient is ever the same. I'm going to get you a referral to a dermatologist and a rheumatologist."

"My insurance is kind of lacking—" I try to explain.

"Don't worry about it. We're calling in a favor and I'll let them know that. We'll figure it out." He gets his phone out and says, "Until then, try to drink enough water, eat good food, and keep your stress under control. Stress is one of the biggest triggers for autoimmune flares."

Why am I immediately stressed thinking about not being stressed?

I can't explain why, but tears start rolling down my face. The doctor keeps using 'we' and it's making me emotional by how much this borderline stranger is on my side. The support and his guess at my diagnosis are fighting for which is making me more emotional—I couldn't pick a winner if you paid me.

"I'm sure this has been hard, but we'll get you some answers and the help you need." He gently puts a hand on the top of my arm.

It's a small gesture—one that shouldn't smash into me like it does. The tears flow freely no matter how much I try to stop the stream.

"I'll give you a minute and call the offices for the doctors I'm referring you to. They're both great—you're in the best hands," he says reassuringly.

Why isn't there a way to pause crying? Like, I'm happy to continue this, but can I get six seconds to tell someone something without sounding like a character from the Muppet show?

"Thank you. For..." I try to take in air to bring my voice down an octave. "Everything. I appreciate you." I grab my shirt and pull it on.

"Lia, we're here for you. You're part of the team." He puts a hand on my shoulder as I let my head fall forward, ugly sobs escaping.

The heartbreak creeps up when the only person I wish I could have is my mom. The woman who has been gone for over fifteen years. I close my eyes and try to catch my breath, but I can't. My hand claws at my shirt, feeling for my heartbeat—it's erratic and too fast. I try to envision waves crashing, one of my go-to visuals for calming myself down. No matter what, it's like the water won't cooperate.

I lay back on the table, throwing a forearm over my eyes and welcoming the pressure. Maybe I can forcibly close my eyes and I'll be able to get a grip. Find the string that brings me back to reality, where I'm okay and things will most likely work out. My brain searches feverishly for the string, and I think I've found it when everything goes silent.

You were made to do hard things.

It's what my mom used to tell me whenever I was hurt, struggling, or complaining about not being good enough at something. It was her go-to mantra: you were made to do hard things. She said it with such conviction, not an ounce of doubt to be found. Her words dripped with love and determination. It wasn't a way to get me to run from an emotion or challenge, but to run at them with full speed instead.

You were made to do hard things.

I cry for myself, for my mom, for the adult relationship I'll never have with her. Tears fall for the unknown, in gratitude for the doctor who spent time with me, for the man who helped me understand that accepting help doesn't make me less.

The sobs subside as my hands press on my chest, feeling the air fill my lungs and then out again. I take my phone and text the person I need more than anything right now.

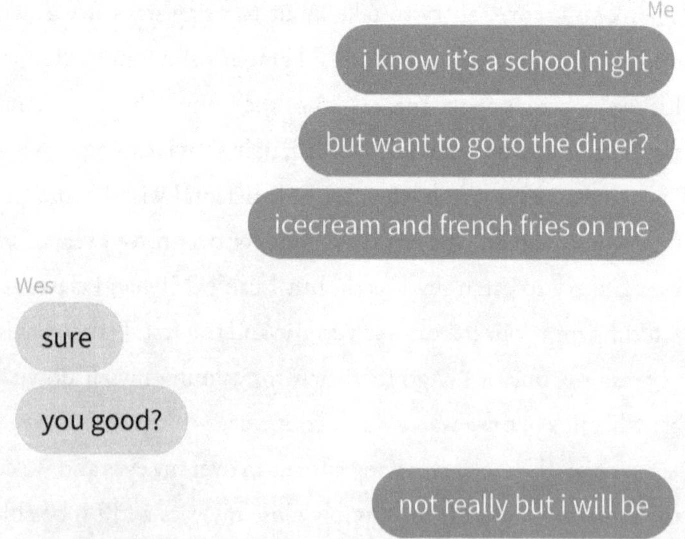

I text Brooks when I'm walking out to the car.

He doesn't ask me about seeing the doctor and I love him even more for that.

Chapter 48
Brooks

I'm almost asleep when Lia crawls into bed, immediately putting her head on my chest. Before I can say anything or ask how the visit with the team doctor went, chest-heaving sobs shake the bed. Rocky moves from his spot at our feet, snuggling up against her back.

"Baby, what is it?" I ask, pulling her to me. I know her back is irritated, so I rub her forearm instead.

She's silent for a while and that's okay. Part of me was a little nervous she wouldn't come back here tonight—that maybe she'd stay with her brother. I'm so fucking glad to see she made it home to me.

When she's ready, Lia sits and rests her back on the headboard. I do the same.

"I was in the training room after seeing the doctor and this tidal wave hit me. Grief. As raw as the first day I woke without my parents. Like, I'd do anything to see my mom. My dad. To have them hold my hand and tell me it's going to be okay."

Fuck. Tears spill from her eyes, red rimmed and swollen.

"I've been relatively healthy my entire life," Lia continues. "I've never been sick. When he was talking about autoimmune disorders, I was thinking about how scary that is and how much I wanted my mom."

Ah, there it is. The doctor gave his best guess before getting her connected with a doctor who can help treat.

"And not only am I fucking scared about what this means, but it made me miss them. Like to my bones. In a way I haven't done in a long time. So, I wanted to go see Wes—"

A sob cracks her voice as she falls into my lap, almost in the fetal position. I let her cry and feel everything. I hold one of her hands and stroke her hair with my other.

"Whenever I was sick, or didn't feel good, my mom would stroke my hair," I tell Lia. "She did it when I was in the hospital recovering from surgery. I can't imagine needing your mom and not having her." I tip down and kiss the tears from her cheek.

She tries to catch her breath but all she can manage are sharp inhales. "It's been so long and..." Lia can't even finish her sentence.

I keep touching her in any way I think will be soothing, doing what I can to make her feel better. Rocky does the same and rests his head on her legs, curled on the side of the bed. "Want me to tell you a secret?" I ask.

She nods her head yes.

"My mom never made it home for Thanksgiving. There was bad weather and her flight was cancelled. I stayed in bed for two days. When everyone asked me what I did, I lied. I didn't have it in me to tell them I'm twenty-seven and all I wanted was my mom."

Lia sits, looking at me with eyes that could bring me to my knees. "Brooks. I'm sorry. I didn't know," she apologizes.

"I didn't tell you. I didn't tell anyone. The point is, you're never too old to want your mom."

She wipes her tears away with her fingertips. When she looks at me, it hurts. Her cheeks are stained with tears, and the red flush makes her forest green eyes even more vivid. Lia puts her lips to mine and it's like we were meant to fit together like this. Tears, grief, secrets and all.

"Let's take a shower," I suggest. "You always feel better after one."

"I still owe you a secret," she replies, watching me rise from the bed.

"There's no rush," I assure her, and she puts her hand in mine. "I'm not going anywhere. Or if I am, it's with you."

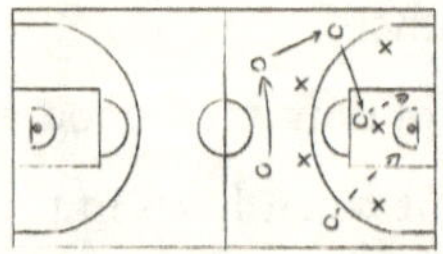

You'd never guess Lia has had a rough two days with the way she looks tonight. This morning, I learned all the tips and tricks for bringing down swelling from crying. I wish I had known some of them when I was back in my jagged, dark depression hole after my knee injury.

Lia is holding a Jags branded mic, standing on the edge of the court and doing sound checks. She's working on the court tonight, getting some interview access with players. It's not for a major broadcast but it's still cool as fuck.

One of my favorite parts is watching the fans and other players interact with her. Many know her from social media or from the DO IT FOR THE DOGS campaign. They want selfies or high fives and it's so fucking wholesome.

Megan stands next to the camera man, testing some shots with Lia. She's fixing Lia's blonde curly hair and giving her tips on where to hold the mic. They laugh loudly enough that I can hear them over the warm-up music, and it makes me fucking smile.

We're only fifteen minutes from tip-off and fans are finding their seats. I look for my special invite, who should be sitting about three rows from the bench.

And there he is.

Wes.

I snooped in Lia's phone, only to get his phone number, and told him I had two tickets with his name on them. He thought I was pranking him and made me FaceTime him to be sure. After he was positive it was really me, he was happy to take the tickets.

I knew Lia would be on court tonight and I thought it'd be nice for Wes to see her. She's doing cool fucking things, and I know she'd want to share this with one of her favorite people. Lia has no idea he's here and I can't wait to surprise her.

When Wes sees me and gives me a wave, Lia walks over for a pregame interview. She's wearing light purple dress pants; they're almost lilac but sort of gray, with a white top. The pants are wide at the bottom of the legs but tight enough on her ass to show the curves I'm going to be salivating over later tonight when she's in my bed. Wait—*our* bed.

Megan gets my attention. "Brooks, are you ready for Lia? It'll only take a second."

I nod but think about how I'd prefer to take my time with her. I never want to rush things, and give her a devilish smirk.

Maybe she knows exactly what I'm thinking because she puts her hand over the mic, turns her head, and says, "Quit that," under her breath.

We get the cue that the camera is rolling, and Lia says, "Brooks Pittman, how's that knee feeling?"

My fingers feel for the tape as I answer, "Good. Probably even better than before the injury. Ready to go out and get a win tonight." My hands rest on my hips as Lia looks at me.

"That's what we want to hear. Now, you're playing one of the top teams in the league, but from the other conference. Some say this could be an early glimpse into an NBA Finals match up. What's the one thing you have to do to win this game?"

She puts the mic in front of my mouth. "We can't turn the ball over," I stress. "Every possession counts and we can't give them any freebies."

"Good luck, Brooks."

"You too, Lia," I reply as the red light above the camera disappears.

Megan and the camera man scurry to the next thing—whatever that is—and I know I only have a second of her time.

"I got you a present. It's sitting behind the bench."

She scrunches her brows. "What do you mean?"

Lia looks from me to the bench, and it takes her a second before she finds Wes.

"You didn't!" she screams.

"I did," I reply with a grin. "Believe me, it wasn't hard to get him here."

"With seats like that, I bet." She smiles at me in the way where I know she wants to say something else. Something more. But this isn't the place. "Good luck tonight."

I watch as she runs over to Wes and wraps him in a hug.

I put up a few shots and when her eyes find mine, I blow her a quick kiss.

Her cheeks are crimson enough for me to see them from here.

Chapter 49
Lia

SLEEPING IN IS THE best. Brooks left early to do rehab before watching film and I'm still in bed with Rocky. No one tells you how hard it is to get out of bed when you have a dog. Like, I'm supposed to leave him here? All snuggled up? No way. The only thing that would make this morning better? Brooks, if he was next to me. And if I had a mug of hot tea or a Dr. Pepper. Any of my favorite drinks would do.

Brooks. The way this man has me down bad. All the way down in the best way. Yesterday he jumped in while I was using icepacks and eye masks to get the swelling down before the game. The way he supports me, without question, is something I'm trying to get used to.

Stretching my arms above my head, I feel the muscle knots in my shoulders. Probably from being nervous at the game. It wasn't as intimidating as being in the booth for a televised game, but it was just as rewarding. Another pinch me moment for the books, *and* my muscles. I melt, thinking about the slow yoga I can do to loosen up. Something about me is I love a yoga session that's only for me—when I'm not in charge of anyone else.

With nothing but time, I sink back into the bed, replaying last night's game. Wes got to see the Jags win in overtime, and I got to do some on-court interviews, all from some of the best seats in the house. He was blowing up my phone last night, freaking out. It didn't help that Brooks signed his jersey and threw it to him, and Jalen's jersey to Wes' friend, after the game.

I'm sure there must be a hilarious social media post where Wes is fangirling and I so badly want to see it. I look for my phone and remember it died last night. I unplug it from the charger and power it on as Rocky comes to lay right next to me. It's like he always has to be touching me. When the screen comes to life, the notifications are nonstop. Like, one after another, differentiating from text messages and social media.

What is happening?

I reach for it but the only thing I see are notification banners, one after another. I open my text messages and go to Shelbie's contact, since she's a favorite and pinned at the top.

Shelbie

> omg are you alright

> how did they get those photos?

> call me

Why wouldn't I be alright? What photos? It's like I'm playing a board game and everyone else knows the rules while I'm flying blind. I see the red bubble next to a social media app, letting me know something is blowing up because that's a lot of notifications.

When I open my account, the one I use for the Jags, I see it. Or some of it. A picture of Brooks and I kissing in the pool. A video of me pulling into his driveway, only for him to meet me at the door. A picture of us at Willow's concert.

Oh my god.

And then I see the headlines.

Foul Play? NBA Star Brooks Caught in Secret Romance with Jags Employee.

Caught on Camera: Brooks and Lia's Heated Pool Night.

Insider Scandal: Did Brooks' Relationship with Lia Influence Team Decisions?

No. No. No. I throw the blankets off and run down the stairs. I immediately call Shelbie, who answers after the first ring.

"Lia, finally! I've been calling!" Shelbie shouts as a greeting.

"My phone was dead. What the fuck is going on?"

Shelbie lets out a slow breath. "Secret's out. One of those gossip accounts released a bunch of videos and pictures. A few anonymous tips." Her voice trails off and I'm a statue.

I can't say anything. My muscles are frozen. My brain stalls.

"Lia? Are you there?"

"No." It's the only thing I can bring myself to say.

"No? You are."

"What?"

"Lia, it's going to be fine," Shelbie insists, trying to console me. "This will blow over. Is Brooks with you?"

"No. Practice. His phone is off. Film day." The voice that comes out of my mouth doesn't sound like me. It's more like a robot than myself.

"Listen, maybe you should call your boss?"

I groan. "Fuck."

"You guys probably need to disable the Jags social media account. I'm telling you right now, it's ugly."

I can't breathe. Megan. What will Megan say? They're for sure going to fire me.

"I gotta go. I'll call you later."

Shelbie tries to say something, but I hang up anyway. I need to get out of here.

I run upstairs, put on a crewneck and leggings and grab my purse. When I open the front door, it's like I've stepped into hell. The flashes of cameras go off, like I'm in the middle of a thunderstorm. They're not in the gated area but they're right outside the fence.

There's nothing I can do. Everyone's already gotten pictures of me.

I don't put my hand in front of my face or do anything to avoid them. What's the point? I've already lost.

I get in my car, slamming the door harder than necessary, and put in the code to the gate. I'm careful while pulling out, as people yell my name while some shout questions. Luckily, I can't decipher one question from the other since they're all on top of each other. I watch the gate close behind me and pull onto the road.

Every one of my movements is being cataloged. Photographed.

Fuck.

Our secret's out.

Chapter 50
Brooks

THE SECOND WE'RE DISMISSED from our film session of a game well fucking played, a trainer is waiting for me. He waves me over as soon as I make eye contact. I already did my rehab, so I'm not sure what they could want. He shuffles his feet and keeps looking down at his phone then back at me.

"What's up?" I ask shortly.

He doesn't say anything but instead shows me something on his phone. It's pictures and videos of me and Lia. A few of them. I swipe, each one feeling like a violation of privacy. The pool. Concert. Her at my place.

"What the fuck?" I shout. "How?"

"They dropped this morning. I saw an account post some pictures of Lia leaving your place a little while ago," the trainer explains.

"Leaving?" Panic starts to roll in my stomach. If they saw her leaving, that means they were waiting for her. *Fuck.* "Where did she go?"

"Brooks, I have no idea." He scrolls through things on his phone and says, "Some of this stuff is nasty."

"What do you mean?" I ask as we walk back to the locker room.

"Besides the typical trolls, there are people mentioning the intern who was fired before her. It's bad. And they're basically saying the only reason Lia's gotten the chances she has is because she's sleeping with you."

The words stop me like a brick wall. I pivot and turn to him. He waves his hands in surrender. "I absolutely don't think any of that," he stammers, stepping away from me. "I'm trying to give you an idea of what's going on."

"Okay, let's think here. I need you to find Megan. Get her to deactivate Lia's account and the Jags one, if it's there too. Just have her figure it out."

"Good idea. I'll do that. But you need to go."

"Yeah. I'll go find Lia."

He's already jogging down the hall towards Megan's office and I take off in the opposite direction, needing to get my stuff from my locker. I damn near sprint because I can't risk being stopped by any other staff or teammates.

I'm trying to think what I would say if anyone stopped me. I don't have a fucking clue.

Did I think this was a possibility? Sort of. I thought someone might see us together, one too many times, and there would be contemplating. But this looks like something that was intentionally held on to in order to make the biggest splash, the sharpest cut.

I'm in my car and I check my phone. Nothing from Lia, which just means I've got stuff from everyone else. I call her and it goes straight to voicemail.

Again.

And again.

And again.

Her phone must be off.

Fuck. Where do I go? There aren't many places I'd think she'd go. I also haven't met any of her friends, so I don't know if that's a possibility.

I'm contemplating my next move while I check my rear-view mirror, trying to see if anyone has followed me from the practice facility. No. I don't think so.

The first place I can check, and I actually know where it is, is her old apartment. With every second that I'm driving, the reality of this keeps settling in. Everyone knows. I'm not sure what more they know but it's definitely that Lia and I are in some sort of relationship. The blurry picture of her and I in the pool comes roaring back. My knuckles are bone white while gripping the steering wheel, and I have to remind myself not to go 100 MPH. The last thing I need is a fucking ticket.

I'm pulling up to her old apartment, wondering what this means for her and I. What happens when I find her? Maybe I should've stayed back and talked to Megan? No. I need to make sure Lia's okay. Fuck, I'm sure she's freaking out.

I park and looking for signs of her car, which I don't see. That would be too easy.

Running up to her door, I knock. No one answers. I go back down to the front of the building and annoyingly ring a doorbell until a neighbor, who happened to be outside the apartment the night of the flooding, opens the door.

"I'm a friend of Lia's," I rush to say. "We were going to check on her apartment progress today. Do you know if she beat me here?"

They shake their head. "No. Haven't seen her."

I go back to my car and doing a quick loop through the parking lot, making sure I haven't missed Lia' car.

She's not here.

I get back in the car, try to call her, and it goes to voicemail. Her phone still isn't on.

Before I can try again, Megan's number flashes on my car display.

"Now isn't a good time, Megan," I snap.

"Are you with Lia? I can't get a hold of her."

"No. I'm not." I don't know what else to say. It feels like I should be careful, or maybe I just say fuck it and tell her everything.

"Are you looking for her?" Her voice is loud over the car speakers.

"I'm obviously looking for her," I shout. "You can yell at me, and fire her, or whatever the fuck you plan to do after I make sure she's safe. And if you think—"

"Brooks. Let me stop you there. The only reason I'm calling is to make sure she's okay. Please let me know when you do find her."

Well, shit. I'm caught off guard and try to switch from the asshole I sounded like to someone nicer, and it isn't easy. But I try.

"Good. Okay. Yeah, I can do that." I practically trip over my words, trying to soften them for Megan, who cares about Lia and is only checking on her.

"We'll talk later about whatever comes next, okay?"

"Okay."

Then she hangs up, and I can't help but hit the steering wheel.

Where the fuck is Lia?

I head back to my house because I don't know where else to go. Maybe she came back? Even as the thought is going through my head, I don't buy it. The pit in my stomach is deep and filled with worry and anxiety. I just want to make sure she's okay.

When I pull down my street and see the paparazzi outside my fence, rage burrows in my skin, hot and fiery. I get into my gate and call the police, letting them know I may need some help.

I get inside and the paparazzi are ruthless, even when the door is fucking closed. Rocky greets me but his ears are back and he's hesitant.

Leaning down, I pet him and pull him to my chest. "You don't like all of this, do you?"

Rocky looks at me, and for the first time since I adopted him, he looks almost like he did at the event when we first met. Scared. Nervous. The pit in my stomach opens.

I walk to the kitchen, making sure all the curtains are pulled shut. I don't know how or when, but someone took photos of us when we were here—in the safety of our own home.

Home. The word feels foreign, like it doesn't quite fit when Lia isn't here.

Sitting on the floor with my back against the fridge, Rocky sits between my legs. I wrap my arms around him and take a few slow breaths.

What does this mean? There's no way Lia can think I'd leak these photos. This has to be something we can work through. What does this mean for the Jags? Will they fire her?

There are too many questions, not enough answers, and a crippling amount of anxiety. This was her fear, or maybe it's worse. People are questioning her work because we may or may not be hooking up? What the fuck is that? She's talented all on her own, and people who work with her know that.

My chest squeezes, thinking about Lia being alone and looking at the comments on these posts. Fucking trolls. They don't know the first thing about her. Or what she means to me.

I have to find her.

Chapter 51
Lia

I DROVE AROUND UNTIL I was sure there was no one following me. I'm far enough from Brooks' place, but there's no way I can handle the paparazzi following me or taking more pictures. They've done enough today. Part of me wanted to go to my aunt and uncles, but I couldn't risk it. Instead, I pull my car into a parking spot on a residential street a few blocks from the diner.

The wind whips around me, stealing my breath and burning my cheeks. Snowflakes dust the sidewalk while clouds hide the sun this morning. I miss the moment when I woke up, rested from sleeping in, before everything fell apart.

It's not that the walk is far, but I forgot my coat at Brooks'. The leggings and crewneck outfit aren't doing me any favors. My fingers ache as I try to pull my sleeves down far enough to keep them covered.

When I walk in, Julie sees me, pours a cup of coffee and sets it at my booth—my favorite one in the back.

"I'll be over when this little rush dies down." She squeezes my shoulder as she passes me, making her way to a table needing her attention.

Slipping into the booth, there's comfort in the worn upholstery. Julie catches my eyes for a split second, and I know she's waiting for me to lose it. To be fair, this *is* my place. I've cried many tears in this diner—and Julie was present for most of them.

Muscle memory takes over as I put a cream and single sugar in my coffee. I wrap my fingers around the mug, letting it warm my fingers.

I've been shivering since I got in the car—it's more than the December temperature.

What do I do now?

For the first time, I think about how someone could have gotten those photos. They were watching us in the pool? Waiting for their moment? I shake off the ick, or try to at least, because this all feels gross.

Part of me thought about how Brooks and I would finally go public—I mean, that would've had to happen eventually. Secrets weren't meant to be kept forever. It wasn't supposed to be in grainy, grimy, gag-inducing photos that someone took without our knowledge or permission.

I sip my coffee, staring at the steam rolling in front of my eyes. Twinkly holiday lights catch my eye, lining the ceiling of the diner. Christmas is only a week away. One of my favorite holidays.

Then it hits me—I don't feel like I have a place. There's nowhere for me to fit. I'm not sure there's anywhere for me to go.

The lights remind me of my apartment, the one currently under construction, which has been my safe space for so long. Brooks quickly assumed responsibility for things he didn't need to. Now it's all complicated and jumbled, and my skin is too tight to fit my bones.

Tears silently fall down my face. I don't try to stop or hide them. Instead, I sit back, grasp the coffee cup like it's the only thing keeping me going, and feel the wave of hurt.

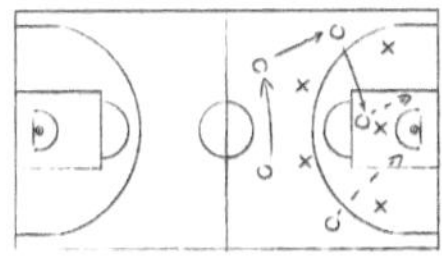

"You need to eat something," Julie protests, sliding a pancake and a few pieces of bacon in front of me.

"No, I'm good. I just—"

"You're not good. And you've been sitting here for hours. Please eat something."

Hours? How?

"Do you want me to call someone for you?" Julie asks with eyes full of comfort, just like old times.

I grab a fork, even though the last thing I want to do is eat.

Someone stands behind Julie and says, "No, I'm here."

Wes.

He's pink-cheeked from the outside and I can smell the snow from his jacket. Julie smiles at him as he slides next to me, not across, and puts a hand around my shoulder.

I tilt my head into Wes' shoulder like he used to do to me when he was little. When he lost a basketball game, hurt himself, or had a nightmare and would crawl into my bed. We've been taking care of each other, in the way it counts, for a long time. He rubs my forearm and if I had tears left, they'd be staining his shirt.

"How did you know where to find me?" I sniffle.

"I just knew," he replies, squeezing me tighter.

Chapter 52
Brooks

I'm pulling into Lia's apartment complex for the second time today—it's been hours but I can't sit here and do nothing. Definitely don't think this is my best idea, but it's the only one I fucking have. I had to delete all the social media apps from my phone because the amount of activity was sickening. Why the fuck do people care so much about things that don't impact them?

Helplessness hits me as I knock on Lia's door, a place I know she can't be. I can basically taste the depression at this point.

I walk to my car after waiting for a few minutes, the snow blowing into my face, and feel the vibration of a text message.

Wes

don't know if you're looking for her

hope you are

but she's at the diner

Finally, I let out a long breath. The diner. She's with Wes. It's like my body was in a vice and its grip has suddenly been loosened. My muscles relax bit by bit, knowing she's okay.

Me

on my way

don't let her leave

I'm in the car and driving across town, and even just having a desti-
nation, fuck, it's making me feel better. She's close. She's not alone. Not
that I know what I'll say when I see her, or how this will end up, but I'll
deal with that later.

All I know is I'll do whatever I can not to lose her.

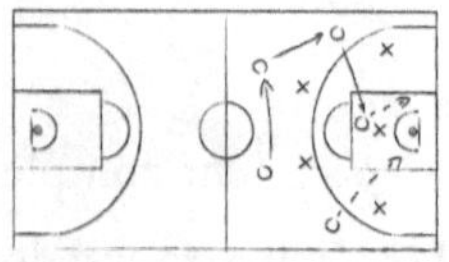

I step into the diner and it's like a magnet—Lia pulls me in her direction
like that. I see Wes before I see her. The same waitress we had before
stands at the counter, and she grins at me, like she's happy I'm there.
Fuck, I hope she's right.

Wes sees me and slides out of the booth as I reach them.

"Where are you going?" Lia asks her brother.

He doesn't say anything but instead moves out of the way. Her eyes
land on me and my heart fucking cracks open in my chest. The way she's
struggled the last few days, and now this? She deserves better.

"Brooks, what are you doing here?" Lia sniffles.

I sit across from her. "I've been looking for you."

"You have?" She seems genuinely confused, like she can't imagine me
doing that. "Aren't you afraid you're going to get in trouble? Can they
suspend you for this? I mean, it sounds ridiculous, but I'm sure there's
some morality clause in your contract and—"

"Lia. Stop." I cover her hands with my own. "I don't care about any
of that. I care about you."

Her rich green eyes look around, darting to the walls before landing
back on me. I feel her knee bouncing and lightly shaking the tabletop.

"This is your career. Your livelihood," Lia tries to argue with me.

"I could say the same for you."

"Brooks." She rolls her eyes and lets her chin fall forward a little. "It's not the same. You have more to lose than I do."

"You're right. I do. But it's not basketball. Lia, I can't fucking lose *you*. You don't get to stroll into my life, on the date from hell, and make me fall in love with you. For this to be it." I learn further on the table. "I need you."

Her eyelids are heavy as she blinks away the tears. "I can't ask you to do that," she protests. Her voice is small and muffled, unlike the bright and confident woman I'm used to seeing.

"Good thing you didn't ask."

Lia's blonde hair falls forward, like her muscles are too sore to keep her head up. I know she's tired; there's no way she's not fucking exhausted.

"They're saying horrible things about me. About you. About the Jags. Even about Megan. It's not just about me."

Lia's need to consider everyone feels heavy, even from here. She's so used to worrying about everyone else and putting herself last. "But what if you let it be about you? And not everyone else?" I ask.

Her voice cracks as she answers, "I don't know how to do that…"

Squeezing her hands even tighter, I quickly reply, "Well, I'm going to fucking teach you how. That way, we can test out this whole forever thing."

"You say that like it's easy." Her hands move from mine, pushing her hair away from her face.

"No, Lia. I say it like it's going to be worth it."

For the first time, I don't feel the push back. There's no retort on the tip of her tongue or doubt in her glare—there's space. It's only a few seconds but they stretch, the string tying Lia and me together pulling tighter.

"What do we do now?"

"First, I'm going to kiss you." I slide out of the booth and kneel so I'm eye level with her. "And then I'm taking you home."

Lia reaches her hand out to me, and I use it to stand us up. My lips crash into hers, telling her more secrets. It's the kind of kiss which feels like the rest of your life. Like you see can the bones of the montage and it looks fucking perfect.

Her lips are full and press back into mine. My hands find her lower back while she grips the front of my shirt. When we break apart, I kiss her forehead, then the top of her head. She falls into me in a way where I feel like I'm holding her up. It's like she's finally given in, and I wouldn't have it any other way.

Chapter 53
Lia

WE'RE IN A CONFERENCE room, one I didn't even know existed, in the Jags arena. Trent scheduled this meeting, and while Megan and some other executive members of the organization will be there, Brooks will not.

I walked the halls like it was high school graduation and it might be the last time I'm in them. The only difference here is I didn't spend nearly enough time here. I'd kill for four years at this organization, but unfortunately, I'm guessing my time has come to an end.

"Lia, thanks for coming in. I'm sure you've been worried about all of this," Trent says as soon as I find my seat.

I take a slow breath, just like I practiced. My fingers squeeze each other in my lap, under the table where no one can see. They ache in a way that's slow and steady. I have a doctor's appointment next week, just like the team doctor promised, and I'm thankful I was able to see him before this all happened.

Keeping my shoulders tall, I nod and say, "Thank you for having me. I know your time is valuable. So I'll kick us off." Surprised eyes land on me, but if there's anything I need right now, it's the small control of doing this my way. "First, I want to say thank you. This job was truly a dream come true. It was better than my dreams, actually. The opportunities I've been given, and the friendships I've made," I look at Megan in that moment, and she nods in understanding, "were better than I could've hoped for.

"Second, I want to apologize. I met Brooks before this job happened, but I'm sure there are other ways I could've handled it. I never wanted negative attention for myself, him, or anyone associated with the organization and—"

"Lia, can I stop you for a second?" Trent jumps in, lifting a hand.

I can't get a read from anyone at the table. They all seem like they are holding their breath, afraid to breathe—in a way I can relate.

"Now, this looks bad. Even if it's not true. We all know, since your situation with Brooks wasn't public knowledge, there's no way you were given a leg up or anything like that. But from the outside? People are drawing their own conclusions." Trent rubs his hands together.

"I wish you would've told me. I could've helped you," Megan says, a touch of disappointment etching her face.

"That would've been best. Now our hands are tied." Trent nods, as do other people around the table. "Unfortunately, we can't let you keep this job."

I'm going to throw up. My barf is going to be on display for anyone who walks by. The nausea rolls through me and my head feels like it's full of cotton. I let my head fall forward, mostly so I can try to get myself together.

"Okay. I get it. Thanks again for—" I start to stand, using my hands to push from the table when Trent interrupts me.

"Lia, no. You can't keep *this* job. The one you're currently in. You can't be leading the project with Brooks."

"I don't get it." I shrug my shoulders because my brain can't put these things together.

Trent smiles. "You've done a remarkable amount of good in the last few months. You work hard, love to learn new things, and love a challenge. You're exactly what we're looking for when it comes to the Jags organization."

People nod along the table.

Raising an eyebrow, I slowly reply, "I feel like this is a joke." It's not the most eloquent thing to say, but it's the only logical thing I can get out.

Megan leans on the table and insists, "It's not. You're a strong, motivating woman in sports, and we want to keep you. We need to do some restructuring and find something else for you."

"What about the intern? The one who got fired before me?"

Megan laughs, putting her hands over her eyes for a flash of a second. "We're talking night and day if we're comparing these situations. The Jags executive in question was married, and his wife came to the facility to confront him, and the intern destroyed his office. That's a great example of what not to do. This is not the same."

Trent jumps in. "If you're uncomfortable working here, with the added layer of your relationship with Brooks, we'll understand. But it's our hope that you'll continue here."

I shake my head. "You're not for real."

Almost everyone chuckles and looks at each other around the table. "Yes, we're for real," Megan insists.

This isn't what I expected. Instead of some bureaucratic "you broke a silent rule" cop out, they're recognizing my value. They're placing what I can bring the organization ahead of who I'm dating, or what that may look like.

"There's such power for people like you in this field. You're inspiring the next generation of girls who love sports, and we're hoping you'll do that in Jags purple," Trent offers, smiling wide and sitting back.

I shake my head, making sure I'm indeed awake, and ask, "Okay. What happens now?"

Someone from HR chimes in, "First, we'll do some paperwork in regard to your relationship with Brooks. Then we'd like to work together on putting out a statement. We can show you a few suggestions but are happy to make adjustments. Plus, Brooks has already made a statement, so—"

My eyes snap upward. "Wait, what do you mean?"

Megan looks to me, brows furrowed. "He gave a statement and it went live a few minutes before the meeting. I thought he would've told you."

The person from HR opens a folder, pulls out a piece of paper, and slides it over to me. "This was all him—a personal statement."

Recently, my privacy was violated when pictures and videos from my home were taken and shared publicly without my knowledge or consent. I've always given everything I have to this sport, this team, and this organization. Now I'm asking for one thing: to keep a piece of my life to myself—the part that includes Lia, the woman who showed up when I least expected but needed her most.

In a sport that's still dominated by men, Lia is the type of person organizations dream of finding. She's smart, hard-working, and loves a challenge. The next time you meet someone like Lia, think about what they bring to the sport and the fans, instead of personal details that aren't yours to examine.

I'm hoping you can respect this request.

Go Jags.

-Brooks Pittman

I look to see everyone watching me. It's overwhelming.

"We can give you some time to think it over. There's no rush," Megan assures me.

My brain is trying to keep up with the mental whiplash I'm going through. I expected to give a heartful apology, thank everyone for the opportunity, and move on gracefully. Instead, they're asking me if I need time to think about keeping my dream job.

I'm about to tell them I don't need time. That I'm one hundred percent in. But suddenly, Brooks barrels through the door.

"You can't fire her. That's ridiculous!" Jaws drop and hands cover mouths with each step he takes further into the conference room. "You know that's not the right thing to do, and you always tell me the Jags get ahead by doing the right things. Trent, you told me that!" He's pointing and standing in front of the general manager. Everyone's eyes are wide and Megan is trying not to laugh.

I should say something, but I can't. My body is frozen.

"Brooks, relax," Trent urges.

"No, I can't relax. I have an ex, one I *wish* would leave me alone for the rest of time, and she's the one who leaked this. She had the pictures taken, but Lia's the one in trouble? How is that okay? No fucking way."

"We're not firing her." Trent's voice is collected and calm.

The look on Brooks' face is absolutely priceless. "You're not?" He sets his hands on his hips. "You're not." This time, it's not a question. His eyes find mine, only to see my lips pressed into the thinnest of lines.

"No. We need to figure it out, but we want her to stay with the Jags. Is that okay with you?" The grin Trent wears drips with playful sarcasm while people laugh around the table.

"Yeah. That would be okay with me," Brooks replies, his chest rising and falling with his fast breath. His eyes find me and the heat that hits my cheeks is impossible to hide.

Megan rolls her eyes and jumps in. "Awesome. Now, I'm sure you have somewhere you're supposed to be, yes?"

Brooks nods and walks out, wearing a smirk and crimson cheeks.

Honestly, this feels full circle. The first time we met, he was jumping in when Little Dick Randall was being rude. It feels on brand for him to run in and try to defend me, even though it wasn't necessary. I still love that he did it.

That he cared enough to do it.

That he loves me in a way that proves I'm worth defending.

Chapter 54
Brooks

"WHAT DO YOU WANT to do?" my lawyer asks, gesturing to the photos scattered across the desk.

Pictures of me and Lia in the privacy of my home. Nothing we asked for or even knew it was happening until it was too late. It only took a couple of calls from my team, and one from Jags' legal team, to figure out what the hell was going on.

Rebecca.

She paid someone to follow us, then immediately turned around and sold those pictures to the press. She didn't get what she wanted and threw a very public—and line crossing—tantrum.

"Let's at least send the formal letter that we're going to sue her for invasion of privacy. I don't know if I'll actually go through with it or not," I admit.

He nods, gathering the photos and putting them in the file. "That's what I'd recommend. Paired with the defamation lawsuit from the Jags, I think she'll understand the severity of her actions."

I fucking hope so.

I'd be in a very different mood if the Jags were going to penalize Lia. She didn't do anything to deserve something like this. I hate how people act like every detail of my life, or hers, is something they should be welcome to. Yes, I'm a professional athlete, but I'm also just a person trying to figure life out.

I'm walking out of my lawyer's office, using the back entrance, when someone shouts my name. How the fuck did the paparazzi follow me here?

I turn and am immediately relieved when I see Zack and my dad. They're standing outside their car while the snow gently falls.

"What are you guys doing here?" I shiver as a burst of cold air whips my cheeks.

Zack hugs me, patting my back. "Lia was on the phone with Willow and Emilie, dishing about the meeting, and she let it slip you were coming here."

My dad adds, "We wanted to make sure you were okay."

They came to check on me.

"You didn't have to do that," I mutter.

"We wanted to. You're one of us, Brooks." My dad steps in and wraps his arms around me.

I let that sink in for a few seconds, before the relief follows. I hug him back and let it say the things I don't trust my mouth to. Zack hates being left out, so he hugs the both of us.

"Our first group hug," he jokes and shakes us.

I'm so thankful for the way they showed up for me, even though I never asked. It's like I'm constantly being reminded that I don't need to struggle alone. There are people here for me.

People that love me.

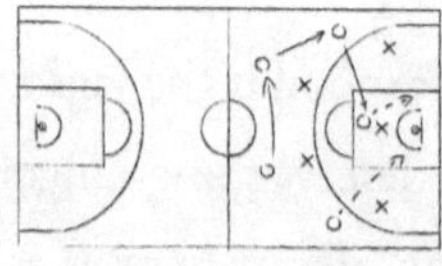

I walk in the house and when I don't hear Rocky running to me, I know they must be outside.

Lia's in the hot tub and Rocky is on his dog bed, equipped with a heated blanket to keep him comfortable against the winter air.

"There she is. Miss Lia Stone, employee of the Jersey Jaguars," I call, and Lia's face brightens the second she hears me.

She pokes me back. "There he is, Brooks Pittman, man of my dreams and meeting interrupter."

I laugh, thinking about my completely unnecessary and impulsive barge in. My coach heard about it and couldn't stop giving me shit at the end of practice.

"I had a nice meeting with HR today, after you met with them." I kneel by the edge of the hot tub, the steam meeting my face.

Lia stands, braving the icy air against her warm skin to kiss me. She almost loops her arms around me but stops herself. "I don't want to get you wet," she pouts.

I shrug my shoulders and step into the hot tub, clothes and all. The water is perfectly warm as the snow still falls gently around us.

"What are you doing?" She laughs through her question.

My nose is almost touching hers. "Kissing my very HR official girlfriend the way she should be kissed." All I feel is her—her lips, her chest against mine, not holding back.

"Thank you. For today. For this. For believing in me the way you do," Lia says, her green eyes damn near glowing in the winter night.

I squeeze her and sway us side to side before placing a kiss on her cheek. "You'd do it for me. And then some."

We stay this way for a moment before I can't hold back. "Want to know a secret?" I ask.

"Always," she replies, a shared breath floating between us.

"You are proof that some secrets are worth keeping."

And before I can say another word, her lips find mine, like they always were meant to. I melt into the kiss, the warmth of the water and her touch making everything else fade away. For the first time in a long time, it feels like forever is right here—something I can reach out and grab.

And never *ever* let go.

Epilogue
Brooks

ELEVEN MONTHS LATER

"This campus is gorgeous," Lia admires while we walk hand in hand.

It's November in Michigan, so naturally, it's freezing. The courtyard is covered in snow but that doesn't mean there aren't enthusiastic college kids with their bodies painted, running to get to the first home basketball game of the season.

"Are you nervous?" I ask, looking over at Lia.

She turns, smiling at me with full brightness—my favorite kind. "Yes, I could throw up, but I won't. I just want Wes to play like I know he can. I love that we can be here for his first college home game."

I pull her gloved hand into mine, putting a kiss to the outside. "He's going to be great. Don't even sweat it," I reassure her.

After I watched Wes play for the first time, I knew he was something special. I called my old college coach about a kid in Jersey that was worth seeing, and he couldn't come to scout him fast enough. He had an offer for Wes a few weeks later, but it wasn't for The University of Alabama. It was for his new school: Great Lakes University. Typically known for hockey, the basketball program was making some moves and found themselves a hell of a coach to build a legacy.

Tonight, we get to cheer Wes on as he takes the court, starting as a highly touted freshman. I can't fucking wait.

Lia shakes her free hand, the way she does when they're sore.

"How are the wrists?" I ask gently.

She looks at me with a hesitant smile. "I'm sore. Maybe from the cold? Or the travel? But I feel like the injections are helping."

It's been a long road over this last year with figuring out what was going on with Lia. We saw a few different specialists, did more tests than I thought were possible, and it seems like we've finally got enough information to try and help her. She was formally diagnosed with severe plaque psoriasis and psoriatic arthritis—both autoimmune conditions that have been wreaking havoc on her body for much longer than she probably noticed.

Everything is a delicate balance. She has days where she seems completely fine, followed by a string of days where she can barely hold herself up because of the pain. The thing we've both been trying to get better at is resting. Lia is learning how important it is to regularly take naps during her flares, and I do my best to make it feel like she isn't missing out on anything.

We don't have all the answers, but I'm damn proud of her for what she's been through and how she takes each day in stride.

"Oh! I almost forgot to tell you," she squeals suddenly. When I turn to look at her, Lia grins like she could lighten the darkest of days or moods. "I'm going to be an extra commentator for NBA TV next week!"

"That's going to be a blast! Can't wait." I love cheering her on as she does the thing she loves—and when she's in the booth, not much can top that.

After the fallout with the leaked pictures and our relationship going public, the Jags pulled together a few other local sports teams in the region and created a subsidiary completely focused on women in sports. They're not employed by a single team, which gives them the freedom to operate similarly to a TV or radio network. Sometimes it's events with like DO IT FOR THE DOGS, or other campaigns which focus on bringing more women into the sports realm. This summer, Lia got to be in the booth for a few WNBA games, and though she'll never admit to it, I feel like she loved it more than any of the NBA games she's done.

"Tell me you see this..." Lia says, nodding ahead.

There's a crowd of people around someone who is signing jerseys and giving high fives. I get close enough to see it's Zack. He's wearing a Great Lakes U Otter jersey, #18—Wes' number. Shaking my head, I laugh and Emilie sees us immediately.

"I told him we could go inside and wait for you, but you know Zack." Emilie hugs Lia just as Zack spots us and lifts his hand in a wave.

Zack breaks away from the group and wraps me in a hug. "You ready to do the otter chant I taught you?" His excitement for Wes makes me want to hug him and never let go. It would be impossible to keep him still that long but, fuck, he has a way of pulling at my heart strings.

"Yes, we're ready," Lia answers and Zack hugs her next.

"Did you wear your championship ring?!" Zack asks, reaching for my hand.

I shake my head. "No, it's not something you wear, like, out in public."

"Fuck that. I wore my Super Bowl ring for basically an entire year."

"You would." I roll my eyes as he lightly punches my arm.

The moment is brief, barely a second long, but it's large enough to bring me to my knees. My life is full and fucking remarkable. I never saw this coming. Zack. My dad. Lia. Rocky. Wes. An NBA Championship.

The dark days still happen, but they're few and far between. And when the claws come for me, there is always someone there to help me get through it.

We walk into the building and the energy is everything. It's electric, sharp and zipping through the air. Before we go to the suite, Lia walks to the first entrance for seats and gets to the railing, looking at the court below.

Immediately she finds Wes and squeals, covering her mouth and jumping and down.

There he is, warming up and locked in. I want him to fucking go off tonight—like I know he can. Just like we talked about.

Lia reaches for my hand and squeezes. "I love you."

I pull her to me, placing a kiss on her mouth that has the fans around us letting out audible "oohs" and low whistles. "Can I tell you a secret?" I whisper. When Lia nods, I look into her shimmering emerald eyes—the ones I plan to gaze into for the rest of my life. "I love you more."

And I fucking mean it.

THE END

Acknowledgments

Here's to the series I had no intentions of writing but AM THRILLED I DID. A shoutout to my girl, Liz, who flat out laughed when I said "I think this should be an interconnected standalone" and she told me she knew this would happen and cheered me on until the end. I LOVE YOUUU.

I love sports—many of these pages were written while I was up late watching west coast NBA games. I'm so thankful I've found readers who love sports romance the way I do. The thing I wanted to do more than anything was work in sports broadcasting and journalism—there's many reasons why this didn't come to be—and being able to experience this through Lia's eyes fills me heart with such joy.

One of my favorite parts of finishing a book is writing this section, looking back at all the support and being in complete awe.

First and foremost, to Shelbie. My main girl. The missing piece of my dark heart. Our meet cute was as described... some college class with an odd icebreaker. Jokes on me because while I was rolling my eyes, I was literally crossing paths with someone I wouldn't be able to live without. Thank you for all of your love, support, love for scary things, and always being there.

Megan, my sweet bookclub find. I love writing bad ass female characters after the real ones in my life. Megan—love you and wouldn't be here without your support. Thanks for always cheering me on.

Author friends who I simply refuse to give up. I don't know what I did to deserve this group of women who cheer me on, hype me up, answer one million questions, and reassure me that I am doing something right... Carly Robyn, Ambar Cordova, Rachel Holm, Cleo White, Grace Pearce, Courtney Corlew, and Stef CR.

My alpha and beta team—Stephanie, Rose, Georgia, Tricia, Keri, Thao, Keona, Sarah, Holly, Brenda, Sam, Kendra. The way you challenged me and helped get this book where it was meant to be. THANK YOU. Your hands are all over this story, in the best way, and I wouldn't have it any other way.

My real life Rocky. The sweetest english bulldog. Not me crying over being able to write him in a way that keeps him alive and with me forever.

Lastly, to Robby, my sweet husband who supports me in this adventure and my obsession with sports. Love you more than everything.

 RACHEL LABERGE is the author of YOUR SECRET TO BREAK, book three in The Play Caller series. When she's not reading or writing, she's probably thinking about donuts, sour candy, or looking for her next hyperfixation. She lives in Michigan with her husband (Roberto), her two Frenchies (Rafa and Ruby), and cat (Riley). You can connect with her on Instagram, TikTok, and Threads **@rachellabergeauthor** (no 'R' name required).

Want to be first in line for updates and bonus content? Sign up for Rachel's newsletter at rachellaberge.com.